Select praise for internationally bestselling author Rachel Reid

"Rachel Reid's hockey heroes are sexy, hot, and passionate!"

—Lauren Blakely, #1 *New York Times* bestselling author of *A Guy Walks Into My Bar*

"It was sweet and hot, and the humor and banter gave it balance. I'm really looking forward to more from Rachel Reid."

—*USA TODAY* on *Game Changer*

"The Game Changers series is a game changer in sports romance (wink!), and firmly ensconced in my top five sports series of all time."

—*All About Romance*

"Rachel Reid writes great hockey romances and has crafted a stellar cast of characters associated with her fictional New York Admirals team . . . If you like M/M sports romance, you will definitely want to dive into the Game Changers series!"

—*Sinfully Good Gay Book Reviews*

Also available from Rachel Reid

Time to Shine
The Shots You Take

The Game Changers Series

Game Changer
Heated Rivalry
Tough Guy
Common Goal
Role Model
The Long Game
Unrivaled

TOUGH GUY

RACHEL REID

HARLEQUIN

HARLEQUIN®

Recycling programs for this product may not exist in your area.

ISBN-13: 978-1-335-00410-9

Tough Guy

First published in 2020. This edition published in 2026.

Illustration by Monika Roe (Violin).

Stock Images: © Good Studio/stock.adobe.com (Whip cream); © StockVector/stock.adobe.com (Face mask); MdJillur/stock.adobe.com (Fruit); © Dedraw Studio/stock.adobe.com (Stars, Mug & Sticker shapes); © vejaa/stock.adobe.com (Paint texture)

Harlequin Enterprises ULC
22 Adelaide St. West, 41st Floor
Toronto, Ontario M5H 4E3, Canada
www.Harlequin.com

HarperCollins Publishers
Macken House, 39/40 Mayor Street Upper,
Dublin 1, D01 C9W8, Ireland
www.HarperCollins.com

Printed in the United Kingdom

26 27 28 29 CPI 10 9 8 7 6 5 4 3

This book is for Matt, who does not like hockey,
but I love him anyway.

Dear Reader,

My only hope when *Game Changer* was first published in October 2018 was for at least one person to read my book and love my characters.

It was the very beginning of what would become an amazing adventure. With each book that was published in the Game Changers series, I received more love from readers. When the *Heated Rivalry* television series based on those books debuted in November 2025, my characters received more love than I could have ever thought possible. I am truly, enormously blessed and grateful for that love and for my readers.

I wrote these books as a lifelong hockey fan, and as someone who wants the culture of the sport I love to be better. The series is based on an idea: that the bravery of one person could create a ripple effect that benefits others and eventually leads to real change. Each book focuses on at least one hockey player, and the man who makes him braver. Stoic New York captain Scott Hunter is charmed by cute and clever history student Kip Grady. Weary Toronto defenseman Ryan Price reunites with bold and beautiful musician Fabian Salah. Distinguished New York goaltender Eric Bennett falls for witty young bartender Kyle Swift. Miserable Ottawa forward Troy Barrett learns how to smile with adorable social media manager Harris Drover. And, of course, despite their best efforts, Shane Hollander and Ilya Rozanov couldn't stop themselves from falling in love with each other.

I love each and every one of these characters, and as I write this letter in February 2026, it feels like the whole world loves them too. It's an incredible feeling, and I'm very aware that none of what I'm experiencing now would have happened without the enthusiastic support from the early fans of my books. The success of the Game Changers series was largely driven simply by readers recommending the books to their friends and online followers. It was driven by booksellers and librarians, by reviewers and bloggers, and by BookTokers and Bookstagrammers. I will always remember and appreciate that support.

Thank you for the love, and I hope you enjoy having these beautiful special editions on your shelves.

Love,
Rachel

TOUGH GUY

PROLOGUE

September 2018

"Are you happy?"

Ryan Price couldn't tell if Coach Cooper was asking the question of him, or of the computer the man hadn't taken his eyes from. The honest answer was that Ryan couldn't quite recall what happiness felt like, but that would be an awkward thing to admit, so instead he just said, "Sure."

"Great," Coach said absently. "Glad to hear it. You found a place to live yet?"

"Still at the hotel, but I'm looking at—"

"I guess you're the expert in changing cities." Coach finally turned his gaze to Ryan, and smiled at him as if he'd just thought of the funniest joke in the world. "You've pretty much got a full bingo card now, right?"

"Yeah." Ryan didn't even try to return the smile. "Pretty much."

Coach leaned back in his chair and folded his muscular arms over his chest. Bruce Cooper was possibly in better shape than any player on the Toronto Guardians roster. He'd never played in the NHL himself, but he kept his body in top form, as if suggesting to his players that he could very easily tie on skates and replace any of them at any time. "Well, you know why you're here. I don't have to tell you what kind of player you are, and what we expect from you. You get what I'm saying, I'm sure." He stopped smiling, and fixed a very pointed look at Ryan.

Ryan got what he was saying all right. It was the same thing every coach he'd had since he was seventeen had told him: we need you to beat the shit out of opponents who threaten our real players.

"Yes, Coach," Ryan said. He had just finished his first skate with the Guardians, and it had gone . . . fine. A few players had shot him curious looks, but no one had been particularly friendly to him. Ryan's reputation had obviously preceded him.

"Protecting Kent is the priority," Coach said. "He's got a mouth on him, but we don't want him getting hurt. Guys might think twice about coming for him if they know they'll have to, you know, *Pay the Price*." He grinned.

Ryan cringed. "Yep. Got it."

"Good," Coach said cheerfully. "Now, the other thing I wanted to talk about was your history of not getting along with your teammates."

Ryan Price ran his tongue along the bottom of his front teeth, scraping off the residue of the four Tums he had crunched down before he'd entered his new coach's office. He wanted to get as much of the antacid into his stomach as possible for this.

"It's not that," Ryan tried to explain. "I mean, it's not that I don't get along with them. I just . . . keep to myself. I guess."

Coach frowned. "The Guardians are a *team*, Ryan. On the ice and off. Teams are built on trust and camaraderie."

"I know. I'll try harder."

"Great to hear," Coach said, as if the matter was resolved. Ryan didn't expect to form any particularly strong bonds to any of his teammates. Something about being naturally awkward, shy, clinically anxious, terrified of flying, and, oh yes, gay, didn't exactly make him a friend magnet in the ol' locker room.

But he *would* try.

"And, listen." Coach dropped his voice and leaned forward. "You're not gonna, like, freak out on us, right? Like before?"

Ryan's eyebrows shot up. *Wow. That's direct.* "I, uh . . . I've been working on that."

Coach narrowed his eyes. "Working on it, like, what? Meditation or yoga or whatever?"

"No. I mean, a bit. But, like, therapy. And I have a prescription—"

"So you have it under control. Good." Coach waved his hand, clearly glad to have the conversation over with. "Let's get through training camp and we'll figure out where you're gonna fit on this team."

"Okay, Coach."

When Coach turned back to his computer, Ryan stood up, nodded, and left the room. The little chat hadn't been much different from the one he'd had with his last coach. Or the coach before that. *We want you to be terrifying on the ice, and normal off of it.*

Ryan headed back to the locker room to get ready for the physical testing the Guardians would be doing that afternoon. In the room, he saw Toronto's star player, Dallas Kent, talking to another star player, Troy Barrett. Kent was short for a hockey player, with blond hair and pale blue eyes. He wasn't what Ryan would call attractive, but that was mostly because his arrogance showed all over his face. Barrett was prettier, with piercing blue eyes and dark hair, but still far from Ryan's type.

Ryan figured he may as well introduce himself to the men he was expected to protect. As he got closer, he could hear Kent describing his previous evening's sexual exploits in great detail to Barrett. Kent didn't even glance up at Ryan when he'd approached, leaving him to stand awkwardly while Kent finished his gross story.

"Swear to god, I thought she was gonna pass out!"

Barrett laughed. Ryan cleared his throat, and Kent finally looked up.

"Oh. Hey." There was a bit of a sneer in Kent's tone.

"Hi," Ryan said stupidly. He thrust his hand out. "I'm Ryan."

Kent stared at Ryan's hand, then shot a look at Barrett. Finally, he quickly shook Ryan's hand and said, "I thought you went crazy."

"No," Ryan said, heat rising in his cheeks and down his neck. "I have it under control."

Barrett snorted. Kent looked at Ryan like he was a pile of dead snakes. "I fucking hope so, Red."

Ryan's jaw clenched. That was *not* a name he was going to answer to.

"Ryan," he corrected him. He straightened his spine, rolling his shoulders back to bring himself to his full height. He let just enough of the monster out to show Dallas Kent that Ryan wasn't someone to fuck with. "Not *Red*."

Kent put his hands up in a placating manner. "Whatever, man." He turned back to Barrett and resumed his story as if Ryan wasn't even there anymore.

Ryan felt his chest tightening as he retreated to his stall. Fortunately, he'd gotten good at talking himself down from these mild attacks.

Inhale for two, exhale for three. Inhale for three, exhale for four. Inhale for four, exhale for five . . .

He was okay. He was fine. Dallas Kent was clearly a fucking asshole, but Ryan was okay.

This is just a job. This is not you. You are more than this job.

Every job has shitty co-workers, right?

He counted one more breath, in and out, then started rummaging around in his gym bag, just for something to do.

"Wanna know a secret?"

Ryan was startled by the unexpected question. He turned to see Wyatt Hayes, who had been Toronto's backup goaltender for years. "Sure?"

"Dallas Kent is," Wyatt leaned in and dropped his voice to a whisper, "a bit of a douchebag."

Ryan sputtered, surprised. "So it's not just me, then?"

"Hell no. But he's the superstar, right, so what can you do?"

Ryan could think of a couple of things he'd *like* to do to him.

Wyatt laughed. "Holy shit, Price. Your face! You can't punch him!"

"I know. I wasn't gonna."

"Well, if you change your mind, make sure you tell me. I wanna watch."

Ryan shook his head, but he was smiling. He decided that he liked Wyatt Hayes. So that was something.

He had thought it might be different, this season. In retrospect, he had no idea why. Since his junior hockey days, Ryan had obligingly filled the role of enforcer on any team he played for. He had never been enthusiastic about it; if he'd wanted to be a boxer, he could have followed in his father's footsteps and been one. Ryan wanted to be a hockey player.

This past summer, after learning he had been traded yet again, Ryan had decided to throw himself into training. He'd worked on his skating, his speed, his lower body conditioning. He'd found a trainer in Buffalo, where he had still been living, and worked his ass off doing sprints, lunges, squats, and a whole nightmare of similar inhuman activities.

He'd shown up for this training camp in Toronto in the best shape of his life with the hope that he might be taken seriously as a defenseman. He would give these fitness tests everything he had, but he doubted it would change anyone's mind about the role he would play on this new team.

God. Ryan wasn't sure he could do this anymore. He *would*, because what else was he going to do? His résumé was pretty sparse.

"Ready to go through hell?" Wyatt asked. Ryan knew he was referring to the fitness testing, but Ryan was thinking about the whole season.

"Sure," he said. "Let's get it over with."

CHAPTER ONE

Fabian Salah *hated* hockey.

Clearly there was some sort of game happening today because the subway train was packed with people wearing blue Toronto Guardians jerseys. Fabian wished he could sit down; he didn't like standing in the middle of these people, being judged by their boring, ignorant brains. There was at least one dull jock who was openly sneering at Fabian in disgust.

Fabian kept his eyes down and resisted the urge to sneer right back at the man.

Three more stops and you're home, he told himself.

A little girl in a pink version of the Guardians jersey—because obviously you can't let your daughter wear something that isn't bubblegum pink—smiled up at him. He forced himself to smile back.

It wasn't her fault he was in a bad mood. It wasn't her fault that he hated hockey and the people who loved it, or that her parents were far too concerned with aggressively gendering their child. She was just enjoying an afternoon out with her parents, cheering on the hometown boys.

Fabian was sure the team was packed with heroic, upstanding

young men. Certainly not a bunch of homophobic alpha assholes who would be celebrating their win by doing very gross alpha things tonight. Fabian had met exactly one hockey player in his entire life of being forced to meet hockey players who wasn't a complete nightmare.

"Is that a guitar?" the little girl in the pink jersey asked him.

Fabian blinked. "It's a violin," he said, as warmly as he could manage.

"Is it yours?"

"Yes."

"Do you know how to play it?"

Fabian smiled. "Yes I do. I think I was about your age when I started learning. Do you play any instruments?"

She shook her head, but then said, "I like to sing and dance."

"Me too."

The girl's mother pulled her closer on their joined seats, and whispered something in her ear that was probably benign, like "Leave the nice man alone" or "Don't talk to strangers," but Fabian couldn't help but imagine it was more like "Don't talk to men who are wearing eyeliner and nail polish."

The girl stopped talking to him, but she watched him intently all the way to Wellesley Station, where Fabian finally removed himself from the hoard of hockey fans.

As he made his way down Church Street, Fabian felt the lingering tension from the subway ride leave his body. He had better things to think about than stupid jocks. For one thing, he had finally broken things off—for good this time—with Claude last night. Claude had been the latest in a long line of self-obsessed snobs that Fabian had, for whatever reason, invited into his bed. He wouldn't call what they'd had a relationship; he'd just kept running into Claude at various events and they would inevitably end up fucking. But Fabian was *done* with that shit.

He was in a good place now. He had some very promising

shows booked, had almost finished his new album, and he'd recorded an in-studio interview and performance for CBC Radio last week. His *parents* had even listened to it, so he had definitely made it big. If things kept up he would be able to quit his part-time job, become super rich and famous, move to a private island, and never see a hockey jersey ever again.

Ryan was pretty sure he had an ugly dick.

The guy jacking off on Ryan's laptop screen right now had a great-looking dick. It was long and straight and not too thick. It was all smooth and cut, with perfectly hairless balls. The shaft jutted proudly out of a tidy patch of dark curls.

Ryan's dick was thick and red, and the hair that surrounded it was even more red. He tried to keep on top of grooming the area, but his pubic hair was as unruly as the hair that covered his head and face. His balls seemed too large and kind of saggy. His dick poked out of a lumpy sleeve of foreskin. The head was fat and dark, and a very prominent vein wrapped around his shaft.

And, unlike the dude in the video he was watching, Ryan took forever to come. He had always been a little slow at sex, but getting off had taken a lot of extra effort the past year or so. He knew it was at least partially the fault of his anxiety meds.

Ryan closed his eyes, blocking out the image of Mr. Perfect Dick, but not the man's happy moans. Ryan took a slow breath—in and out—then looked down at his dick.

"All right, buddy. We can do this. No pressure, just whenever you're ready. But let's try to get there this time, okay?"

He went easy on it, stroking himself with loose fingers and a lot of lube. Sex these days, even with himself, required a lot of patience. For this reason, he rarely dragged anyone else into the ordeal.

The guy on the screen was having a lovely time, swearing and gasping and promising a huge load very soon. "Show off,"

Ryan muttered. He started scrolling through the recommended videos that were listed under this one because he knew he was going to need another.

He wasn't even sure what he was looking for. He liked jerk-off videos because he could kind of pretend he was sharing an experience with someone. He could pretend he was the one making the beautiful man on his computer screen moan with pleasure.

Instead he was alone in his apartment, offering encouraging words to his barely interested dick.

Why couldn't he do this? He was horny as fuck, that was for sure. He hadn't been with anyone for months. He hadn't come for over two weeks. The situation was getting desperate.

"Just one little orgasm, buddy. How 'bout it?"

It felt nice, stroking himself like this. It certainly didn't feel *bad*. He could keep this up for a long time and just enjoy the ripples of pleasure that never fully crested—and he often did just that, stroking himself for an hour or more without getting off. It was frustrating, though, and this time he was determined to come.

"Oh shit," the video guy gasped. "Oh fuck, I'm gonna come I'm gonna come . . ."

And then he did. The asshole.

"You know what?" Ryan snapped at his dick. "I'm calling the shots today. I'm going to put on another video, and we're both gonna watch it and I'm gonna start from scratch. I'll go slow, but we are fucking coming tonight."

It's not like coming was impossible, but he needed to be relaxed. He couldn't be distracted at all, but he also couldn't be overly focused. The circumstances needed to be exactly right—everything lined up like the perfect shot at an open net. If he could find that sweet spot, he could achieve orgasm. But it was a tall fucking order.

It was time to bring out the big guns. He went to his favorites folder and brought up a video of a porn star that he particularly liked named Kamil Kock. He was small and slim and a bit femme, with an elaborate peacock feather design tattooed down the left side of his torso. He had gorgeous dark eyes and light brown skin. Ryan had a lot of his videos saved.

"Look," he said to his dick, "it's Kamil. We love Kamil."

His dick gave a halfhearted twitch. It was something.

Ryan spent the next twenty-seven minutes watching Kamil Kock pleasure his lean, elegant body while Ryan punished his own. Kamil had a musical lilt to his voice, and his long, slender fingers were covered in elaborate rings. He was beautiful in a way that Ryan never could be.

Ryan had a type, no question. He liked men who . . . blurred the line, a little. He found androgyny very sexy, and it wasn't just the physical beauty of a dazzling, decorated man that attracted him; he was in awe of their *confidence*. Of their bravery to openly be themselves and *dare* anyone to say anything about it. It turned Ryan on like nothing else.

He had been quietly out for years, which meant he didn't actively hide his sexuality, but he didn't talk about it either. Chatting online and hooking up in various cities had been Ryan's go-to method of getting laid for most of his hockey career. His teammates didn't ask him many questions about who he was hooking up with because they likely didn't care. Playing for a different team every season had made it difficult for Ryan to form any close bonds with his teammates anyway.

And that's how Ryan had flown under the radar as a sexually active gay NHL player for nearly a decade. And now, in this new era where Scott Hunter was kissing his boyfriend on live television after winning the Stanley Cup, it didn't seem as necessary to hide. Hunter had been brave enough to come out first, and now being a queer NHL player was barely interesting. One of Vancouver's goaltenders married his longtime boyfriend over the summer—a rugged older man who built cabins for a living. And a Swedish guy who played for Los Angeles had started posting photos on Instagram of him and his boyfriend, who was a model. Or an Instagram model. Or something. He was a ripped hot guy anyway.

One thing Ryan had noticed about the boyfriends of NHL players: they were all very *masculine*. Scott Hunter's boyfriend was cute, but he wasn't what Ryan would call a twink. And twink wasn't even an accurate description for what Ryan was into.

So maybe it was suddenly acceptable for an NHL player to have a boyfriend, but Ryan suspected that hockey players were expected to have a certain *type* of boyfriend. And while Ryan mostly didn't care what other people thought—he didn't even *have* an Instagram account—he really didn't want to have to explain his choices.

His other problem was that he was fucking *shy* around beautiful men. He couldn't imagine they would want to look at him, let alone touch him, so he rarely pulled the kind of men he actually wanted. He settled for men who he felt were more in his league.

There had been one guy in New Jersey—a stunning young man named Anthony—who had been surprisingly hot for Ryan. He'd seemed to love Ryan's size, and his strength, so they were a good match for a little while. But he'd wanted Ryan to hurt him during sex. Not actually injure him, but he'd wanted pain, and Ryan couldn't give it to him. Ryan spent too much of his life causing physical pain to others, and the thought of bringing that into the bedroom made him sick.

So that had been it for Ryan and Anthony.

He hoped Anthony had found what he needed with someone else. Someone who didn't have Ryan's mountain of baggage.

Ryan realized that he had zoned out, and was just blankly staring at the screen where Kamil was teasing his asshole with a vibrator. Ryan's hand was loosely holding his softening dick, unmoving.

Damn it. He'd gotten distracted. It was over.

He released his dick and it slumped, exhausted, against his thigh.

He closed the video and slammed his laptop shut. *Stupid fucking meds. Stupid fucking anxiety. Stupid fucking porn stars and their perfect functional dicks.*

He scrubbed his hand over his face. What a fucking catch he was. He'd taken down his Grindr profile a few months ago, and now wondered if he should reactivate it. Maybe provide an updated description: *Looking for a disappointing time with a shaggy oaf who probably won't come even if you blow him for an hour?*

Fuck it. Ryan needed to go to sleep.

"We're trying this again tomorrow night," he warned his dick. "You, me, and Kamil. We're gonna do this thing."

His dick seemed to actually retreat *farther* into his foreskin.

"I should chop you off, all the good you do me," Ryan grumbled.

CHAPTER TWO

Fabian wondered if he could pull off the Stila Enchantress Glitter & Glow liquid eye shadow. It was really fucking pretty.

He brushed a little of the tester on the back of his hand.

So pretty.

He tilted his hand under the florescent lights of the store and watched the eye shadow shimmer. The color really worked with his olive skin.

He set the tester bottle back on the shelf and returned to his stool behind the cosmetics counter. He perched himself on the edge and swivelled back and forth, bored out of his mind. There were only forty minutes left in his night shift at the Savers Drug Mart, but the store had been mostly dead for the past hour and Fabian was beyond ready to go home.

He checked his own makeup in the mirror that sat on the desk in front of him. Everything was still totally on point. He'd done a particularly good job on his liquid liner today.

He was, he supposed, grateful he had a job that allowed him to wear some pretty wild and experimental makeup looks to work. He wore a black button-up shirt and black pants—

the uniform for all Savers beauty department employees—but he could get creative with his face. The job was far from glamorous—it wasn't even *mall cosmetics store* glamorous—but there were jobs that would have been far more soul-crushing. At least here he could be himself.

The automatic sliding doors opened, and Fabian glanced up. It was his job to warmly greet as many customers as he could when they entered the store, but he had a feeling this guy wasn't here to buy cosmetics. He was an enormous man, with a full bushy beard and long red hair sticking out from under his gray toque. He looked like an autumnal Santa.

"Good evening," Fabian said cheerfully. The man looked startled, and glanced around until his eyes landed on Fabian. "Can I help you fi—?"

Holy. Shit.

"Ryan?" Fabian blurted the name out before he could stop himself. Even if it *was* Ryan Price, it's not like he would recognize Fabian. Probably wouldn't even remember him.

The man who was possibly Ryan Price stared at Fabian, his mouth hanging open and his eyes wide. "Yeah?" he said finally.

"Sorry," Fabian said quickly. "You probably don't recognize me at all. It's—"

"Fabian," Ryan said, barely above a whisper.

Fabian beamed. "You remember!"

Ryan nodded. "Fabian," he said again.

Fabian walked out from behind the counter and stopped a couple of feet in front of Ryan. Ryan didn't move at all.

Ryan. Fucking. Price.

"Look at you," Fabian said. "You look . . . humongous."

He was even taller than Fabian remembered. Obviously he probably had grown since he was seventeen, but so had Fabian. Sort of. Fabian still had to be a foot shorter than Ryan. And the beard—his whole look, really—gave Ryan a rugged biker/ Viking vibe. When Fabian had last seen him, his red hair had been short and his face had been smooth.

Ryan's face finally relaxed into a shy smile. "I almost didn't recognize you," he said quietly. It then occurred to Fabian that Ryan might be a little weirded out by his (flawless) eye liner and shadow. The thought alone, whether warranted or not, made Fabian stand a little straighter, daring Ryan to say anything about it.

But all Ryan said was, "You look good."

Oh.

Fabian relaxed his shoulders, since it seemed there wouldn't be a fight, and said, "So what brings Ryan Price to Toronto?"

Ryan's smile widened, and his eyes grew warmer. "Hockey. I play for the Guardians."

Well, that's embarrassing. "I probably should have known that," Fabian said. "Sorry. I'm still not a hockey fan, I'm afraid."

Ryan laughed. "S'okay." For a moment, they just stood in awkward silence, and then he said, "You still play music?"

Fabian lit up. "Oh yes. This," he gestured at the store around him, "is just my side hustle. Music is my main thing."

"Like . . . your own songs? Songs you wrote?"

"Mostly, yes."

"That's awesome! Do you play shows?"

"I do. I play here in the Village a lot. But all over town. Sometimes in other cities. I have a show at the Lighthouse next Saturday."

Ryan frowned. "There's a lighthouse here?"

Oh no. Ryan Price is still adorable. "No," Fabian laughed. "It's a bar, just in the neighborhood here."

"Oh." Ryan's face turned pink. "Yeah, that makes more sense."

"Yes. The show is a fundraiser for a shelter, and it's a big venue. It should be good."

"Oh. Cool." Ryan looked at the floor. Then up at Fabian. Then behind him. "Uh, I have to pick up a prescription, so . . ."

"Right! Don't let me stop you!"

"Yeah. So, um . . . it was nice seeing you again."

"You too. And congratulations? For playing for the Guardians? I understand that is a very big deal."

That earned Fabian another warm smile. "Thanks." Then Ryan turned and headed for the back of the store.

Fabian hugged himself because suddenly he felt very exposed and weird. He hadn't expected to ever see Ryan again, but suddenly he was transported right back to being seventeen with a confusing and ridiculous crush on the hockey player who had lived with his family for less than a year.

Fabian's parents had housed members of the Halifax Breakers junior hockey team for years. Young Fabian had always resented it, and had actively avoided interacting with the obnoxious jocks who'd invaded his home every winter. To be fair, the hockey players hadn't seemed at all interested in Fabian either.

Except Ryan.

Ryan had been different, and it had completely thrown Fabian off balance. Teenage Fabian had been all thorns, unable to hide his queerness, so he'd guarded himself by being a self-important grouch. Mostly, he'd just kept to himself, practiced his music, and dismissed anyone who'd tried to talk to him. A big dumb hockey player couldn't hurt him if Fabian didn't give a shit about him.

Which was why Ryan had been so fucking dangerous.

Ryan, who was *in Fabian's store right now.*

Something occurred to Fabian: if Ryan was picking up a

prescription at this pharmacy, it meant he probably lived in the neighborhood, which was not only where Fabian lived, but it was also Canada's largest queer village.

Which didn't necessarily mean anything. But it was interesting. Maybe.

Fabian spotted Ryan as he was leaving the store, a small paper bag in hand. Just as he was about to step through the doors, Ryan paused and looked over at Fabian. Ryan gave him a bashful little smile and a wave, and then he was gone.

CHAPTER THREE

Ryan looked straight ahead as he entered the plane. He did *not* look at the bolts on the aircraft's exterior, or the intricate mechanics visible around the open door. He didn't think about how crucial it was for *every single one* of those bolts and wires and thin plates of metal to stay together; that the slightest malfunction could cause the fiery death of everyone on board.

Ryan couldn't think about any of that. Instead, he ran through his usual preflight list of sensible, calming thoughts.

Millions of people fly every day without issue.

This plane has probably taken off, flown, and landed hundreds, if not thousands, of times without issue.

The pilot wouldn't fly this plane if it weren't safe.

The flight attendants are calm and happy and smiling. This is their job every day.

Your teammates are calm.

Flying is safer than driving.

Ryan knew all of these things were true, but he couldn't stop the intense dread that gripped him every time he boarded an airplane. He couldn't stop thinking that he was the only one who *knew* everyone on board was doomed. That they all needed to get off this plane *right now* because *couldn't everyone see how dangerous this was?*

Ryan exhaled as he squeezed his large body along the narrow aisle. His suit felt too tight. Why did they have to wear suits on these plane trips? He tugged at his necktie as he searched around for an empty aisle seat.

"Pricey!"

Ryan looked toward the back of the plane and saw Wyatt Hayes waving at him from behind a seat. Ryan nodded in response, and moved toward him.

"How ya doing?" Wyatt's tone was cheerful. Definitely not a man who was worried about dying today.

"Good as always, I guess," Ryan said. He set his backpack on the seat next to Wyatt and opened it. He rummaged around and pulled out a crisp new paperback novel by one of his favorite authors, a small bottle of Tums, and a battered copy of *Anne of Green Gables*. He stuffed the items, along with his phone, into the seat pocket in front of him, shoved the backpack under the seat, and sat down.

"That's why I like sitting with you, Pricey," Wyatt said. "You're a reader." He gestured to his own seat pocket, where Ryan could see the top of a thick graphic novel sticking out. Wyatt loved comic books and superheroes. Ryan didn't know anything about them. Maybe Ryan could ask Wyatt for entry-level comic book recommendations. That would be a friendly thing to do . . .

"Should be a smooth flight. I was looking at the weather between here and Nashville." Wyatt said this conversationally, but Ryan knew he was doing his best to help. Maybe it was because he was Toronto's backup goalie and spent more time watching games than playing them, but Wyatt was remarkably observant and considerate. Ryan nodded in response. He wished he could find comfort in Wyatt's weather report, but there was really nothing that would make his brain calm down. His anxiety meds helped a bit, and were probably what was keeping him from running screaming off the plane right now, but no amount of common sense would make him stop imagining worst-case scenarios.

It's a short flight. You'll be in Nashville before you know it.

Ryan longed for the days when NHL teams traveled mostly by bus. When he'd played junior hockey, all travel had been by bus. He knew he was in the minority, but he would take a fifteen-hour bus ride over a two-hour flight any day.

He removed his phone from the seat pocket and sent a text to his sister, as he did before every flight. He told himself it was only because he liked hearing from her and *not* because he worried he may never see her again.

RYAN:
Heading to Nashville.

COLLEEN:
Who are you sitting with?

Ryan glanced over at Wyatt, who was pulling down the window shade in a gesture that was almost certainly for Ryan's benefit.

RYAN:
Wyatt Hayes

COLLEEN:
He's cute! You should date him!

Ryan flushed and angled his phone so Wyatt definitely wouldn't be able to see the screen.

RYAN:
Straight. Married. And shut up.

COLLEEN:
Aw. He's cute, though, right?

Ryan stole another glance at Wyatt, who caught his eye and grinned at him, all dimples and blond curls. He was attractive, no question, but . . .

RYAN:
Not my type.

Wyatt wasn't the one who Ryan couldn't stop thinking about. It had taken a long time and a lot of distance for Ryan to almost forget about Fabian Salah. And now a chance reunion in a Toronto pharmacy, over thirteen years later, had opened a floodgate of memories.

Even as a teenager, Fabian had been stunning—far from macho, and even farther from apologizing for it. He'd always been short, and couldn't have weighed more than a hundred and twenty-five pounds at the time, but Ryan had been thoroughly intimidated by him.

He had also been thoroughly *infatuated* with him.

A flight attendant was shutting and locking the plane door. Ryan's stomach clenched. He sent another text to his sister. Taking off soon. Gotta go.

COLLEEN:
Do you have Anne with you?

Ryan smiled, and touched his fingers to the frayed edges of his ancient copy of *Anne of Green Gables*.

RYAN:
Always.

COLLEEN:
Then you're safe.

RYAN:
I know. Thanks.

COLLEEN:
Love you. Text me when you land.

RYAN:
Ok. Love you.

He tucked his phone into the seat pocket so he didn't risk crushing it in his hand during takeoff. Thank god for Colleen. His sister was only three years younger than him, and they'd been thick as thieves growing up together in a town of less than two thousand people. Leaving her behind had been one of the hardest parts of turning pro.

The plane began to move, and Ryan gripped the armrests. He closed his eyes, and went through his breathing exercises. *It's fine. Everything is fine.*

When he opened his eyes, he could see the grinning, idiotic faces of Dallas Kent and Troy Barrett peering at him from around their aisle seats. As soon as he caught their eyes, they started laughing. Even though several rows divided them from him, Ryan could hear Dallas say something like "He looks like he's going to have a heart attack."

Assholes.

"Hey," said Wyatt, who probably guessed what was happening. "Did you ever play for Nashville? I forget."

"No," said Ryan. "Haven't played for any Western teams."

"Ah. I thought I was going to be drafted by Nashville. My agent thought it was going to happen. But then . . . Toronto."

"Were you disappointed?"

Wyatt grinned. "A little. But then I met Lisa in Toronto, so it all worked out."

Ryan had only met Wyatt's wife, a doctor, once, at a team dinner. She and Wyatt had met when Wyatt had been in the hospital with a broken collarbone. Ryan wasn't surprised that he had managed to charm her in such a short time.

"Not that I ever get to see her," Wyatt added. "The only thing worse than marrying a hockey player is marrying a doctor. Don't do it."

"Okay." Since Ryan hadn't even been on a *date* in over a year, it definitely wasn't a problem he was worried about.

The plane turned, and then stopped, and Ryan knew they were about to take off. He hated this part. He hated all the parts, but he *really* hated this part.

"You can tell me to shut up if you want," Wyatt said, "but does it help if I talk right now?"

"Yeah," Ryan gritted out. "Keep talking."

"You should come with me next time I visit the center." Wyatt was a regular visitor to a community center in a low-income area of Toronto. He would hang out with the kids, playing floor hockey and distributing Toronto Guardians merchandise.

"You really think kids would be excited to meet me?" Ryan asked dubiously.

"Sure. Why not?"

"Wouldn't they rather meet Kent? Or Barrett?" Ryan nodded his head in the direction of the two jerkoffs who also happened to be NHL All-Stars.

"I don't think those shitheads should be allowed within a hundred yards of children. Or anyone. Bad influences."

The plane's engine roared to life and jolted forward, and Ryan shut his eyes and listed NHL teams alphabetically in his head. In seconds, he knew, this would be over. He just needed to get through it.

"I mean, they've mostly been getting visits from the backup goalie, so I'm sure a defenseman who plays actual minutes would be exciting for them," Wyatt continued, politely ignoring Ryan's increased state of distress. "Plus, you're enormous. Kids love that."

Ryan grimaced, but forced himself to reply. "Kids are scared of me."

"Nah. You're like Chewbacca. They'll love you."

By some miracle, Ryan actually laughed while being on a plane during takeoff. "Thanks a lot."

Wyatt kept talking, telling him about some of the kids he'd met during his visits. Ryan didn't respond much, but he listened intently. After a few minutes of Ryan listening silently with his eyes squeezed shut, Wyatt said, "I think we've leveled off, by the way."

Ryan opened one eye, and then the other. It always astonished him how calm everyone around him seemed on a plane. His teammates were just chatting and joking around, or putting on headphones, or flipping down their tables to play cards. Some were asleep. Ryan couldn't even fathom being relaxed enough to *sleep* on a plane.

"We made it!" Wyatt smiled at him.

"Great," Ryan said tightly. *Nothing to worry about when you're forty thousand feet in the air.*

Wyatt shook his head. "I can't believe you put yourself through this. Is it always this bad?"

Sometimes it's worse. "Yeah. It is."

"There isn't a pill or something you can take?"

"I do take something. Sort of." Ryan didn't really feel like getting into the details of his anxiety meds or therapy. No point in weirding out the one guy on the team who seemed to enjoy talking to him. He decided to change the subject. "What are you reading?"

Wyatt hauled his colorful book out of the seat pocket. "It's a collection of Jack Kirby's *Mister Miracle* comics. It was a series that spun out of his *Fourth World* comics for DC. Amazing stuff."

Ryan had never heard of Jack Kirby, Mister Miracle, or the Fourth World, so he just nodded.

"If you ever want to borrow any books, let me know. My collection is pretty ridiculous at this point. Our basement is basically my comic lounge now. You should come over and see it some time."

"Sure, yeah. That would be cool." It would probably also never happen, but Ryan didn't say that.

"Did you move into your new place yet?"

"Yeah. I still need to buy furniture for most of the rooms, but I'm in."

"Cool. Apartment, right? Downtown?"

"Yep." Ryan knew he could be doing a better job with the back and forth of this conversation, but he didn't want to tell Wyatt where his apartment building was. Not that living in a sky-rise in the heart of Toronto's Gay Village meant anything necessarily—it was a downtown neighborhood with expensive properties where lots of different people lived—but Ryan knew for sure that none of his teammates lived there, so his address might raise questions. And Ryan did not like answering questions.

The plane hit a bump and he gripped the armrests. *Normal. This is all normal. Like a bump in the road. Like waves under your uncle's boat. You're safe.*

He tried to imagine that for a while, that he was on a boat instead of a plane. He'd grown up on boats back in Ross Harbour, Nova Scotia. His mother's father and brothers were all lobster fishermen, and almost everyone in the small village owned some sort of boat. Boats comforted Ryan, even though they were probably statistically more dangerous than planes.

Thinking about boats made Ryan's brain call up one of his favorite memories: a chilly April night, standing close enough to Fabian that their arms brushed as both boys leaned on the railing of the Halifax-Dartmouth ferry and watched a giant container ship pass in front them. Its massive hull had blacked out the lights of the city across the harbor, and Ryan had said something embarrassing about feeling small. Fabian had said *something* back, but Ryan could only remember the way Fabian had smiled up at him.

That smile.

It had been so sweet and shy. Ryan didn't know—would never know—if he'd imagined the invitation in Fabian's eyes. If they had actually moved closer together. If Fabian had tilted his head slightly, and parted his lips . . .

When Ryan opened his eyes, he could see Kent and Barrett were grinning at him again. They turned back around as soon as he met their eyes, because they were both fucking cowards.

Ryan pulled his book out of his seat pocket, determined to ignore his idiot teammates, and to stop daydreaming about Fabian.

And Fabian's eye makeup.

Ryan had not been at all prepared to see Fabian with his eyes painted like that—jade-green shadow and black winged liner that made the dark brown eyes and long lashes that had enchanted Ryan as a teenager even more striking. It was an image he wasn't going to be forgetting anytime soon.

God, he'd looked good.

He wasn't much taller than he'd been as a teenager, but his jaw was sharper, his chest and shoulders broader. He was still very slim, but it was a *man's* body. When Fabian had crossed his arms over his chest, Ryan could make out the slight bulge of lean muscle in his arms.

Nope. Stop thinking about Fabian.

Fabian, the first boy he'd *almost* kissed.

The first boy he'd desperately *wanted* to kiss.

Fabian had mentioned a show he was playing. At a place called the Lighthouse? Ryan was pretty sure he'd said it was next Saturday. Ryan was playing a game in Toronto that night, but maybe it would be over early enough that he could check out Fabian's show.

But Ryan couldn't go to *that*, could he? It's not like Fabian had invited him. It would be weird if Ryan showed up. What would he even say? *Hi, it's me. The guy you were probably just being polite to in the drugstore the other night. I'm stalking you now.*

Nope. Absolutely not.

But he did say it was a fundraiser. Maybe Ryan should go. As a good and charitable citizen. That wouldn't be weird. Right?

Good god. Ryan was losing his mind. And that certainly wasn't something he could afford to do. Not again.

CHAPTER FOUR

Fabian blinked awake and had to stifle a groan when he saw who he was snuggled up against.

All of the events of the previous evening came flooding back. Fabian having a wonderful time at Ian's Halloween party. Fabian running into *Claude* at the party. Claude looking so fucking good in a slim-cut dark denim shirt and tight black jeans, because Claude was too cool for costumes. Claude's breath tickling Fabian's ear when he leaned in to tell him how much he missed him, his Québécois accent sounding a whole lot less ridiculous than when Tarek did his impression of it. Fabian's hand slipping into Claude's, as if he had no control over it.

And then Claude coming home with him, back to the apartment that, while shitty, Fabian didn't have to share with anyone. He often felt that Claude mostly liked him because he had a place to himself. They'd made out forever on Fabian's bed, and Claude had told him that he missed him. In the moment, that had sounded great. It had sounded great again later when Claude had been fucking him.

But now . . .

Fabian shifted carefully away from Claude, not wanting to

wake him. Or maybe he *should* wake him so Claude would *leave*.

Fabian studied Claude's face. When he was sleeping instead of talking, Claude was . . .

Oh god, he was pretty. His silky brown hair was covering the eye that wasn't hidden by the pillow, and his full lips were parted. Claude's lips were . . . well, they were distracting.

He had an artist's body, slim to the point of almost appearing malnourished. His skin was pale, like a young, sexy vampire. And he may as well have been one because Fabian certainly seemed to be ensnared by him.

Fabian grabbed his phone from the nightstand. The screen was full of missed texts from Vanessa.

I saw you leave the party with Claude.

Did you go home with Claude???

DID YOU SLEEP WITH CLAUDE???

FABIAN! ARE YOU HAVING SEX WITH CLAUDE RIGHT NOW???

Stop having sex with Claude, Fabian. Right now.

Goddammit.

We are TALKING ABOUT THIS at Bargain Brunch. Don't bring Claude.

Fine. You can bring him. But he's not allowed to talk. Make this CLEAR.

Fabian snorted at that last one, which caused Claude to stir awake.

"Fuck," Claude croaked. "What time is it?"

"Nine thirty," Fabian said.

Claude made a face like the hour of nine o'clock was the grossest thing in the world. Fabian wanted him gone. He wanted to erase this entire bad decision.

"It's Bargain Brunch day," Fabian said. "You can come if you want."

"*God* no."

"Well, I'm leaving soon, so . . ."

"*Fine*." Claude made a whole production of hauling himself out of bed and into the bathroom. When he came back, he started aggressively searching for his clothes. "Fuck, where are my smokes?"

"I don't know, but you're not smoking them in here."

Claude snatched his jeans off the floor. "I *know*." He glanced around. "I had a jacket."

"On the chair," Fabian said helpfully. He wanted Claude to leave so he could take a shower. He was more than ready to wash the sins—and residual glitter—of last night away.

Claude stopped grumpily throwing his clothes on and reached for Fabian. Fabian sighed, and stepped into his embrace. "We can keep doing this," Claude said in that infuriatingly sexy voice. "It can just be casual."

"I *can't* keep doing this," Fabian said. "It isn't what I want. We have to stop."

"You say that, but . . ."

He shook his head. "I mean it. I'll see you around, all right?"

Claude stepped back, and gave him an obnoxious, knowing grin. "I am sure you will."

Fabian cursed himself after Claude shut the door behind him. He had *finally* broken things off for good with Claude, and then he'd run into Ryan goddamned Price of all fucking people. Like, what the fuck, universe? *Hi, Fabian. Remember that hockey player you were obsessed with when you were seventeen? Well, here he is! And he's a giant, sexy lumberjack wet dream now!*

Not that seeing Ryan had anything to do with sleeping with Claude again.

Okay, Fabian pledged to himself as he stepped into the dingy shower stall, *no more Claude. No more thinking about Ryan Price. Just music, and normal, healthy things from now on.*

Fabian's friends had a semi-regular Sunday tradition that they affectionately called Bargain Brunch. The three major components were: frozen waffles, cheap skin masks from the drugstore, and gossip. Everyone brought a topping that they thought would elevate the frozen waffles to haute cuisine. After the week Fabian had been having, friends and facials were exactly what the doctor ordered.

He hit the buzzer on the door to an apartment that was next to the door for a vape shop and heard footsteps bounding down the stairs immediately. When the door opened, he was greeted by a very enthusiastic Vanessa.

"Fabian! Yay!" she said, and threw her arms around him.

Fabian laughed and hugged her back. "Miss me since last night?"

"You smell like Claude."

"Fuck off. No I don't."

"You do. You smell like cigarettes and condescension."

"Shut up."

Bargain Brunch was hosted by Vanessa, Marcus, and Tarek, who lived platonically together in a two-bedroom apartment they had converted into a three-bedroom apartment. *Converted* was perhaps too fancy a word for it: the living room was also Marcus's bedroom. Vanessa led Fabian up the stairs and through the front door that opened directly into the living room/Marcus's bedroom. Fabian slid his backpack off as he made his way to the futon where Marcus and Tarek were both sitting already.

"What did you bring?" Tarek asked.

"Pears."

"And . . ."

Fabian pulled four thin packets out of his backpack. "Face masks! I have clay, avocado, sea kelp, and, uh . . . oh, grapefruit." He spread them out on the coffee table like playing cards.

"What does sea kelp do?" Marcus asked.

"Moisturizes, nutrifies, and makes you glow like Zendaya," Fabian said, with all the authority of someone who worked in the cosmetics section of a Savers Drug Mart.

"Sold." Marcus leaned forward and snatched the sea kelp mask. He really didn't need any help glowing; his dark skin was flawless.

Vanessa emerged from the kitchenette with four mugs, which she lined up on the coffee table. Marcus jumped up and went to the fridge to retrieve a container of orange juice, and a chilled bottle of Baby Duck Canadian "champagne."

"The kettle is boiling for tea and coffee," Vanessa said. She dropped into the worn-out armchair opposite the futon, draping one leg over the arm. "Mimosa me, Marcus."

Marcus carefully filled the mugs with Baby Duck and orange juice, and distributed them. Fabian had barely taken a sip before Vanessa said, "I can't believe you fucked Claude again."

Fabian narrowed his eyes at her. "Moment of weakness," he grumbled.

"I thought he was moving back to Montreal," Tarek said.

"Well, he hasn't yet. Obviously. And every time I see him I just . . . forget why he sucks."

"I could make you a list," Vanessa offered helpfully. "And you could carry it around with you."

"That's okay."

"One!" she said, ignoring him. "He has absolutely no interest in you or anything you do."

"He . . . is interested in me. Sometimes."

"Two," Marcus piped up. "He hates Bargain Brunch."

Fabian pressed his lips together to keep himself from smiling.

"Three," said Tarek. "He's a snob."

"All right, I get it."

"Four." Marcus again. "He is a filmmaker who is bad at making films."

Fabian had to swallow his sip of mimosa quickly to stop himself from doing a spit-take.

"Five," Vanessa said. "He complains when food isn't organic, but he smokes cigarettes."

Fabian was laughing now. He couldn't help it. "Shut up. I know he's awful, all right? He's just . . . there. And I kind of needed someone last night."

Vanessa stopped teasing him. "What's wrong, babe?"

"Nothing really. I'm just burnt out, a little. I took some extra shifts at the drugstore this week, and I've been trying to finish some new songs. And get ready for the fundraiser show I'm doing this Saturday."

"Oh, right! I'll be there for sure," Vanessa said. "I don't work on Saturday at all!" She worked at a very cool lesbian-owned sex toy store in the Village, only a couple of blocks away from her apartment.

"I'm working that night," Marcus said. "Sorry." That was no surprise; he was a bartender at Force, the biggest gay nightclub in town.

"No problem."

"I can go," Tarek said. He was the only one of the four of them who had a nine-to-five job. He worked as an office assistant for an immigration services organization.

"Cool. It's a good lineup."

"Yeah, but *you're* the one I'm going to see," Tarek said.

"He's the one *everyone* is going to see," Vanessa said.

"As if," Fabian said. He took a sip of mimosa from his tacky Niagara Falls souvenir mug. "I think I might debut a new song at the show."

"Yay!" Vanessa said. "Oh my god, is it *so beautiful*? Am I going to cry?"

"Probably."

"I'm totally going to cry. I still cry whenever you play 'Ravine.'"

"That song is eight years old, Van."

"Every. Time."

Later, after their waffles were eaten, and the Baby Duck bottle was empty, the four friends lounged around with skin masks on their faces.

"I know I ask this every week," Tarek said, "but is it supposed to burn this much?"

"Yes," Fabian said. "It burns because your face sucks. It has to work extra hard to fix it."

Tarek flipped him off.

"Oh!" Vanessa said suddenly. "I have something for you, Fabian." She grabbed her messenger bag from the floor. It was covered in patches and buttons that loudly identified her as the queer, sex-positive feminist that she was.

"Does it vibrate?" As well as working at a sex shop, Vanessa also had a reasonably popular sex toy review blog. It wasn't unusual for her coerce her friends into being product testers.

"Honey, it does so much more than that." She produced a shiny purple box from her bag and handed it to him. "Be sure to tell me what you think."

"Do I have to?" Fabian peeled his mask off, crumpled it into a ball, and set it on his empty waffle plate.

"Come on. I don't have time to review *all* of these toys myself! And it's not like I have a prostate!"

"You get bullet points," he said. "If I even use the thing."

"You'll use it. It does all the stuff. And it's purple!"

"Does that . . . make it better?"

"It makes it *cuter*. Be a better lover than Claude, probably."

Fabian glared at her.

"More pleasant to talk to, for sure," she added, grinning. "Better Instagram posts."

"*Anyway*," Fabian said, desperate to change the subject to anything else. "How was work last night, Marcus?"

He rolled his eyes dramatically. "Exhausting. I hate it when Halloween is a Thursday because it turns it into a week-long festival. The club was packed with barely legal kids in devil horns being sloppy all over the place. I was so done when we finally closed I couldn't even be bothered to go home with the Cillian Murphy-looking guy who'd been flirting with me all night."

"Tragic," Fabian said.

"No one looks like Cillian Murphy except Cillian Murphy, but okay," added Tarek.

"He was hot, he was into me, I turned him down." Marcus glowered at them. "Now I'm eating waffles with you assholes instead of sharing a morning shower with Cillian-light."

"Mm," Tarek said. "I was going to fuck Nick Jonas last night but I didn't want to."

"Fuck. You," Marcus said. But he was laughing.

Fabian *almost* mentioned running into Ryan to his friends, but it was too confusing to explain and too insignificant to bother with. He'd run into someone he hadn't seen in over a decade, and now he would probably never see him again. The end.

It's not like he'd been thinking about Ryan since running into him. It's not like he had been secretly looking for him whenever he was walking around the Village.

God. Enough. Ryan was a *hockey player.* He wore one of those blue jerseys Fabian hated so much to *work.* And Fabian didn't need any distractions right now, no matter how tall they were, or how adorable their smile was.

So he thanked his friends for yet another lovely time, grabbed his bag—now heavier, thanks to the dildo—and headed home to hopefully lose himself in music.

And, he supposed, if he got bored, he had a new toy to play with.

CHAPTER FIVE

Ryan wrapped his hand around the other man's arm, pulling him close in a firm grip. He dipped his head, and brought his lips close to the man's ear.

"You sure you wanna do this, kid?"

When Ryan pulled back, he could see the fear in the young man's eyes. Hell, he could *smell* it coming off him in waves.

"F-fuck you," the man spat out.

So Ryan punched him across the jaw. And the crowd went wild.

Ryan had hoped the one punch would do the trick, and the younger player would fall to the ice. Then the refs could step in and break it up, the kid would get to say he fought Ryan Price, and Ryan wouldn't have to hurt this rookie too badly.

But the kid didn't go down. Instead, he pulled back his right fist and hit Ryan in the shoulder, which probably hadn't been where he'd been aiming, because Ryan could hear his knuckles cracking against the hard plastic of his shoulder pad.

The kid—a twenty-two-year-old rookie for Minnesota named Corkum—stared in horror at his own fist for a second, and then turned his wide eyes to Ryan's face. Ryan sort of shrugged and gave him an apologetic look before landing a second punch to the right side of his face.

This time, Corkum hit the ice. Ryan made a show of covering him with his much larger body and pulling his arm back as if he might hit him again. He wouldn't—the kid was turtling now, and Ryan would never hit a guy in that position—but he wanted to get the ref's attention.

It worked. In a moment, one of the linesmen was roughly hauling Ryan off of Corkum. The crowd was chanting now as Ryan was ushered to the penalty box.

"Pay. The. Price."

Ryan hated that chant. Truly, and deeply despised it. It had followed him from his junior hockey days to the eight different NHL teams he had played for, and now to his ninth team.

"Pay. The. Price."

He settled into the box, took his helmet off, and shook out his long, sweaty hair.

"I was starting to miss you," the penalty box attendant joked. Gerald was in his sixties, and chattier than most of the attendants around the league. Ryan would know; he was very familiar with them.

"You're going to be expecting a proposal soon, I'll bet," Ryan said. "All this time alone together."

Gerald laughed, but Ryan found himself wondering how many hours of his own life had been spent in penalty boxes. How many days, if he added up all the two-minute and five-minute intervals.

Well, less than Gerald. Maybe.

When the crowd had settled down, and the play was underway, Ryan heard Corkum yelling at him from his own penalty box. "Hey, Price!"

"Yeah?"

"Thanks!" Corkum was *beaming*, and flushed like he'd just had the best sex of his life. Ryan snorted and shook his head.

"You made his night!" Gerald said cheerfully.

"He's an idiot," Ryan grumbled. He grabbed a water bottle and squirted it over his head, then finger-combed his damp hair, pulling it away from his face before putting his helmet back on. It wasn't unusual for young players to challenge him to fights; Ryan was known to be one of the toughest fighters in the league. A youngster could quickly earn a little respect by challenging him. It was probably Ryan's least favorite kind of fight, though. The last thing he wanted to do was truly hurt someone, so he had to concentrate on pulling his punches, and making sure they didn't land on the guy's temple or his nose or eyes. At six-foot-seven and almost two hundred and sixty pounds, Ryan was usually the biggest guy on the ice, so evenly matched fights were rare.

Ryan inspected his left hand before putting his gloves back on. He'd probably have a bit of bruising on his knuckles, but nothing serious. He was more concerned about the fact that his back had been bothering him again.

He glanced up at the clock. He doubted he'd see more ice time tonight; his team was up by two goals with a little over eight minutes left to play, and he had done his job for the night.

When the five minutes were up and play had stopped, Gerald opened the door to let Ryan out of the penalty box. He quickly made his way to the Toronto bench, where he wedged himself between his defensive line mate Marcel Houde and Wyatt.

"Good fight, Pricey," Marcel said halfheartedly when Ryan sat next to him.

"Thanks." Ryan didn't mind the lack of enthusiasm; it hadn't, truthfully, been a good fight. But fighting was all his teammates expected of him, and if he didn't get perfunctory acknowledgments for punching people, Ryan would never hear praise at all.

"Who do you think the stars will be?" Wyatt asked with a grin.

"I don't know. Maybe—"

"I mean," Wyatt continued, "obviously the first star of the game will be me, but who will the second star be?"

Ryan laughed. "You and me, buddy. One and two."

Wyatt shook his head. "I'm one, the Zamboni is two. You're three."

"I'll take it," Ryan said. The game was now into its final minute, and Ryan realized he was in a good mood. His team was going to win at home, and it would be days before he inevitably started worrying about the next flight he needed to board.

The game ended and Ryan joined his teammates on the ice in celebration. Wyatt, in his ball cap and clean, dry uniform, had launched into his usual routine. "Whoosh, that was a tough one, boys. Couldn't have done it without me! Where are we drinking?"

The celebration continued into the locker room. Ryan sat in his stall in one corner and quietly removed his gear as his teammates whooped and hollered and made plans for later that night.

It was Wyatt who thought to ask him. Of course.

"You comin' out with us?" Wyatt, who hadn't played and thus hadn't needed a shower, was already dressed in a dark gray suit, ready to leave the arena.

"Oh, uh, I think I'm gonna head home, actually. I . . ." Ryan didn't finish his sentence because he didn't want to tell Wyatt about his plans. He had decided to go to see Fabian's show that night. He had been wrestling with the idea all week, and he'd finally decided that his desire to see Fabian perform outweighed his anxiety about going out.

Thankfully, Wyatt didn't require an explanation. He wouldn't have been expecting Ryan to accept his invitation anyway. Ryan was sure of that. "See you Monday, then," Wyatt said. "Have a good day off."

"Right. Okay. You too."

Ryan needed to hurry. It was already after ten o'clock. He took the fastest shower ever, and cursed the rule about wearing suits out of the arena after games. He wouldn't have time to stop at home to change; as it was he needed to haul ass to the club and hope he hadn't missed Fabian's set entirely.

When Ryan arrived at the Lighthouse, Fabian was already onstage, but it looked like he was just setting up. The room was quite full, which was good for both the charity the concert was raising money for, and for Ryan, because he would rather Fabian didn't see him. He didn't want *anyone* to see him, really. Especially since he was wearing a full suit, which made him stick out even more than he would have anyway. Everyone in the room was dressed casually, but in a way that suggested their outfits had been carefully put together. He saw everything from button-up shirts with loud prints on them, to overalls, to plain white T-shirts and skinny jeans. Definitely no other suits, though.

He stood at the back of the dark room, mindful of his size and not wanting to block anyone's view, and watched Fabian fiddle with a complicated-looking setup that included several floor pedals, a laptop, and a keyboard. He could also see Fabian's violin case on the floor behind him. Fabian moved quickly and efficiently between each of the components, occasionally chatting with people in the audience near the stage.

Ryan saw him smile and laugh, and he was struck by how surreal it was to see him again as a beautiful and confident adult.

And that was before Fabian was even performing.

The first song started with a simple drum track that Fabian played from his laptop. To that he added layers of music from the keyboard, which he seemed to record and loop using the floor pedals. When he was satisfied with how that sounded, he would add another layer, building a wall of sound all by himself. He moved away from the laptop and keyboard, and picked up his violin, and when he stepped in front of the microphone, Ryan felt like the wind had been knocked right out of him. Fabian stood, alone, under the stage lights in a black, transparent shirt, sleek black pants, and several sparkling necklaces. He was also wearing dramatic makeup—Ryan could tell, even from the back of the room—and it all made him look like a mythical creature or an angel.

Ryan may have gasped a little when Fabian brought the bow to the violin and played the first notes. Ryan had loved listening to him devotedly practice his instrument as a teenager, and hearing it again now was bewildering. The slow, dreamy melody was recorded and looped with the pedals, and then Fabian rested the violin and its bow at his sides, one item in each hand. He turned to the mic, closed his eyes, and sang.

It was the most beautiful thing Ryan had ever heard; haunting in a way that sent sparks dancing down Ryan's spine and into his abdomen. Fabian's voice was kind of soft and high, but also clear and confident. The music could probably be called pop, but it was so complex that Ryan wasn't sure it fit any category. Fabian's lyrics were cryptic, but they were also unmistakably sexy. Ryan couldn't quite follow the story of the song, but he definitely *felt* every word.

He held his breath, not wanting to make even the faintest

sound that might compete with this perfect gift Fabian was giving the audience. Ryan couldn't believe this was actually happening in front of him and that there were people in the world who were *not* here witnessing what was surely humanity's most impressive achievement.

The song ended, the audience erupted into cheers, and Ryan, gobsmacked, nearly forgot to clap. And then he realized that was only the *first song*.

"Thank you," Fabian said quietly, as if he hadn't just done something completely amazing. "This next song is new. I haven't named it yet, but I wanted to try it out tonight, if that's all right with you."

There was scattered applause and a few whoops of appreciation. Ryan had considered, as he'd been walking to the club, just staying for a song or two, but there was no way he was going anywhere now. He stood, barely moving, for however long it took Fabian to finish his set. Thirty minutes? Forty? Ryan had no idea how much time had passed because he was transfixed. When the last song finished, Fabian sort of half bowed and blew kisses at the crowd.

The show was over, and Ryan should leave, but now he really wanted to talk to Fabian. Just to tell him how much he had enjoyed the show. Fabian hopped off the stage and Ryan lost sight of him for a while. He considered getting a beer, or maybe finding a table to sit at, now that some of the people were starting to clear out. Instead, he leaned back against the wall and stared at the floor for a few minutes, just to keep himself from obsessively scanning the crowd for Fabian.

It was probably twenty minutes later when Ryan saw Fabian standing alone next to an empty table, drinking from a bottle of water. Ryan decided this was his chance, and took a step toward him. He ran a hand quickly over his beard, hoping he looked all right.

He stopped in his tracks when he saw a man wrap his arms around Fabian. Fabian beamed at the man, and kissed him quickly on the mouth. The man was stocky, with skin slightly darker than Fabian's, and he was wearing a stylish outfit complete with dark-rimmed glasses. He was *cute*. And of course Fabian had an adorable boyfriend.

The man's hand stayed on Fabian's arm as they chatted. *Possessive*, Ryan thought. He didn't blame him. But he did hate him a little.

Jesus. What the hell gave him the right to think badly of Fabian's boyfriend? Ryan didn't know the guy. Ryan didn't know *Fabian*. Ryan needed to get out of this bar. He didn't belong here. This was why he never went anywhere. This was why he was so fucking lonely. He was about to turn away when Fabian suddenly locked eyes with him.

Shit.

Fabian's face broke into a smile, and he gently tapped the other man's arm before making his way to Ryan.

"I *thought* that was you," Fabian said. He was still smiling—a full, delighted smile that showed his teeth. Ryan realized his own mouth was just sort of hanging open, like a dead fish.

"Hi. I, um, was just—you mentioned you were playing here. Tonight. When we were talking last week. In the, um . . ."

Fabian stepped closer. "I remember. I didn't expect you to actually come."

"Sorry. I probably shouldn't have—"

"No! No, I'm glad you're here. It's . . . really sweet. Actually."

"Oh."

"I perhaps should have been clearer about the dress code." Fabian's gaze swept over Ryan's light gray suit, and his lips twisted into a teasing smile.

"I came straight from the arena. I didn't have time to change. I know I look ridiculous."

"Not at all."

For a few seconds, they stood in silence, and Ryan wanted to both run away, and to reach out and touch his fingers to Fabian's gorgeous face. Standing as close as they were, Ryan could now clearly see the artistry of his makeup; Fabian's eyelids were painted in smoky layers of black and silver, and there was an iridescent shimmery powder on his face that highlighted his sharp cheekbones.

"Did you enjoy the show?" Fabian asked.

Fuck, Ryan. How rude are you? "Holy god. Yeah, it was unreal. You are . . . really good."

Fabian pressed his lips together, then said, "Thank you."

Ryan wanted to say more, but he couldn't find the right words to describe how incredible Fabian's music had been. So instead he said, "Well, I should let you get back to—"

"Come sit with us," Fabian interrupted. "You can meet my friends. I have drink tickets. What can I get you?"

"Oh. You don't have to—"

"Come on. You can tell me some more about how great I was."

Ryan laughed at that. "Okay."

Fabian led him back to the man he'd been hugging, and kissing, and touching a few minutes ago. "This is my friend, Tarek. He lives with my other friends, Vanessa, who is here . . . *somewhere* . . . and Marcus, who isn't here because he's working tonight."

Friend. "Nice to meet you, Tarek." Ryan extended his hand. "Ryan."

Tarek's face clearly expressed that he had no idea who Ryan was, but not in a rude way. "Ryan," he repeated back as he shook his hand.

"Ryan used to live with my family," Fabian explained. "When we were both seventeen."

"Oh!" Understanding dawned on Tarek's face. "You're a hockey player!"

"Yeah." Ryan fiddled with the button on his suit jacket, and wished for the millionth time that he'd had time to change.

"Do you still play?" Tarek asked politely.

Ryan wasn't famous, exactly, but it was unusual for him to be speaking to anyone who didn't know who he was. Unusual, and kind of nice, to be meeting people who had no expectations about him. "I play for the Guardians. For now, at least. I get traded a lot." *God. Shut up, Ryan.*

"That must be tough," Tarek said, and he sounded truly sympathetic. "I moved a lot as a kid. It sucks."

Ryan nodded. "It does." He desperately tried to think of something to ask Tarek, but was spared when a woman *attacked* Fabian with the kind of hug that was normally reserved for game-winning goals.

"Fabian! That was so fucking good!"

Ryan couldn't see Fabian's reaction, because his face was covered by the woman's voluminous, curly blond hair. She turned her head to look directly at Ryan, without letting go of Fabian. "Wasn't that incredible?"

"Yeah," Ryan replied. "Amazing."

She released Fabian and turned fully to face Ryan. "Who are you?"

The question was so blunt, it startled a laugh out of him. "Uh, Ryan. Just . . . we used to, ah . . ."

"Hi, Ryan! Are you a fan of Fabian's?"

"I, um . . ."

Fabian came to his rescue. "This is Vanessa, by the way. She's kind of a *lot*."

"Definitely true," she agreed. "I like the suit."

"Oh. Thanks."

"What can I get you, Ryan?" Fabian asked, tilting his head toward the bar.

"You don't have to—"

"A beer? I'm going to guess beer."

There was a quirk to Fabian's lips that let Ryan know he was being playful. Ryan answered in kind. "You shouldn't make assumptions about people."

Vanessa punched Fabian's arm. "That's *right*. You should know better. Ryan, I happen to know that the bartender tonight makes the most amazing lemon drop martinis. Give me the drink tickets, Fabe. You stay and keep your *friend* company."

Fabian fixed a look on Vanessa's face that probably said a lot of things that Ryan couldn't translate, and handed her a strip of paper tickets. "I'll have one of those martinis."

Vanessa pointed at Tarek, and then Ryan. "Martini? Martini?"

"Sure," Tarek said.

"Ah, I actually *would* just like a beer," Ryan said shyly.

"Ha!" Vanessa looked delighted. "Beer it is. Tarek, come with me."

"Subtle," Tarek muttered as he turned to follow her.

Fabian watched his ridiculous friends make their way through the crowd to the bar, before turning his attention back to Ryan. "They might be a while," he said. "Vanessa has a crush on the bartender."

Ryan's hair was tied back in a little bun tonight, which only accentuated the poofiness of his beard. "I don't know how you write songs like that. Or play onstage in front of people."

"Don't you play hockey in front of, like, a million people all the time?"

"It's not the same."

"It's not?" Fabian genuinely didn't understand how it wasn't the same thing.

Ryan shook his head. "I can play hockey in front of a crowd, but I could never, like, sing the national anthem, y'know?"

Fabian tried to picture that, and smiled to himself. "That's because you're *good* at hockey. I'm good at this." He gestured toward the stage. "And my audiences don't tend to boo me when I make a mistake. I've heard that sports fans are less forgiving."

Ryan's mouth turned up a bit at that. "They can be pretty harsh for sure. And I'm not so sure I'm *good* at hockey."

Okay. Well this was just dumb. "You play in the *NHL*, Ryan. Is there a higher league I'm not aware of?" He frowned. "Honest question. There actually might be one."

Ryan laughed. "No. The NHL is the highest. But I'm not—" He stopped himself, and Fabian wondered what he had been about to say. He was startled out of his wondering when Ryan blurted out, "I like your outfit."

Fabian smiled. He was proud of his look tonight—a sheer T-shirt with black, baroque-style velvet flowers on it, black tuxedo pants, and a whole pile of sparkly necklaces he'd bought at Forever 21. He noticed Ryan's gaze catch on Fabian's chest, where the piercing in his right nipple was visible through the shirt. "Thank you."

"I feel so ordinary," Ryan said, then immediately looked embarrassed about saying it. He ran a hand through his hair and over his beard, a gesture that Fabian already recognized as a nervous habit.

"Just an ordinary seven-foot-tall hockey star. So boring," he teased.

Ryan blushed. "I'm not seven feet tall."

"Did I underestimate?"

"I'm six-seven."

Oof. Six fucking seven. Fabian had never been with a man anywhere near that tall. What would it be like? Was kissing even possible? He would dearly love to find out.

Not that he was going to be hooking up with Ryan Price. For so many reasons.

"Come sit." Fabian gestured at the empty table next to them. Sitting would at least remove the distraction of Ryan's height. And of how well he filled out that suit.

Once they were seated, Fabian propped an elbow on the table, leaned forward, and rested his chin on his fist. "Tell me all about yourself, Ryan Price."

His tone was probably a tad too flirtatious, because Ryan laughed nervously and looked away. "Not much to tell."

"Do you live in the neighborhood? The Village, I mean?"

"Uh, sort of. Like, not right here, but a few blocks south. Near the drugstore there, where you work."

"So . . . yes, then? You live in the Village?" Fabian couldn't help his teasing smile, but it seemed to put Ryan at ease. He smiled back at him.

"Yes. Sorry. Long answer to a simple question."

Fabian had to push this. He was burning with curiosity. "Did you *know* you were moving into the queer neighborhood?"

Ryan's brow furrowed, as if he was trying to decide how to answer the yes-or-no question. "Yeah. I knew."

No further information was offered, so Fabian backed off. He was intrigued, though.

They sat in silence for a moment, Fabian looking toward the bar as if he was extremely interested in the progress of their drink orders. He decided he would let Ryan ask the next question.

Instead, Ryan broke the silence by suddenly blurting out, "I'm gay."

Even though Fabian had kind of guessed this might be the case, hearing Ryan say the words was . . . "Holy shit."

"Surprise," Ryan said with a shrug.

"Are hockey players even *allowed* to be gay?"

Ryan laughed. "It's only a five-minute major now."

Fabian looked at him blankly.

"Sorry," Ryan said. "Hockey joke. A *bad* hockey joke. Yes, there are gay hockey players."

Fabian considered this. "I guess there's that guy in New York. The hot one."

"Scott Hunter. Yeah. I'm the other one. The not-hot one." Ryan smiled at his self-deprecating comment.

Fabian wasn't so sure about *that* assessment, but he ignored it for now. "So why have I heard about the New York guy being gay, but not you?"

Ryan snorted. "Because I'm not a superstar. And I didn't kiss my boyfriend on live television after winning the Stanley Cup."

Ryan saying the words *kiss my boyfriend* made Fabian's head spin a little. Did Ryan *have* a boyfriend? Ryan dated *men*. Ryan *kissed* men. Ryan played hockey and he also *kissed men*.

"I also don't talk about it much," Ryan continued. "Being gay, I mean. Or anything, really."

Well that was certainly true. Ryan didn't seem to be any chattier now than he had been as an awkward teenager. "Your teammates don't know?"

"Some of them do. Did. I get traded a lot, like I said."

"Are they dicks about it?"

Ryan shrugged. "Most of them don't seem to care. Or maybe it just helps that I'm big. I dunno."

At that moment, Tarek returned to the table with a martini glass in each hand and a bottle of beer tucked in his elbow. "Vanessa is flirting with Callie."

"Ah," Fabian said, accepting his martini glass. "We probably won't see her again."

"Probably not," Tarek agreed.

Fabian watched Ryan take a sip of his beer. He was turned away from them a bit, but he didn't seem to be looking at anything in particular. Fabian was struck by how bizarre it was to be sitting at a table in one of his regular bars with his best friends . . . and Ryan Price. Ryan Price, who was apparently every bit as queer as Fabian, Fabian's friends, and this bar they were in.

But he was still a hockey player, and Fabian had been very glad to eliminate all traces of hockey from his life as soon as he'd moved to Toronto to start university over a decade ago. Having Ryan here, in one of Fabian's favorite spaces, should have been annoying him more than it was.

Ryan was *different*. Fabian had felt it when they'd been seventeen, and he still felt it now. Unlike every other hockey player who had entered his family home, who Fabian had gone to school with, who had been coached by his father, Ryan had never made him feel uncomfortable. When they had lived together, Fabian had actually enjoyed Ryan's quiet presence. When they'd done their homework together at the kitchen table, or watched *Finding Nemo* together with Amy (again), or walked to school together, it had always been in almost total silence. But Fabian had always liked having him around. He was like . . . a big, sweet dog.

Fabian grimaced at the unflattering thought, and took a sip of lemon drop martini.

For several long minutes, no one at the table said anything. Ryan was still looking away, his back half turned to Fabian, and Tarek was engrossed in his phone.

"How do you get all of your gear home?" Ryan asked suddenly.

Fabian was surprised by the question. "Usually a friend or two helps me. I have a system: all the pedals and cords go in a backpack with my laptop, so it's just the violin, the keyboard, and the stand that need to be carried. Sometimes I take a cab, but I only live a few blocks away from here."

Ryan nodded.

"About that," Tarek said slowly. "I've been messaging with this guy, Mario . . ."

"Mario the flight attendant?"

Tarek smiled dreamily. "The very same. He's in town and he's got a *hotel room*, so if you've got someone else helping you, I'm gonna . . ."

Fabian waved his hand. "Go. Enjoy Mario. I'm sure I can—"

"I can help," Ryan said quickly. "I'll carry your gear. I don't mind."

Fabian stared at him, then smiled. "Cool. Thanks."

Tarek stood and kissed the top of Fabian's head. He waved at Ryan and said, "Nice meeting you" before making a quick exit.

"And then there were two," Fabian said, his voice more sultry than was appropriate. There was a trace of alarm in Ryan's eyes, so Fabian leaned back in his chair and returned his voice to normal. "You don't have to walk home with me. Really."

"Oh."

God, he looked *disappointed*. "I mean, you *can*. Of course. I'd like that."

Ryan's face brightened. "You would?"

"Sure. Big, strong man carrying my gear for me? Who wouldn't like that?"

Ryan snorted, but he looked less enthused than he had a second ago. "Right."

Fuck. "I'd like to talk to you. Away from this noise," Fabian clarified. "It would be nice to catch up."

That seemed to do the trick, because the beard area around Ryan's mouth curved up.

Twenty minutes later, Fabian was making sure he hadn't left anything near the stage when Vanessa planted herself in front of him. "Time to go?"

"Yes, but you don't have to walk with me."

Vanessa frowned. "Uh, yes I do. Tarek bailed and you need help. Unless you're taking a cab."

"It's fine. You can stay and hang out with Callie. Ryan is going to help me."

"Oh," she said. Then, "*Ohhhhhh.*"

Fabian rolled his eyes. "Nope. Just friends. Or whatever."

"Sure."

"As if I'm going to fuck a *hockey player*."

Instead of laughing, or arguing, Vanessa made a weird face that Fabian interpreted as *Ryan the hockey player is standing right behind you.*

Shit.

CHAPTER SIX

Fabian turned and, sure enough, there was giant, sweet Ryan, holding the keyboard in one hand, the stand in the other, and had the heavy backpack full of gear slung over one shoulder.

"Is there, uh, anything else?" Ryan asked. He was very obviously pretending he hadn't heard Fabian's awful comment. The parts of his face that weren't covered in beard were flushed and he was looking at the floor.

"Nope!" Fabian said, overly cheerful. There was no reason to address what Fabian had just said. It wasn't like sex was on the table anyway. Ryan was a hockey star, and Fabian was . . . the worst. "I've got the violin." He raised the hand that was holding the case, waving it around as if it were hard to see.

"Okay. Should we head out?"

"Yes. Bye Vanessa! Have fun tonight!" Ugh. Fabian did not like the shame that was coursing through him like fire.

"I will. And thank you, Ryan, for helping. You seem like a *great guy*." She glared at Fabian when she said those last words. Fabian wanted to die.

He turned his attention to Ryan with a forced smile plastered on his face. "Shall we?"

The crisp November night air didn't do much to relieve the heat in Fabian's cheeks. He wrapped his wine-colored pashmina scarf around his neck and buried the lower half of his face in it.

They made it one block, in silence, before Fabian couldn't take it anymore.

"I'm sorry I said that. It was very rude and I feel like an asshole."

He glanced up at Ryan's profile, and he could tell he was deciding whether or not to acknowledge that he had, in fact, heard what Fabian had said earlier.

"It's okay," Ryan said finally.

"It's *really* not. You came to my show, you're helping me carry my gear home, you don't even *know* me, really. I made a stupid joke and it was shitty and I'm sorry."

"All right."

They walked another block in silence, and then Ryan said, "I wouldn't fuck a hockey player either."

Fabian's laugh sounded like a honk, which was humiliating, but he was relieved and delighted by Ryan's joke. Ryan smiled down at him and it occurred to Fabian, in that moment, that this guy was fearlessly—and seemingly happily—walking beside a man who was wearing a full face of dramatic makeup. That wasn't nothing.

Fabian nudged him with his shoulder, which hit Ryan somewhere just above his elbow. "So we have something in common. Besides being gay Nova Scotians in Toronto."

"Yep."

It only took a few more minutes to reach the street where Fabian's shitty apartment building was. It was only then, relieved of some of his previous embarrassment, that he realized how imbalanced the load was between them. "Oh my god. Let me at least take the keyboard stand. I can't believe I let you carry all of that."

"It's fine," Ryan grunted. But then he stopped and held out the stand. "Actually. Yeah. Sorry. My back has been bothering me a bit lately."

Maybe a meteor could land on Fabian right now. The perfect end to a perfect evening. "Let me take the keyboard too. Or the backpack." He managed a flirty smile. "I'm stronger than I look."

"Nope. I'm good. Thanks."

"Well, my apartment is just right there anyway." Fabian gestured ahead of them with his violin case. "Ground floor too. Totally easy delivery job."

A minute later they were standing together on the step at the front of Fabian's apartment building as he struggled with the key. It was in an ancient two-story building that used to be an orphanage or a children's hospital or something. Either way, it was, as Vanessa had put it, for sure haunted.

"This stupid fucking lock," he grumbled, jiggling the key until it finally turned. They were greeted by the familiar cocktail of smells that Fabian now recognized as home: musty walls, garlic-heavy vegan cooking, and weed. There was a wooden staircase with worn carpet directly in front of them, leading to the three apartments on the second floor. On the ground floor, there was a door to each side of the staircase, and Fabian directed Ryan to the door on the left.

"This is me," he said, turning the key in a lock that was only slightly less stubborn than the one outside. "Get ready to be dazzled by opulence."

Ryan followed him into the tiny studio apartment. Fabian set the gear he'd been carrying against one bright red wall, and gestured for Ryan to do the same. "Thank you again. That really was very nice of you."

"No problem." Ryan carefully placed the keyboard and backpack on the floor with a quiet grunt.

"How's your back?"

"Good as ever." He looked enormous in the confines of Fabian's apartment. He also looked extremely uncomfortable and out of place. Fabian waited for him to say something, but instead Ryan just stared at his hands, flexing them and rubbing his knuckles.

"Oh my god!" Fabian exclaimed. Without thinking, he took Ryan's left hand in his own. "What happened?" There was dark bruising on the knuckles, and Fabian ran his fingers delicately over them, back and forth. "I can't believe you carried all that stuff when your hand is busted up! Does it hurt? It must hurt."

"Uh," Ryan said quietly. Fabian glanced up and saw that Ryan was staring at Fabian's fingers.

Fabian dropped his hand and stepped back. "Sorry."

"It's okay. They don't hurt too much." Ryan shoved his bruised hand in the pocket of his wool coat and looked at the floor. Quite a lot of hair had escaped from the bun he'd tied it back in, and the loose tendrils were hanging around his face. It was a good look.

"So that's normal for you? Bashed-up hands?"

Ryan shrugged. "Pretty normal, yeah."

Fabian remembered noticing similar bruising on teenage Ryan's hands. He was pretty sure Ryan had tried to hide it from him then too.

"Well," Ryan said. "I should probably get going." He said it at the same moment that Fabian said, "Can I offer you a drink?"

"What?" Ryan said.

"I have most of a bottle of wine in the fridge." Fabian pulled his own scarf off and draped it over a chair that already had several scarves on it. "Or tea, if you prefer. I might have one of those grapefruit sparkling waters left . . ."

"I—no. That's okay. I'm pretty tired after the game. I should go."

"If you're sure." Fabian ducked his head and slipped the necklaces off, laying them over the scarf. He wondered what Ryan would do if he removed his shirt next.

"I'm sure. But . . . it was nice. Seeing you again."

Fabian stepped closer to him. He smelled *good*. "Likewise."

Fabian wasn't sure what his plan was here. He didn't want Ryan to leave, but he also had no idea why he wanted him to stay. If he and Ryan had never met before tonight; if Ryan had just been a big, strong, attractive stranger who had offered to walk Fabian home, Fabian would be tearing his clothes off right now. But Ryan wasn't a stranger, and while part of Fabian really liked the idea of tearing his clothes off, he just . . . couldn't.

Not even when Ryan was gazing down at him in a way that took Fabian right back to that night on a ferry all those years ago. To that moment where he'd thought for a wild second that Ryan was going to kiss him. Fabian could kiss him *now*. He could go up on his tiptoes and brush his lips against Ryan's. It didn't even need to be a big deal. It would be a simple thank-you kiss, the kind Fabian gave his friends all the time.

But instead, Fabian said, "We should do this again sometime."

Ryan blinked and jerked back a bit. "What?"

"I mean, we should hang out. Get coffee. You know. Catch up some more."

Ryan's brow furrowed, but then he nodded. "I'd like that. Can I get your number?" They traded phones and entered their numbers. "I haven't really explored the neighborhood too much."

"Well, let me be your guide." Fabian's tone had gone silky again. Much too flirtatious.

Ryan froze, and Fabian mentally kicked himself. Ryan was not the kind of guy you were casually flirtatious with. When they'd been teenagers, Ryan had gotten so easily flustered whenever

Fabian had attempted to tease him. It didn't seem like that had changed.

It was still inconveniently charming.

"I'll wait to hear from you, then," Ryan said stiffly. He raised one hand, as if he was going to offer a farewell handshake, then seemed to think better of it and stuffed his hand in his coat pocket instead. "Good night."

"Good night, Ryan Price. Take care of those hands."

Ryan nodded, and left. When the door closed, Fabian cringed. Did *take care of those hands* sound flirty? It definitely sounded dumb.

With a sigh, Fabian fell back onto his bed. What a weird night.

CHAPTER SEVEN

"Can I move in with you?"

Ryan smiled at his sister's pained expression. He'd slept late that morning and had been awoken by Colleen's FaceTime request. "You don't want to move to Toronto," he said.

"I totally do. I'll get on a plane tomorrow. Today, even. This town is smothering me."

"You love it, though. And what would all those poor third graders say when their teacher disappears?"

"They'd be thrilled. Seriously. Let me mooch off of you in Toronto for a few months. Or years."

Ryan would honestly love to have Colleen closer to him, but he knew she was kidding about this. "You should come visit soon."

She sighed. "I want to. If you don't come home for Christmas, maybe I could go there for a few days."

"I'm going to try," Ryan said. "I want to come home this year."

She smiled. "That would be awesome. But I still want to visit you in Toronto. I want to go *out*. Have you been to any of the clubs?"

"Um . . ."

"*Ry-an*," she whined. "You are a young, rich gay man in Toronto's Gay Village!"

"I'm not that young," Ryan argued.

"You're thirty-one. That's not old."

"I have the body of a seventy-year-old, though."

"You have the body of an Olympian. What the hell are you talking about?"

"My back's been bothering me."

Her expression softened. "Sorry. I'm being a dick. So you really haven't been going out at all?"

"Well." Ryan braced himself, because he knew his sister was going make a *thing* about this. "I actually ran into someone recently. From Halifax."

"An old teammate?"

"No. Do you remember when I lived with the Salahs?"

"I think I only met them once, but yeah. You liked them, right?"

"Yeah." He bit his lip, which his sister noticed immediately.

"Oh my god. What?"

"I liked *one* of the Salahs in particular."

"Please don't let it be the dad."

"No!" Joe Salah had been an attractive man, but no. Absolutely no. "Their son. Fabian."

"Ohhhh. And that's who you ran into in Toronto?"

Ryan nodded. "Yeah. And we were catching up a bit. You know."

"Catching up like . . ."

"Just talking. We're friends. We're not . . ." Ryan shifted so he was sitting more upright against the headboard. "He's way out of my league."

Her eyes narrowed. "Way out of your league how? You are literally a star athlete and a millionaire."

"Yeah, but he's beautiful. And charming. And has a ton of friends who all do interesting things. And he plays music that's, like, the most amazing thing I've ever heard."

"Okay, so this charming, beautiful man has been hanging out with you?"

"We haven't really been hanging out. I went to his show last night, though, and I . . . walked him home after."

Colleen's face lit up. "Ryan! That's adorable! Did you carry his books?"

Ryan flushed. "I carried his gear."

"Aw. Did he kiss you good night?"

"Let's change the subject."

"Come *on*. The last date I went on was with Andy Hart, and it turned out we're distant cousins. I need some big city romance stories."

Ryan laughed. "Isn't he Mom's cousin's son?"

"I don't know. Something like that."

"Yeah, that's not that distant."

"Oh, look at you, Toronto. So fancy just because you aren't dating your cousins."

They both cracked up. Ryan loved his sister, and he hated thinking that she was lonely back in Ross Harbour. She deserved to be loved by someone wonderful.

"Have you bought furniture yet?" she asked when they'd stopped laughing.

"Not really. Still just in the bedroom, basically."

She looked dismayed. "That's sad. Please order some furniture. I know there's an IKEA in Toronto."

"Yeah, I know."

"What if you *did* meet a guy? You can't bring him back to a weird empty apartment!"

"I *know*, I said."

"They can probably do next-day delivery in Toronto!"

"There's no point in buying furniture if I'm just gonna be traded again!"

Ryan thought that outburst would end the argument, but Colleen persisted. "Yeah, that's no way to live, buddy. Buy a sofa."

"I have to go."

"Don't be mad at me. I'm just—"

"I'm not mad at you. I just have stuff to do," he lied.

"All right. Love you. We'll be watching the game tomorrow night."

"Love you too. Say hi to Mom and Dad."

"Call them soon, will you? Mom has been complaining about you forgetting about them."

"Will do." God, it hadn't even been a week since he'd last called them. "Bye."

Ryan yawned and stretched. He wasn't surprised he had slept in. After returning home from Fabian's last night he'd been up for hours, staring at the ceiling and replaying every detail of the evening in his head.

And now he was awake with nothing to do. Colleen was right; his life was sad.

He grabbed his laptop from his nightstand and opened the IKEA website in his browser. It wouldn't hurt to order a few things; his apartment really did look ridiculous. And what if he did want to invite a man back to his place? It wasn't a *likely* scenario, but it wasn't impossible either.

As Ryan added more items to his cart, he found himself getting excited about his new furnishings. When it was time to check out, he went hog wild and opted for the extremely expensive express delivery so he would get the stuff the next day.

He tried not to imagine, as he entered his payment information, what Fabian would think of the colorful throw pillows he had ordered.

★ ★ ★

"Prepare to have your minds blown," Fabian said cheerfully as he plunked his backpack on Vanessa, Marcus, and Tarek's kitchen counter. "I hit the discount Halloween table at the grocery store and bought . . ." He paused for dramatic effect, and then quickly pulled from the backpack. "A caramel apple!"

"Oh my god! Oh my god, Fabe," Vanessa said. "Are you suggesting we *slice up* the caramel apple and layer it on top of the cinnamon cream cheese I bought? Because that is fucking genius."

"I am suggesting exactly that."

"What about my blackberries?" Marcus complained.

"Fuck you and your blackberries," Vanessa said. "Caramel apple plus cinnamon cream cheese for the win."

"I'm putting blackberries on mine," Marcus grumbled.

They all ate delicious waffles and drank coffee and cheap mimosas, and to her credit, Vanessa waited until the food was gone before mentioning Ryan. "So you want to tell us about that hockey lumberjack or what?"

"Hockey lumberjack?" Marcus asked, setting his phone on the coffee table facedown in a gesture of absolute interest in the conversation.

"He was at the show last night," Tarek explained. "Some hockey player who is in love with Fabian."

"That is so wrong, I don't even know where to start," Fabian protested.

"As if," Vanessa said. "He's completely in love with you. He carried your gear home."

"Right." He rolled his eyes. "I forgot that means we're engaged now."

"Can someone tell me what the fuck is happening?" Marcus said.

"It's *not* a big deal. Remember I told you my parents used to billet hockey players? Like, every year a different teenage hockey player would live with us?"

"Yeah. You hated it. Who wouldn't?"

"Right. So, I did hate it. They were all homophobic jock assholes who almost definitely would have beat me up if they hadn't been living under my parents' roof." Fabian chewed his lip before continuing. "But one of them . . ."

Marcus's face lit up. "Oh my god. You hooked up with one of the dumb hockey bros!"

"No," Fabian said quickly. "Not at all. It was just that this one guy, Ryan. He was . . . different. He was nice to me. And . . . I liked him."

"Aw, you had a crush on your hockey player housemate!" Vanessa said. "This is good shit, Fabian. Continue."

"Nothing happened, like I said. We just . . . got along. Not that we were hanging out or anything, really, but we would do homework together. Watch TV. Sometimes walk to school together. Stuff like that."

"Cute," said Tarek.

"And . . . okay. This is the thing I kind of can't forget about. I had this recital. An end-of-year thing at the conservatory. My sister had a playoff game that night, so my whole family went to that instead."

"Yeah, well, of course," Vanessa said flatly. "Who gives a shit about their insanely musically talented son when there's a hockey game to go to?"

"Right. So the thing is, no one in my family was at my recital. But Ryan was."

Vanessa covered her mouth with both hands. "Fuck. Off!"

Fabian's cheeks heated. "I know."

"That is the sweetest thing I have ever heard," Tarek said.

Fabian's belly fluttered at the memory of spotting Ryan Price at the back of the auditorium. "I couldn't believe he was there."

"And you *didn't* run off the stage into his waiting arms?" Vanessa exclaimed.

"No. Oh my god. As if." He hesitated, then said, "But . . ."

Vanessa leaned in. "You have my undivided attention."

"We took the ferry home together. And it was this beautiful night where all the stars were out, and the moon was full. Just ridiculous. And we had . . . a moment. I think."

"A moment? Like what?" Marcus asked.

Fabian was sure his face had gotten a little dreamy as he remembered that night. "There was a second where I thought . . . I mean, I was sure he was going to kiss me. Or that he was waiting for me to kiss *him*. But then it passed and that was that."

Vanessa leaned back in her chair. "That story sucked, Fabian. I hate that story."

Fabian shrugged. "Sorry."

"Okay, but why was he at your show last night?" Marcus asked.

"I ran into him at work last week. I told him about the show."

"Did he *recognize* you?" Vanessa asked.

"Yeah. We talked for a bit. He . . . he definitely remembered me. He looked at least as stunned as I was."

"This story is getting good again," she said.

"So what's he doing in Toronto?" Marcus asked.

"He, um, he plays for the Guardians now, I guess? And yeah. He looks good."

"He plays for the *Guardians*? Are you *kidding me*?" Marcus pulled his phone out. "What's his last name?"

"Price."

He tapped at his phone for a few seconds, and then his eyes bugged out. "Hello, Daddy."

"I know."

"So, is he gay, or . . ."

"Yeah. He told me last night."

"Seriously?"

"Weird thing for a hockey player to lie about, so I assume he's actually gay, yes."

"So what we know," Vanessa said, "is that he liked you enough to go to your recital when you were both teenagers, he remembered you after thirteen years, he went to your show last night, he carried your gear home, and he's totally gay."

"Right."

"That," Marcus said, "is fucking romantic."

"That," Fabian corrected him, "is not anything."

"It's the best, right?" Vanessa said gleefully. "Like, this is the most interesting thing ever. I am fully invested in this."

"Completely," Tarek agreed.

"There is nothing to be invested in," Fabian said wearily. "I'll probably never see him again. We exchanged numbers, but you know how that goes."

"You exchanged numbers!" Vanessa said in a voice so high it was almost inaudible.

"So, new plan," Marcus said, clapping his hands together. "Fabian breaks up with Claude, and then he marries the gay hockey player and they have big, dumb babies together."

"You're an idiot. And Claude and I are *not* together."

"Your mouths were together last week," Tarek pointed out.

Fabian closed his eyes, drawing strength from the universe. "It's not happening again. It was a mistake. I'm done with him."

"Sure," Tarek said.

"Totally," Marcus said, nodding.

"Whatever. I hate you guys."

"Does that mean you are going to make out with us?" Vanessa

asked. "Because it seems like—" Her sentence was cut off when Fabian tossed a cat-shaped pillow at her.

"Who wants more coffee?" he asked. He needed a break from the room after that conversation. Everyone raised their hands, so he busied himself in the kitchenette for the next few minutes.

"Next order of business," Vanessa announced, when Fabian returned with a French press full of coffee, "is Tarek's birthday."

Tarek let out a long groan. "If you don't mention it, it might not happen!"

"Sorry, babe. You're turning thirty. Deal with it." She shoveled two heaping spoonfuls of sugar into her coffee.

"So, obviously we're going out," Marcus said. "May I request that we go anywhere other than—"

"Force! Force! Force!" Vanessa started chanting. Tarek joined in, followed by Fabian.

"Fuck you guys," Marcus grumbled. "Fine. It's in three weeks, right? I'll make sure I'm not working, at least."

"Remember when you were a stripper?" Vanessa said. "And we'd visit you at work? That was the best."

"That was the *worst*, actually," Marcus corrected her. "But I do miss that gig sometimes. Stupid fire."

"Stupid arson, you mean," Tarek said.

"Yeah. It was a good club."

"It totally was," Vanessa agreed. "Remember that time you fell down?"

"I did *not* fall down! I *stumbled*. And recovered. And you are awful."

They all laughed. Fabian scheduled in the night out at Force on his phone. He could really use a night of dancing. It had been an age.

"You should bring your hockey boyfriend," Marcus teased.

"I'm gonna bring your *dad*."

"You should. My dad is a smoke show."

"ABC," Tarek said. "Anyone. But. Claude."

That caused Vanessa to howl with laughter, and Fabian couldn't help but join in.

"ABC," he agreed. "Definitely."

CHAPTER EIGHT

"Got big plans for the day off?" Wyatt nudged Ryan playfully as they were getting ready to leave the arena after another win at home.

Ryan laughed. "Yeah. I got an IKEA delivery this afternoon. Gonna put it all together tomorrow."

"Wow. That's a fun day."

Ryan smiled sheepishly. "My apartment is pretty empty. I thought I might try to make it more of a home, y'know?"

Wyatt looked like he was about to make a joke, but instead said, "You need a hand with putting that shit together? I've assembled a few Billy bookshelves in my day. Or maybe you could ask Anders. He should be an expert, right?"

The idea of asking Anders Nilsson, Toronto's star goalie and only Swedish player, to help Ryan assemble IKEA furniture was unimaginable. Nilsson had said maybe four words to Ryan all season. "I should be all right."

Wyatt nodded. "Okay, well. See you in a couple of days then."

He turned to leave, and Ryan cringed at himself. This was *exactly* the sort of opportunity his therapist would want him to seize. He ignored the knot in his stomach and said, "Hey, uh, Hazy?"

Wyatt turned back, probably just as surprised as Ryan was.

"If . . . I mean, if you aren't doing anything, and you really don't mind, it would be nice to have some help tomorrow."

Why the fuck was that so hard?

Ryan waited, stomach churning, and was about to tell him to forget it when Wyatt smiled and said, "You buy the beer."

Ryan nearly slumped forward with relief. God, he was pathetic.

"Deal."

"Okay, so we've got some work to do." Wyatt stood in front of the mountain of boxes of flat-packed furniture that Ryan had piled in his living room.

"Yeah," Ryan said, running a hand anxiously over his beard. "I basically just have a bed, and the stools at my kitchen counter. Everything else is in these boxes."

"I can see that. Where the hell have you been sitting?"

"The stools."

Wyatt shook his head. "Well, let's start with the couch, and then the coffee table." He grinned. "And speaking of coffee . . ."

Ryan flushed. Why hadn't he offered some as soon as Wyatt came in the door? "Of course. I'll just . . . I made some. I can make a fresh pot, if you—"

"I'm not fancy," Wyatt said easily. He was crouched in front of the boxes, head tilted as he read the labels. "I'll drink your leftovers."

"Okay." Ryan rushed off to the kitchen. He hated how jittery he was. Through all his years in the NHL, and all the teams and all the apartments, he had very rarely invited anyone into his home. But he liked Wyatt, and he really did need help with this furniture. Plus, he *wanted* to be the kind of guy who could invite a friend over without completely falling apart.

He pulled one of the matching navy blue mugs he'd bought at the dollar store down the street out of the cupboard. He started to pour the coffee, then realized he had no idea how Wyatt took it.

He poked his head out of the kitchen. "Hey, um, do you want milk or sugar or . . . ?"

"Cream if you have it," Wyatt called back.

Oh god. Ryan did *not* have it. "I, um . . . I can go get some. Sorry. I didn't even think—"

"Fuck's sake, Pricey. It's fine. Milk is great. Make it a good splash, though."

"All right." Ryan fetched the milk, which he thankfully had plenty of, from the fridge. *That wasn't so bad. You didn't have cream and it was fine.*

"Sorry," Ryan said as he handed Wyatt the mug.

"For what? Free coffee?" Wyatt smiled at him, and placed a hand on his shoulder. "Relax!"

"Sorry," Ryan said again. If only he could obey that command.

"How about we do the coffee table first so I have somewhere to put this mug?" Wyatt suggested.

Ryan nodded, probably too enthusiastically. "Sounds good."

They worked together for about an hour. Wyatt did most of the talking, but Ryan enjoyed listening to him. He was funny, and he told great stories. At the end of the hour they had the coffee table, the sofa, and an armchair built.

"So," Wyatt said, grunting the word as he sat down hard on Ryan's new sofa, "I noticed that your choice of neighborhood is . . . unusual."

"Oh." Ryan sat in the armchair that faced Wyatt across the

coffee table. "Yeah, well. I just thought I would give it a try. It might . . . be a good fit for me." He forced himself to hold Wyatt's gaze. He *wouldn't* look at the floor as he braced himself for Wyatt's reaction.

But Wyatt just nodded. "I think you'll like it. My sister moved to the Village after college. She said it changed her life. Well." He gave Ryan a sad smile. "*Saved* her life, is what she said."

"Is she still here?"

"No. She's in Vancouver now. Her wife works in the film industry. Production design. Here, just a sec." Wyatt snatched his phone off the coffee table and thumbed through it for a few seconds before turning the screen toward Ryan. "Here they are. That's Kristy, my sister, and her wife, Eve. And this little guy is their son, Isaac."

Ryan smiled at the chubby-cheeked toddler in Kristy's arms. "You're an uncle!"

"Best uncle in the world," Wyatt said proudly. "I visit every time we play in Vancouver. And in the summers."

"That's awesome."

"And that," Wyatt set his phone back on the table, "is my way of telling you that I am totally cool with you being . . . whatever."

Ryan couldn't help teasing him a bit. "So cool you can't even say it."

Wyatt looked outraged. "I can say whatever word you want! I just wasn't sure which one you preferred. This is me being sensitive and knowledgeable."

Ryan laughed, and then said, "Gay. And thank you for . . ." He was suddenly at a loss. He'd played on eight NHL teams before this one, and exactly zero of his teammates had openly accepted his sexuality. In fact, most of them had ignored any hint that Ryan may have given them. "It means a lot," he finished.

"I'm a, whatchacallit, an ally!" Wyatt said, beaming. "So if anyone wants to fight you about it, they gotta come through me."

They both laughed, because Ryan had roughly eighty pounds and nine inches on Wyatt.

This burgeoning friendship with Wyatt was, without question, the best thing about playing for the Guardians. It was always hard for Ryan to feel enthusiastic about hockey when he didn't like his coach, and after a couple of months playing for Bruce Cooper, Ryan was pretty sure he didn't like his coach. He embodied a lot of Ryan's least favorite things about hockey culture: he was short-tempered, used a lot of tired sexist and homophobic adages, motivated his players by using fear and threats, and generally made Ryan uncomfortable. Frankly, Ryan was long past the point of wanting to sit straighter and bark "Yes, Coach!" whenever an aggressive man holding a white board was tearing a strip off him. These days, he kind of felt more like walking out of the room. Maybe just keep walking until he was back home in Nova Scotia.

It was tempting.

There had been a time, he was sure, that he had loved being a part of a team, of helping that team win games and championships. But he couldn't quite recall that feeling. Even his memories of winning the Stanley Cup with Boston weren't as golden as he would have thought they'd be when he'd been a kid.

For most of his NHL career, hockey had just been a thing he did because he didn't have anything else. And because he'd *made* it, when so many others hadn't. Every boy he'd grown up with had dreamed of making the NHL one day, and Ryan was the only one who had. It would be pretty fucking stupid of him to throw that away.

It wasn't until most of an hour had passed, and the two men were finishing up a dresser, that Wyatt asked, "Do you have a boyfriend?"

There wasn't a trace of scorn in the question, but Ryan flushed anyway. "No," he said quietly.

"Has there ever been one?"

Ryan smoothed a hand over the top of the dresser, and followed its path with his eyes. "Not for a while now, but yeah. A couple." He glanced up to meet Wyatt's eyes. "Why? You have someone in mind?"

Wyatt's face split into a huge grin. "Is that *flirting*? Are you *flirting* with me, Pricey?"

"No! Jeez! It was just a joke, and I didn't mean—"

Wyatt punched Ryan's arm. "I know. I was kidding. And I'm sure you'll do just fine here in Toronto. Guy like you," he stood back to eye Ryan critically, "tall, huge arms, got the whole rugged Viking thing going on. Plus the hockey butt. And the NHL salary. And . . ." He waved his hand around at Ryan's living room. "The luxury apartment in the middle of the Gay Village. Do you have a Grindr account?"

"Oh my god," Ryan grumbled, bending to open the next furniture box, not even looking to see what it was.

"You must, right? I mean, there's gotta be a billion guys here looking to score with you!"

Ryan slid the contents of the box onto the floor. It appeared to be a bookshelf. "I doubt it."

"Fuck that. You're a giant, orange teddy bear with deep pockets! And, I couldn't help but notice, you're hung like a—"

"All right. Enough," Ryan mumbled. "Let's build this thing."

CHAPTER NINE

It turned out that Fabian's music was available online. Ryan had discovered this on the Thursday after Fabian's show, and he'd immediately purchased and downloaded everything he could find. He'd spent most of that day listening to all of it. When he'd decided, late in the afternoon, that he really needed to get some groceries for dinner, he brought his earbuds so he could continue to listen as he walked to the store.

He focused on the intricacies of Fabian's music, which was providing a nice soundtrack for the beautiful autumn day in Toronto. Since the end of the game he'd played last night, Ryan had been slipping pretty steadily into preflight panic mode. The flight to Ottawa would barely be anything—they would be landing almost as soon as they hit cruising altitude—but it still involved a takeoff, a landing, and way too much space between the plane and the ground. Which was exactly the sort of thing he should *not* be thinking about. He tried to appreciate the cheerful rainbow flags that decorated almost every business on this section of Church Street, and the attractive men who were just *everywhere* around him. Men who were openly and fearlessly holding hands and, yes, this was a good place. Ryan felt at least a little bit at ease here.

Of course, the idea of actually *talking* to one of the many attractive men—or god help him, *flirting* with them—made Ryan want to curl into a ball. Except that ball would still be enormous and, no doubt, noticeable on the busy sidewalk.

Good things. Focus on good things.

Tea was a good thing. An iced chai latte was an even better thing, so Ryan decided to stop into the fancy-looking coffee shop that he'd almost passed by.

There were two people in line in front of him, so Ryan stared up at the menu, confirming that they had iced chai lattes. He mentally rehearsed placing his order. Ordering food was always one of his most embarrassing problem areas; he tended to stammer, and sometimes ordered the wrong thing, or the first thing he saw. If a server suggested something to him, he would order it even if he didn't want it. But surely even *he* could order a fucking latte.

When he got to the counter, the cute barista smiled at him. "Hello. How are you today?"

"Chai—I mean, good. I'm good." *Come on, Ryan.*

"What can I get you?"

"Uh. The, um, chai latte. But with ice."

"An iced chai latte? What size?"

"Oh." Ryan glanced back up at the board, where there were two prices listed next to iced chai latte but no actual sizes. "The, um . . ."

The barista helpfully held up two different sized plastic cups. "Regular and large."

Ryan pointed to the larger one. "Large. Thanks."

He paid by tapping his bank card because he *loved* the tap feature. He loved anything that ended a transaction faster. He selected the highest suggested tip amount, as usual.

"You can wait at the end of the counter there. It will just be a minute. Thank you!"

Ryan was grateful for the instruction. He hated not knowing where to stand. He found a spot where he wouldn't be *too* in the way and waited.

"Ryan?"

Ryan looked first at the counter, thinking his drink had been made already. But he hadn't given them his name, so that was dumb. Then he turned toward the tables in the café and saw Fabian.

"I thought that was you!" Fabian beamed at him.

"Yup. Hi." *Jesus, what are the odds?*

"Large iced chai latte?" someone called from the counter. Ryan turned and accepted his drink. When he turned back to Fabian, Fabian gestured him over.

"Come sit. Unless you're rushing off somewhere."

Ryan maneuvered himself through the narrow spaces between tables until he got to Fabian. There was a notebook open in front of him on the table, the pages full of words scribbled in pencil. There were also loose pages of handwritten sheet music. Fabian tidied everything into a neat stack as Ryan sat in the chair across from him.

"Good choice," Fabian said, nodding at the drink.

Ryan didn't reply. He was completely distracted by Fabian's face. Unlike the other two times Ryan had seen him, Fabian wasn't wearing any makeup today. At least, none that Ryan noticed. His hair was tucked under a black toque, and he had dark stubble on his jaw. He looked so different, but no less beautiful. His dark brown eyes were still fringed by the same long, full lashes that had fascinated Ryan as a teenager. His plush lips were quirked up in a playful little smile. Probably because Ryan was staring at him.

"Sorry," Ryan said. "What?"

Fabian waved his hand dismissively, and Ryan noticed the dark blue polish on his nails. "Nothing. What are you up to today?"

"I was heading to the grocery store. Just to get something for dinner."

"Ah. I should probably do that myself."

"What's all this?" Ryan asked, gesturing to the stack of papers. It was weird to be talking to the person whose music he had just been enjoying.

"Oh, I'm just working on something. I was struck by inspiration today, but I needed a change of scenery. As you saw, my apartment is a little grim."

"I liked it," Ryan said, remembering the red-painted walls, the deep plum bedspread and curtains, and the eclectic pile of cheerful pillows. "It was . . . colorful."

Fabian pressed his lips together, then said, "Mm. I'll give you the complete tour next time. You may not have seen all four corners."

Next time. "I just mean, it looked like you, y'know?"

Fabian rested his chin in his palm, obviously amused. "You know me already, do you? And here I thought I was complex."

"You are!" *Oh god.* "I mean, I don't know you. You're right. Not really." Ryan's face burned like the sun.

Fabian laughed. "It's okay. I wouldn't exactly say we're strangers, would you?"

Ryan smiled shyly back. "No."

He took a sip of his latte, and Fabian asked, "So, you . . . played a hockey game last night?"

That made Ryan laugh. "I did. Yes."

"Did you win? Sorry I didn't ask about it before."

"It's okay. We did win."

"Hey! Good for you! Go Guardians." He waved his hands in the air what Ryan assumed was supposed to be a celebratory manner.

"You're mocking me."

"Never. I am nothing if not a sports fan."

"Do you know where the arena is?"

"*Yes.*" Fabian mocked offense. "I saw Beyoncé there, so . . ."

Ryan laughed, and then said, "I saw her in Boston."

Fabian's eyes went wide. "You're a fan?"

"Isn't everyone? And I'm not sure what part of *I'm gay* you didn't understand."

"Honestly?" Fabian said. "All parts of it. I'm afraid I've developed a bit of a prejudice against hockey players, and it *may* have caused me to make some false assumptions."

"That we're all super-straight aggressive jocks?"

"Well, yes."

"You don't have to be straight to be an aggressive jock. Believe me."

Fabian seemed to consider this as Ryan took another sip of latte. "You're not. An aggressive jock, I mean. You never were."

Ryan felt a pleasant warmth bubble inside him at Fabian's kind assessment, but he had to be honest. "I know you don't follow hockey, but do have any idea what my job is?"

"Playing . . . hockey?"

"Yeah. But my job on the team—on every team—is being, ah, intimidating. I'm a fighter, mostly." Ryan kept his eyes on his drink. "So aggressive jock might be a good description for me, actually."

He glanced up, and Fabian looked *sad*. "Do you *like* it? The fighting?"

Ryan sighed. "It's hard to explain."

"Do you get in fights *off* the ice?"

"No. I've broken up a few in my life. Bars, parties, that sort of thing. But I don't fight people when I'm not being paid to do it, no. I've never wanted to either."

"You must be good at it, if you've made a career of it."

Ryan shrugged. "Yeah. I'm good at it. About the only thing I *am* good at."

They sat in silence for a minute. Ryan finished his drink and then figured he should probably leave. He was about to say so when Fabian asked him, "You said you're going to the grocery store?"

"Yeah. Thought I'd pick up something from the frozen aisle for dinner."

"That does sound incredible, but have you ever been to the ramen place on the corner here?"

"No."

Fabian leaned in. "Wanna go?"

"Now? With you?"

"Yes. I'm *starving*. Sometimes I get lost in writing and I forget to eat. I realize that makes me sound like a moron."

Ryan was pretty sure he had never forgotten to eat in his entire life. "No. It doesn't."

"So you want to go?"

"Uh . . ."

"I said I'd show you the neighborhood." Fabian stood up and shoved his papers into his bag. "We can start with ramen."

Ryan grinned. He really liked this idea. He liked anything that gave him a chance to be around Fabian. He was . . . comforting. "Okay."

It wasn't until they were seated at an intimate table in the corner of the ramen restaurant that Fabian realized he may have just invited Ryan on a date. Or, at least, what Ryan might perceive to be a date. In truth, Fabian had just wanted ramen and conversation.

And, yes. He liked looking at Ryan.

Ryan, who was studying his menu as if there would be a test

on it, *wasn't* looking at Fabian. Even at the coffee shop, Ryan had seemed tired. Or stressed, maybe. Now he seemed like he was already regretting his decision to follow Fabian to a second location.

"Hey," Fabian said gently, as if Ryan might spook if his voice were too loud. "If you don't want to eat here, I won't be offended. It was just a suggestion."

Ryan finally looked up from his menu. "No! No, it's fine. I just . . . what do you usually order here?"

"I always get the Tonkotsu ramen because the broth takes forever to make. Like, I'd never boil bones for hours at home. And it's delicious."

Ryan closed his menu. "Okay."

"But," Fabian said quickly, "they have lots of stuff. Some of the ramen has beef, or seafood, or some have spicy broth, if you prefer."

"The first one you said is fine."

They sat in silence for a moment, and then Ryan started drumming his fingers on the table. He stopped when the server came to take their orders. Fabian ordered first, and then Ryan grunted, "I'll have the same."

As soon as the server left, Ryan returned to drumming his fingers. Finally Fabian asked, "Are you all right?"

The drumming stopped, and Ryan moved his hand off the table, into his lap. "Sorry."

"You seem nervous about something. I hope it isn't me."

Ryan grimaced. "No. I have to get on a plane tomorrow. That's all."

Fabian was surprised. "Don't you have to get on a plane, like, every day?"

"Pretty often, yeah. You'd think I might have relaxed about it by now."

"You're scared of flying?"

Ryan nodded. "Always have been. I hoped I'd get over it, but . . ."

"So you fly like a zillion times a year, and *every time* you're terrified?"

Ryan nudged his chopstick holder with his finger. "Yep."

Fabian wanted to reach out and place a hand on Ryan's arm, or maybe find his hand under the table. He did neither. "God, that sucks."

"It's stupid, I know. There's no reason for me to be . . . like this. But I can't help it."

"Is there anything you can take for it? Or have you tried, like, hypnotism?" Fabian cringed inwardly. He really had no idea what he was talking about.

But Ryan nodded. "I've tried just about everything. It's not only flying. I'm . . ." He seemed to consider his next words very carefully, but before he could say them their server returned with glasses of water for each of them. By the time the server left, Ryan apparently decided to change the subject. "Why don't you tell me about your favorite bars here in the Village?"

Fabian was disappointed, but he could be a distraction, if that's what Ryan needed. He launched into an animated and probably overly detailed description of the types of men Ryan would be likely to meet at each bar.

The conversation continued until their food arrived and beyond. He discovered, as he was telling Ryan about one of the pubs that usually showed hockey on the big screens, he didn't particularly like the idea of Ryan hooking up with other men. But that was ridiculous.

He soldiered on. "So if you're looking for older guys, or guys who are kind of more," he waved his hand in Ryan's direction, "masc, or whatever, that's a good place to go."

Ryan sucked a tangle of noodles into his mouth and then said, "A chill vibe is good. But those guys aren't really my type."

Fabian's eyebrows shot up.

"Not that it even matters," Ryan said quickly. "I don't really pick up. At all."

"Wait. *Never?*"

Ryan poked at something in his bowl with his chopsticks. "Not for a while, no."

Fabian was intrigued. "Are you, like, not into casual sex? Or sex at all? It's cool if you aren't. I have friends who—"

"I like sex," Ryan said, this time looking Fabian right in the eyes. There was an intensity there that made his stomach flip.

"Oh. So . . ."

"I'm just bad at talking to people."

Fabian nudged Ryan's foot under the table. "You don't seem so bad to me. I like talking to you. If this were a date I'd say it was going very well."

Ryan looked back at his soup. "Thanks."

They ate in silence for a bit, and Fabian used the time to consider the new information he had gathered from Ryan. He liked sex but didn't have it very often, he didn't go out much, and he maybe didn't like traditionally masc guys? That would actually make sense, given the way Ryan had obviously appreciated Fabian's flamboyant stage outfit the other night.

Fabian didn't have any particular type. It was actually wild to think that, just over a week ago, he had woken up with Claude in his bed. And now he was having dinner with a man who was the opposite of Claude in almost every way. Fabian found both men attractive, but he almost certainly had more in common with Claude. In theory, Fabian really shouldn't have much to say to Ryan.

"Do you like to dance?" Fabian asked.

"Sort of. I'm not good at it, and I usually feel stupid doing it, but I like it sometimes."

"My friends are going out to celebrate Tarek's birthday in a couple of weeks. It will be fun. You should come."

Ryan's brow furrowed. "Me?"

"Yeah!" This wasn't a terrible idea, was it? "We're going to Force, which is the biggest gay nightclub around. It's very loud and busy, but you are guaranteed to see hot men in every flavor. And if you don't want to dance, that's cool, but you should come."

"Um. Maybe."

"I'll remind you closer to the date. I haven't been to Force in ages. I'm excited."

"I'll bet you're a good dancer," Ryan said.

"Oh god, I'm the best. Totally amazing. Just wait."

Ryan laughed. "I've always admired your confidence."

"Really? Even when I was a grumpy teenage shit?"

"Yes," Ryan said earnestly. "Even then."

"Huh." Fabian was honestly pretty touched by Ryan's words. He hadn't thought of himself as particularly admirable when he'd been a teen.

"Are you supposed to eat everything in the bowl?" Ryan asked. It was a clear attempt to change the subject. "I still have a lot of corn left."

"I think only the most hardcore ramen eaters clean the bowl," Fabian said. "So what do you have planned for this evening?"

Ryan set his chopsticks on the table and pushed the bowl away. "Go home. Rest up for tomorrow."

"Are you actually going to rest, or are you going to start worrying about your flight the moment you're alone?"

Ryan sighed. "Probably that second thing."

"Well then . . ." Fabian leaned in. "How about I distract you some more?"

Okay. He could admit that was just blatantly flirtatious, but he wasn't actually suggesting anything . . . untoward.

Ryan's mouth hung open for a second, and then he said, "Distract me how?"

"Well, we could walk off this ramen. I could show you the neighborhood. You probably don't get enough exercise, right?" Fabian teased. He had no idea why he was doing this. He should let Ryan get back to his own life, and Fabian should go home and figure out these songs. He had already taken up far too much of Ryan's time.

"Sure," Ryan said, lips curving into one of his adorable shy smiles. "A walk sounds good."

The sun was low in the sky when Ryan and Fabian left the restaurant. They walked north, up Church Street together, both with their hands in their coat pockets. Ryan knew this thing wasn't a date, but if it was it would be the best one he'd ever been on.

"How's your family?" he asked. "God, Amy must be grown up now."

"She's eighteen," Fabian confirmed. "Just started university."

"That's wild," Ryan said. "I can only picture her as a five-year-old. How about Sonia?" Fabian's older sister had been the hockey star of the family. She hadn't been living at home when Ryan had been there, but she'd joined the family for dinners, and came by the house to do her laundry sometimes. Most people would say that she and Fabian were total opposites, but Ryan thought they were actually pretty similar, just into different things. Both were confident, opinionated, and extremely talented. Unfortunately for Fabian, Sonia was the one whose talents were celebrated in the Salah household.

"Are you ready for this? Sonia is married and *pregnant*."

"Wow, really?"

"Yep. She announced it last month. She's also a hockey coach now, which is kind of badass: a pregnant woman behind the bench."

Ryan smiled at that. It did sound pretty awesome. And he could imagine Sonia daring anyone to suggest she shouldn't be there. "That's cool. What about your parents?"

"They're fine. Dad is still coaching. Mom is still working. I don't talk to them very often. There's no rift or anything. We just . . . don't have that much to say to each other, I guess."

Ryan wasn't surprised by this. Joe and Maya Salah had always seemed a little bewildered by their only son. Ryan was sure that they had expected to be raising a future NHL star and instead had gotten . . . Fabian.

"Are your parents cool?" Fabian asked. "Do you get along with them, I mean? I've never met them."

"They're great," Ryan said sincerely. "I don't get home as much as they'd like, but we talk all the time."

"That's good. Do they know you're gay, then?"

"Yeah, they know. I think they were pretty surprised when I told them, but they were good with it. I mean, Dad never says much, but . . ."

"Are you telling me your father is a quiet man, Ryan? I'm shocked."

Ryan laughed. "Dad makes *me* seem chatty. Colleen, my sister, was maybe *too* excited. It's like having a gay brother is the most interesting thing that's ever happened to her or something."

"That's kind of sweet, though, I guess," Fabian said. "Was your dad a hockey player too?"

"No. He played a bit, I think, but he was a boxer. A good one. One of the top-ranked boxers in Canada back in his day. He has a little gym back in Ross Harbour where he teaches kids."

"Is that where you learned how to fight?"

Ryan shrugged. "He taught me the basics. My heart was never really in it, and I think he knew it. The skills have come in handy, though."

They were silent a moment, and then Fabian said, "I'm going home for Christmas this year. I don't always, but I thought with the pregnancy and all, I should probably go."

"I don't usually make it home for Christmas," Ryan said. "I feel bad about it, but it's a lot of travel for two days, y'know?"

"Especially when you hate flying."

"Yeah." Ryan didn't want to talk about flying. At the moment, he was the most at ease he'd ever been the evening before a flight. He wanted to keep it that way. "So where are you taking me?"

"What do you want to see? There's a cool bookstore on the next block, and a record store. On the next block there's a great little cocktail bar, not that I am trying to be a bad influence."

Ryan chuckled. "I *do* have to play a game tomorrow night."

"Next time."

He liked the sound of *next time*. "For sure. How about we check out the bookstore?"

Fabian grinned at him. "I forgot that you're a book lover. You'll love this place. It focuses on queer lit and political nonfic, but they have a bit of everything. And the staff is super awesome. I should take you to Vanessa's store sometime. It's closed now, but it's rad."

"Is it a bookstore too?"

"They do have books, but it's mostly a sex shop. But, like, a very sex-positive, queer-positive one. Vanessa has been working there for years. I think people think she owns it."

"Oh." Ryan had spent very little time in sex shops. None, actually. The only toy he'd ever owned had been purchased online, and he'd always bought the rest of his supplies at drugstores.

"They've got everything. Talk to Vanessa. She'll hook you up with whatever you need," Fabian said casually, as if he were talking about a sporting goods store. Ryan would definitely *not* be asking Vanessa to *hook him up*. "Here's the bookstore."

They spent a half hour or so looking around the store, which seemed to double as a community space for speakers and workshops. There were posters throughout the store that listed upcoming events. Ryan liked it, and he planned to come back again sometime soon.

After that they strolled to the northern most corner of the Village, crossed the street, and walked back down toward Ryan's apartment building. Fabian pointed out the bars, shops, and restaurants that he liked as they walked and talked. It was one of the most enjoyable evenings Ryan had ever experienced. When they reached Ryan's building he felt an inappropriate urge to kiss Fabian good night. Or invite him up.

"So hockey is paying you okay, then?" Fabian asked wryly as he glanced up at the gleaming tower where Ryan lived.

"Pays all right," Ryan muttered, embarrassed. In a perfect world Fabian would be making at least as much money playing music as Ryan did playing hockey.

"I liked this," Fabian said. "I'm glad we reconnected."

"Me too," Ryan said. God, Fabian's lashes were long. Makeup or no makeup, he was gorgeous.

"You know," Fabian said, and his lips curved into the playful, seductive smile that both thrilled and terrified Ryan, "of all the hockey players who lived with us, you were my favorite."

Ryan snorted. "I was the best of the worst, was I?"

"Oh yes. By far."

"I liked living with your family. With . . . you."

"Did you?" Fabian was so close to him, Ryan worried he would be able to hear the hammering of his heart. "When are you back in town?"

"Next Friday. I play a game on Saturday night."

"There's an open mic on Mondays at the Indigo Café—I pointed it out to you on our walk—and I'm planning on playing it that Monday after you're back. I want to work out some of these new songs."

"Are you inviting me?"

The playful smile returned. "I am casually dropping that information in the hopes that you will come. I couldn't possibly *invite* you to watch me fumble my way through some new material. That would be rude."

Ryan laughed. "I'll be there."

"I won't be offended if you change your mind."

And then Fabian stretched up and kissed Ryan on the cheek. Ryan was caught so off guard by it that he just stood there stiffly, barely registering what was happening until it was over. "Good night, Ryan."

Fabian turned and walked away so quickly that Ryan could only mumble "good night" to his retreating back as he brushed his fingers against the spot where Fabian had kissed him.

CHAPTER TEN

There were two interesting things about the game in Ottawa. One was that Coach Cooper had announced that Wyatt would be in nets because the Guardians' star goalie, Anders Nilsson, needed a rest, and, frankly, Ottawa had a terrible team. Coach had, in fact, described the Ottawa team's abilities using some very vulgar and homophobic language that Ryan was trying not to dwell on.

The other interesting thing was that this was the first time Toronto had played against Ottawa since the former Boston superstar, Ilya Rozanov, had signed with them over the summer.

The first period had barely made it to the five-minute mark when Rozanov started getting into it with Dallas Kent. Both players were known for their trash talk as much as their goal scoring ability, but neither of them was much good at finishing what they started. That was Ryan's job.

Rozanov had just very obviously shoved Kent during a stoppage in play. The officials either hadn't seen it, or were choosing to ignore it. Ryan skated over to where the two superstars were shouting at each other and very halfheartedly pulled Rozanov away from Kent.

Rozanov turned and beamed at Ryan like he was delighted to see him. "Price! Thank god you are here. This goblin is bothering me."

Ryan pressed his lips together. Goblin was an amusingly accurate description of Dallas Kent.

"Eat my nuts, Rozanov!" Kent snarled.

Rozanov made a face. "No fucking thank you."

Behind him, Ryan heard Wyatt bark out a laugh. Ryan turned and shook his head at him.

"Sorry!" Wyatt held up his giant glove. "Sorry. I shouldn't laugh."

Both Rozanov and Kent had skated off to their benches, so Ryan said, "Don't encourage Rozanov."

"I think I might love him."

Ryan had no beef with Rozanov. He'd played with him in Boston—had won the Stanley Cup with him, in fact—and while they hadn't exactly been friends, Rozanov had always been nice enough to him. He was the opposite of Ryan in almost every way—flashy, and confident to the point of being obnoxious—but Ryan respected him.

Despite Rozanov and Kent sniping at each other throughout, the game was pretty relaxing for Ryan. Fun, even. Ottawa didn't really have a proper enforcer, so he'd known it was unlikely he'd be getting into any actual fights. He spent most of the game pulling Ottawa players away from Toronto players after the whistle, and chatting with Wyatt.

And, oddly, Rozanov.

"How's Toronto?" Rozanov asked him during a break in the second period.

"Not bad."

"Sucks that you have to play with Kent, though."

Ryan didn't reply to that. "How's Ottawa?"

"Not as bad as I thought it would be."

Ryan didn't think Ottawa suited Rozanov at all. He'd been as surprised as everyone else when Ottawa had announced Rozanov's signing in July. Ilya Rozanov was flashy and loud, with his European sports car collection and his reputation as a ladies' man. Ryan would have expected him to go somewhere like New York or L.A. or maybe Florida, since a player as talented as Rozanov could choose who he signed with. Ottawa was a seemingly random and baffling choice.

In the third period, something incredible happened: Ryan scored a goal. He'd had the puck at the blue line and, not seeing any better options, had just fired the puck at the net, hoping someone would get a rebound opportunity out of it. But the Ottawa goalie had missed it, and it had ended up streaking over his shoulder and hitting the back of the net.

"Holy shit, Price," Rozanov chirped as Ryan skated past the Ottawa bench. "I didn't know you could do that!"

Ryan bit his lip, but he couldn't stop the goofy grin that took over his face. He'd scored only a handful of goals during his NHL career, so each one was pretty exciting. When he reached his own bench he was met by a chorus of "Attaboy, Pricey!" and "Nice one, Pricey!" He knew, as he sat on the bench, that there would be a close-up of his face on the televised broadcast right now. He tried to look cool.

The game ended with Toronto winning 5–2, and the team just had time to shower and put on their suits before they needed to board a plane to Montreal. Ryan was not a fan of days that involved two flights and a game, but it was probably better to get the flight over with now than to spend a night worrying about it. He didn't understand why teams needed to fly from Ottawa to Montreal anyway. It was such a short drive.

He was exhausted, mentally and physically, by the time he fell on his bed in his Montreal hotel room. Unlike Ottawa, Montreal had a very good team, thanks in part to their star player,

Shane Hollander, having an outstanding start to his season. Ryan would have to get as much rest as possible before the game tomorrow night.

But there was a text message on his phone.

From Fabian.

You scored a goal!

Ryan checked, and then double-checked, to make *sure* the message was from Fabian. Because it didn't make any sense that he had watched the game. Then Ryan texted back, You watched the game?

FABIAN:

I was at a bar to see a friend's band and the game was on.

RYAN:

And you watched it?

FABIAN:

Not closely. But I saw a blue jersey with "Price" on the back so I watched for a bit.

Ryan smiled and replied with, How did I look?

He wished he could take the question back, but Fabian was already typing a reply. It seemed to take forever for his response to show up on Ryan's phone.

FABIAN:

Tiny, mostly. But there was one close-up shot of you where you looked kind of . . . intense. And sweaty.

Oh. Ryan had no idea what to say to that. But Fabian added, It was a good look with a winky face emoji.

Ryan snorted and wrote, If you say so.

FABIAN:

I do say so. And then I saw you score that goal. It might be the first time I felt excited about a hockey thing.

RYAN:

Happy to be your first.

Oh god. What the fuck, Ryan? What was it about Fabian that made Ryan *playful*? He was never playful.

FABIAN:

Where are you now?

RYAN:

Montreal. We flew here right after the game. Another game tomorrow night.

FABIAN:

At least the flight is over.

RYAN:

Yep. Where are you?

FABIAN:

Home. Trying to figure out a song.

RYAN:

It's late.

FABIAN:

I know. But I won't be able to sleep until I work this out.

Ryan smiled, and wished he could see Fabian right now. He imagined his hair being disheveled from Fabian running his hand through it as he worked. Maybe he was wearing pajamas or something cozy.

RYAN:

Don't stay up too late. I'll see you on Monday, ok?

FABIAN:

Ok, superstar.

Ryan took his tea the same way his mother did—orange pekoe with a big splash of milk. Unfortunately, his Columbus hotel room only had powdered coffee whitener, so the tea tasted terrible.

He sat on the edge of the bed, staring at the wall and trying to process everything he had just discussed in his Skype session with his therapist. Or, more importantly, what he *hadn't* discussed with her. Like the fact that Fabian brushing his delicate fingers over Ryan's bruised knuckles had nearly made Ryan's knees go out. Surely it had more to do with how long it had been since Ryan had last been touched by another man, but god, it had affected him. And then there'd been that chaste kiss Fabian had pressed to Ryan's cheek last week, which Ryan swore he could still feel on his skin.

He could have also talked about the fact that he was feeling real sexual desire for the first time in a *very* long time. Or the fact that, as much as he liked imagining laying Fabian on top of the clothing that was strewn all over the mattress in his charming little apartment and kissing his elegant neck, Ryan was too insecure to actually attempt intimacy with anyone.

He *should* talk about these things, but he just couldn't. It was too embarrassing to get into, even with a professional therapist. So when she'd asked if he had anything else he wanted to talk about, he'd just said, "Nope. I think that's about it for today."

Coward.

Fabian hadn't texted him since their brief conversation in Montreal the other night, which wasn't surprising. Frankly, the surprising thing was that he had texted Ryan in the first place. That he had *watched Ryan play hockey*.

Ryan picked up his phone now, just in case.

There was a message, but it was from Wyatt. I can't believe our day off is in Columbus.

RYAN:

Bored?

WYATT:

Did you know there is a Drainage Hall of Fame here?

Ryan grinned, and wrote, I heard the lines are pretty crazy this time of year, though.

Wyatt didn't respond right away, and Ryan started to worry that he didn't get his joke.

WYATT:

Maybe we can buy a speed pass. Skip the lines.

RYAN:

What are you really doing today?

WYATT:
I was thinking about doing literally anything else. Wanna grab lunch?

RYAN:
Yeah!

"Holy shit! Check it out, Pricey!" Wyatt held up a seemingly random issue of a comic book that he'd pulled out of a long box crammed full of comics. When Ryan didn't respond with the level of excitement Wyatt obviously thought this treasure warranted, Wyatt explained, "I've been looking for this for years. It's the only Norm Breyfogle *Batman* comic I don't have."

"Oh. Cool."

Wyatt kissed the plastic wrapper on the comic. "I love Columbus!"

Ryan laughed and followed Wyatt to another box of comics. It had, in fact, been an enjoyable afternoon. Wyatt found a really nice brewpub for the two of them to have lunch at, and after lunch (and a couple of beers) they'd wandered around downtown Columbus, which wasn't a bad place at all. Then Wyatt had led them to this comic shop, which Ryan suspected had been his plan all along.

The afternoon had been a good distraction. If Wyatt hadn't invited him out, Ryan probably would have spent the day in his hotel room, daydreaming about Fabian. He needed to stop wishing for impossible Fabian-related things, like kissing his sexy mouth. Fabian, he was sure, hadn't wanted to kiss him now any more than he had when they'd been teenagers. Fabian probably had a boyfriend. Or a lineup of beautiful men who wanted to kiss him. Or, most likely, both.

And Ryan was still a dumb hockey player. Still much too large, much too awkward, much too boring for brilliant, gorgeous, confident Fabian.

"You heard about the party, right?" Wyatt asked as he inspected another bagged comic.

"Party?"

"Yeah. Kent's birthday party."

Ugh. "Oh. I think I heard some of the guys talking about that. Are you going?"

"Sure. Team party. Of course I'm going. Aren't you?"

He almost said no, but he remembered his coach's warning that he wanted Ryan to be a team player off the ice, as well as on. "When is it?"

"Next Friday at Kent's house. Kent's *mansion*, I should say."

Next Friday. Why did that seem like a significant day? Ryan pondered it as Wyatt moved on to examining the shelves of colorful books that lined one wall of the comic shop. Ryan pulled a book with a bright pink spine off the shelf and flipped through it. The story looked very weird and confusing, full of bizarre-looking alien characters and floating heads yelling things in outer space. He put it back.

"Maybe there will be a cute guy at the party for you," Wyatt said with a grin. Ryan rolled his eyes. "What? You never know."

"I'm not going to meet someone at Dallas Kent's fucking birthday party."

Birthday party. Right. Next Friday night was when Fabian and his friends were going to that club to celebrate Tarek's birthday. Damn. It was probably unlikely that Ryan would have actually joined them at that club anyway. But it sure sounded more appealing than a party celebrating Dallas goddamned Kent.

"You should read this," Wyatt said. He handed Ryan a thick book that said *Daredevil* on it. "It's about a sad sack who sacrifices his body every night to save others. You'd like it."

Ryan attempted a menacing glare. "I'm not a sad sack," he lied.

"You know what? Most superhero comics are about self-sacrificing sad sacks, now that I think about it."

"You saying I'm a superhero?"

"No question." Wyatt grabbed another book off the shelf and added to a small stack he had built on the floor. "Speaking of, have you thought any more about visiting the community center with me?"

Ryan hadn't thought about it at all. "You still want me to?"

"Definitely. Like I said, the kids will love you. I'll let you know next time I go, okay?"

"Sure. I guess. If you really think they'd want me there."

"Trust me, it'll be great. You'll love them." Wyatt hefted the stack of books off the floor and handed it to Ryan with a playful smile.

Ryan rolled his eyes and accepted the heavy pile. "How are you even going to fit these in your suitcase?"

"Easy. I'll throw some of my clothes in the garbage."

Ryan snorted and shook his head. He took the books to the counter so Wyatt could pay for them.

"Well," Wyatt said a few minutes later when they were standing outside the store. "We could just go back to the hotel. Or . . . we could go check out the *world's largest gavel*."

"What?"

Wyatt looked at his phone. "It's outside the Supreme Court Building." He frowned. "Oh. It's only the *second-largest* gavel now. They built a bigger one in Illinois."

"That's disappointing."

"Yeah. Fuck that. I'm not lugging these books around Columbus just to look at the *second*-largest gavel. Largest or nothing. Let's head back."

It seemed Ryan would have time to daydream about kissing Fabian after all.

CHAPTER ELEVEN

When Ryan arrived at the café on Monday night, Fabian was nowhere to be seen. There was a small stage—really just a slightly elevated corner of the room—which was empty besides a stool and a microphone stand. A few patrons sat at tables, but it was mostly quiet in the room.

Ryan did not like *this* situation at all.

Maybe he should text Fabian to confirm that this open mic was still happening, and that Fabian would indeed be coming to it. Maybe Ryan had gotten the location wrong. Maybe he should just leave and apologize later if he needed to.

Oh god. Ryan had just been standing, frozen, at the café entrance and now people were staring at him.

He made a decision, and went to the counter to order something. He could sit and nurse a beverage for a bit, and if Fabian didn't show up, he could leave.

The barista was a young woman who looked far cooler than Ryan could ever hope to be, but she smiled warmly when he approached the counter. "You here for the open mic?"

"Uh, yeah. I was worried I was in the wrong place maybe."

"Nope. It's not usually a big crowd. Mondays, y'know?"

"Right."

"Are you playing tonight?"

For a moment, Ryan thought she recognized him and was asking about a hockey game. Then he realized what she was actually asking him.

"Me? God, no. No. I'm here to see a . . . friend."

"Ah. Can I get you something?"

Ryan ordered a tea, and wished he had noticed before that the café was licensed. He would have preferred a beer. But she was already preparing his orange pekoe, so he didn't say anything.

He found an empty table, sat, and waited, staring at the steam rising off his tea like it was the most fascinating thing in the world. Then he remembered that he had an e-book on his phone he could read. Thank god for books.

He had been comfortably reading for about half an hour when he heard Fabian's voice behind him. Ryan turned and saw both Fabian and Vanessa, and a third person—a young Black man—who Ryan didn't recognize.

Fabian spotted him immediately and waved. He seemed to have brought only his violin tonight.

"You came!" he said cheerfully when he reached the table. He fell into the chair next to Ryan while Vanessa and the other man pulled chairs over from nearby tables to join them. "Have you been waiting long? I should have warned you that this thing always starts late."

"It's okay. I was reading."

"Oh good. You remember Vanessa? And this is Marcus, her roommate and one of our very best friends. Marcus, this is Ryan."

Marcus extended a hand. "Oh, I have been *dying* to meet *you*."

Ryan warily shook his hand, and Fabian slapped Marcus's arm. "Don't listen to him, Ryan. He's just trying to embarrass me."

Ryan tried not to think too much about what that might mean. Instead he said, "It's a lot quieter here than it was at your show." He noticed that Fabian was dressed very casually—jeans, a black sweater, and just a trace of eyeliner. When Fabian leaned forward, Ryan could see his collarbone peeking out of the wide neck of the sweater.

"Oh, this place is dead," Fabian said casually. "I like that, though. It's a good place to try stuff out."

"The place would be packed if people knew he was playing tonight," Vanessa said.

"As if." Then Fabian smiled. "Well, yes. Probably. But it's a very small room."

"So you play for the Guardians?" Marcus said.

"Yes. Last I heard anyway." It was a joke that would work better in hockey circles, but Marcus smiled politely.

"You played Saturday night. The bar I work at shows the games early in the evening. I didn't see the end. Did you win?"

"We did. It was a good one."

"What are you drinking?" Fabian asked. "I'll buy a round."

"Um, tea."

"You're not buying me anything, Fabian," Vanessa scolded. "Sit down."

"I'll buy," Ryan said. "I was thinking of getting a beer, and hockey pays pretty well, so . . ."

"I'll bet it does," Marcus purred. "I like your new friend, Fabian."

Ryan stood, and Fabian offered to go with him. Ryan was grateful because he was worried he would forget everyone's orders. When they were away from the table, Fabian said, "Sorry about them. They're sort of . . . overly interested in you."

"Really? Why?"

And for a moment it really looked like Fabian might be blushing a bit. "I don't know. I guess because they know how I feel about hockey players and they probably think it's funny that I—" He shook his head. "They're just being dumb. You're a curiosity because you're new."

"Okay."

They ordered everyone's drinks and Ryan paid. Everyone had ordered a beer or a wine, so they didn't have to wait long for them. Ryan picked up two pints of beer and was about to carry them to the table when Fabian put a hand on his arm. "Wait."

"What?"

"Just . . . before we join those two idiots—who I love—I just want to thank you for being here. Sincerely."

"Oh. No problem. To be honest, I've been looking forward to it."

Ryan held his breath and waited for Fabian's reply. There was something in Fabian's eyes—surprise or maybe confusion. But then he smiled and said, "Me too."

Ryan truly had no idea what this was anymore. It seemed almost like a date, but that would be ridiculous. And impossible. Ryan liked spending time with Fabian, and he loved watching him perform, but someone as beautiful and happy as Fabian had no place in Ryan's miserable world. And Fabian was showing Ryan kindness by offering himself as a guide to the Toronto scene. It didn't mean he wanted anything to do with Ryan beyond that.

They brought the drinks back to the table and they had barely sat back down when Vanessa said, "Have you tested that vibrator yet, Fabian?"

Fabian struggled to swallow his wine, then glared at her. "What is *wrong with you*?"

She spread her hands. "What? Are we shy about vibrators

now? Is this a church supper? I need to get a review of that thing on my site."

"We can talk about this *later*."

She turned to Ryan. "Sorry. Are you an adult who is aware of the existence of sex toys?"

"Yes."

"Great. Fabian, have you used the vibrator?"

He shook his head slowly, eyes narrowed. "You are so inappropriate. No. I haven't used it, okay?"

"Well, use it! Or find someone to use it on." She very deliberately tilted her head in Ryan's direction after she said this. Ryan looked at his beer. Marcus started laughing.

"All right, enough," Fabian grumbled. "I am going to ask if I can play first, and you two are going to be nice to Ryan."

Fabian left, and Ryan decided he could try out being cool. "You review sex toys, Vanessa?"

"I do! But sometimes I have to outsource the ones for parts I don't have. A lot of the guest reviews are anonymous, so if you ever want to—"

"No, I'm not—I mean. I wouldn't be any good at that."

She shrugged. "Offer stands. Just let me know. It's a great way to get free toys."

"Um. Thanks."

"Oh my *god*," Fabian said when he returned to the table. "Are you still talking about sex toys?"

"It's okay," Ryan said quickly. "I asked about her website."

Fabian looked suspiciously at Vanessa, then he must have decided to drop it. "I'm going on in a minute. Raksha says there's only three people signed up for tonight."

The place had filled up a bit since Ryan had first arrived, but it was still a relatively small crowd, the kind where Fabian would be able to see each individual face when he was on the stage. Ryan felt ill just imagining it.

"Good luck!" Vanessa said. "I can't wait to hear what you've been working on."

Marcus turned to Ryan. "He totally disappeared last week. He does that. He'll be struck with inspiration and go into hermit mode."

"I wasn't a hermit," Fabian protested. "I worked two shifts at the drugstore, went to see a show, and I even bought groceries."

Marcus flicked his hand. "Go. Show us the fruits of your labor."

Fabian made a show of grabbing his violin case and turning dramatically toward the stage. Ryan found it oddly sexy.

Even with the small crowd and the minimal setup, Fabian was a commanding presence when he took the stage. He took a moment to get himself and his instrument ready, plugged his phone into something-or-other, and then he nodded at the barista—Raksha—to kill the music that had been playing through the speakers. There was chatter after the music stopped, followed by a moment of almost perfect silence when Fabian stepped to the mic.

Ryan thought he would greet the crowd or introduce the first song, but instead Fabian just started singing, a cappella. The first note was so strong and clear, it was startling. And maybe that was the point; Fabian obviously knew how to get an audience's attention.

After a verse and a chorus, a backing track from Fabian's phone accompanied him, and he started to play his violin. He couldn't sing and play the violin at the same time, so he would just switch between voice and violin, like a magical conversation he was having with his instrument. Ryan didn't think his own heart beat even once during the entire song.

"Wow, right?" Vanessa whispered to him when the song was over.

"Yeah," Ryan said stupidly. Fabian smiled at the crowd and

tugged the shoulder of his sweater, which had slid halfway down his arm while he'd been playing, back up. He was so fucking beautiful Ryan couldn't stand it. As stunning as Fabian had been onstage in the club at the last show, with the wall of sound he'd created and the dramatic costume and lighting, there was something even more enchanting about this moment. The intimacy of the room—the small audience, the warm lighting, and Fabian's casual attire—made Ryan feel special, like he was one of the chosen few who were permitted to watch a prince perform.

For about the millionth time that week, Ryan remembered the fleeting touch of Fabian's soft lips on his cheek. It had been so chaste—nothing, really—but it had absolutely consumed Ryan's thoughts for days. Was it possible for your heart to hold on to a ridiculous crush for thirteen years? And if so, why would his heart choose someone so unattainable? Why would it want someone who was so wildly incompatible with Ryan?

But Fabian, for whatever reason, gave Ryan the impression that he enjoyed his company. He didn't seem to notice or care that Ryan was starved for the light Fabian radiated effortlessly. He didn't know that, if he got too close, Ryan would no doubt extinguish that light and drag him down into the shadows with him.

Fabian played four songs and then thanked the audience for listening. The applause was surprisingly enthusiastic for such a small group. A couple of minutes later, Fabian had rejoined the table, violin case in hand.

"Don't say anything," he said. "I don't want to hear a word."

"Hm?" Marcus said, pretending to be engrossed in his phone. "I'm sorry, I wasn't paying attention. Did you play yet?"

Fabian rolled his eyes. "Okay, asshole."

"That was terrible," Vanessa said. "I can't believe you made us listen to that."

"You guys are such fucking dicks."

He glanced at Ryan, and Ryan knew he should say *something*, but Fabian's sweater had slipped again, exposing an entire shoulder. Ryan wanted to sink his teeth into it.

"Speechless," Fabian said, waving a hand at him. "Ryan is my new favorite."

"We *know*," Marcus muttered.

"That was really—" Ryan started.

Fabian cut him off. "Incredible. I know. Let's talk about something else. Are you going to come dancing with us on Friday?"

Vanessa lit up. "Oh my god! Yes! You have to!"

"Actually, I can't." He looked at Fabian. "Sorry. There's a team party—a birthday thing. I just found out about it a couple of days ago. Otherwise I would have gone."

Fabian actually looked disappointed by this. "Oh. Well, that's too bad. If the party sucks, be sure to drop by the club. We'll be there until it closes, I suspect."

"Right. Okay." Ryan wished he could say no to the party. He didn't want to go to Dallas Kent's stupid house. He definitely had no interest in celebrating Kent's birthday. But he'd promised to be a team player this year, on and off the ice. Skipping the star player's party would likely be a bad move.

It was probably for the best. Going to a dance club with Fabian and his beautiful friends would be torture. Ryan could envision how the night would go: he would be standing against a wall, trying not to be noticed. He wouldn't be dancing, and he'd be overheated and uncomfortable. The music would be too loud. Fabian would be on the dance floor, pressing his lithe body against some other gorgeous man. And then they would start touching, and kissing, and Ryan would be unable to look away.

And then Ryan would go home alone to unsuccessfully jerk off.

Well, fuck that. Ryan could unsuccessfully jerk off just fine *without* the trouble of watching Fabian seduce another man on a dance floor.

The other open mic performers were both women with guitars, and both were talented with interesting songs and strong voices. But Ryan was getting anxious to leave. If he weren't worried about being rude, he would have left after Fabian's set. With each minute that passed, Ryan was increasingly overwhelmed by the feeling that he did not belong here. He wished he could fit in with these sparkling, creative people, but he didn't. He was a dark cloud, and it was time he drifted away.

"I'm gonna head out," he said, after the last performer left the stage.

"Oh," said Fabian. "Are you just going home?"

"Yeah. Thanks for inviting me out, though. It was great to hear you again."

Without warning, Vanessa clamped a hand on Ryan's wrist. "Wait. Which way are you walking, Ryan?"

"South."

"Oh good! Marcus and I are walking north, so you can walk with Fabian. We don't like him walking alone at night."

Ryan glanced at Fabian, but he was glaring at Vanessa. "You don't have to, Ryan," he said, his eyes not leaving her face.

"No, it's okay. I can walk with you."

"Great!" Vanessa said. "Fabian really appreciates it."

Marcus snorted, and Ryan wasn't sure what that was about, but for now he could focus on the noble and completely non-sexual task of making sure Fabian got home safely.

CHAPTER TWELVE

Ten minutes later, Fabian was saying his goodbyes to his friends out on the sidewalk. He kissed both of them on the cheek, and Ryan felt a stab of embarrassment over how much that meaningless gesture had affected him last week.

"Shall we?" Fabian asked him, after Vanessa and Marcus had left.

Ryan half expected Fabian to loop arms with him, but he didn't. Instead, he said, "So that wasn't too terrible, then?"

"God, no. That was awesome. I had, like, goose bumps." Ryan held his arm out, as if to prove it, before realizing he was wearing a heavy coat. He put his arm down. "Is it weird playing in front of a small audience like that?"

"Not really. I like how intimate it is. It wasn't so long ago that I was only playing open mics like that."

"And you miss it?"

Fabian laughed. "No. I worked damn hard to get where I am now. I played open mics while working shitty retail jobs and occasionally playing with a string quartet for hire. Then I started recording my music and getting it online. I was asked to open for a few local artists, which eventually led to my being able to book my own shows. Now I'm on an indie label." Fabian quickly added, "Just a small one. Medium-sized, if we're being generous. I'm not making piles of money, but at least the label does a lot of the tedious stuff so I can focus on making music."

"That's cool. What's the next step?"

"Super Bowl halftime, obviously," Fabian said wryly. Ryan laughed.

They walked in silence for a bit, and Ryan said, "I like your friends."

Fabian snorted, but Ryan could see that he was smiling. "Vanessa can be a bit much sometimes. She's pretty unapologetic about, well, everything. When she meets someone new, she tends to come on strong, like she's testing them. She's a total sweetheart, really. Like, the best friend you could possibly have, but she isn't shy about who she is or what she believes in."

"No, I can see that."

"So that's why she started talking about sex toys right out of the gate. I don't think she would have if you weren't there. Which I know is kind of fucked, but her thinking is sort of like . . ." Fabian seemed to search for his next words, so Ryan offered some.

"If you can't stand the heat, get out of the kitchen?"

Fabian smiled. "Right. If you can't stand her belief that sex is a positive and natural thing, then get out of the group."

Ryan considered this. "You don't seem as comfortable talking about it as she is."

"Oh, I am. I mean, no, no one is as comfortable as *she* is, but in the right company I have no problem. I appreciate that not everyone is comfortable talking about sex, though, whether or not they enjoy it."

"Right."

"I agree with her about it being natural. I think sex is fun. It *should* be fun anyway."

Ryan couldn't honestly remember the last time sex had been fun for him. The rare times over the past few years that he'd actually had sex, it was more or less an act of desperation, especially if it involved another person. Even with the men he'd had relationships with, the sex had always been stressful for Ryan. Performance anxiety, his own body issues, and being completely unsure of what to say, or what his partner wanted from him, had always tripped him up. Jerking off was just easier. Or, at least, it *had* been, before he'd started taking the meds.

But Ryan had always held on to the belief that sex *could* be fun, with the right partner. Or if he could ever let go of some of his hang-ups. He liked the general idea of sex a whole lot.

"You're quiet," Fabian observed. "Am I being as bad as Vanessa right now?"

"No," Ryan chuckled. "I just get lost in my own head a lot."

The night was cold and there was a brisk wind howling up the corridor the buildings made on both sides of the street. There was an ominous weight in the air of impending rain, and Ryan hoped it held off until they were both safely indoors.

"Do you, um . . . are you . . ." Ryan silently cursed himself for sounding so stupid, then tried again. "Is there someone that you're . . . with? Now?"

Fabian batted his lashes at him. "Ryan Price. Are you asking if I am spoken for?"

"No," Ryan said quickly. "I'm just curious. You never mentioned anyone, but I wasn't sure."

"I am currently unattached." They walked for a minute in silence, and then Fabian added, "I've never been particularly good at finding men who deserve me, as Vanessa likes to say."

Ryan didn't like the idea of some bozo who didn't appreciate Fabian getting to touch him. "No?" he said.

"I don't know if you've noticed," Fabian said wryly, "but I sort of love attention. And I get plenty of it with a healthy dose of adoration from my fans. I realize this makes me sound pompous, but it's the truth. I'm sure you understand, given who you are."

"Sort of. I guess." Ryan wasn't sure his NHL career had ever actually been the reason a man was attracted to him. His height, and the muscular body hockey had given him, had definitely been factors, but no one he'd ever hooked up with had seemed at all interested in hockey. Ryan hadn't even bothered to mention his occupation to most of them.

"Right, so it wouldn't be hard for me to find a man who loved my music and was thrilled to have sex with me."

"Sure. Easy," Ryan said dryly.

Fabian nudged him with his shoulder. "Listen. I'm just saying, I *could* find a nice boy who was already half in love with me just from watching me onstage, but I tend to gravitate toward the men who have almost no interest in me beyond appearances. Men who are usually so into their own creative pursuits that they couldn't care less about anyone else's. They just want to fuck me and tell me about their brilliant idea for an art installation, or show me their photography, or complain about publishers not understanding why their book is so great."

Ryan's brow furrowed. "Why would you want to be with those guys?"

"I don't know!" Fabian gave a high, frustrated laugh when he said it. "Believe me, if I knew I would stop."

"You *should* stop."

"Yes, thank you, *Vanessa*. What about you?"

Ryan froze for a second, and then scrambled to catch up with Fabian. "What about me what?"

"Do you get a lot of hockey groupies?"

"Uh, no. The kind of guys I'm into . . . aren't usually hockey fans."

They stopped at an intersection, waiting for the walk light, and Fabian turned to look up at him. "And what kind of guys are you into?"

You. Exactly you. "Um."

"Sorry." Fabian took a step back, and looked at the sidewalk. "It's none of my business. I won't judge you, believe me. I have friends who are into just about everything you can imagine. But you don't have to answer me."

"No. It's okay. I'm not that adventurous. But I like men who are . . . the opposite of me, basically."

Fabian seemed to study him a moment, as if trying to calculate what the opposite would be. "So, small guys?"

Ryan shuffled his feet nervously. He'd never talked about his personal tastes out loud to anyone before. Even his past partners. "Usually, yeah. And other stuff."

The walk light came on, and they crossed the street. When they reached the other side, Fabian picked up right where they'd left off. "Twinks?"

"Not exactly, no. But that's close, I guess. Age doesn't matter. It's not even a body type. It's more about . . . how they present themselves."

"Okay, now I really am intrigued."

Ryan could not believe he was trying to describe his perfect man *to* his perfect man. "Okay. This is it: I like men who sort of look at what men are *supposed* to be and say 'fuck you.' I like men who have the confidence to be themselves, even if it means a lot of people are gonna look at them funny."

For an agonizingly long time, there was no reply. Ryan was sure he'd just spouted a bunch of nonsense at Fabian, and Fabian was now wondering why he'd allowed such a weirdo to walk him home. It wasn't until they had approached Fabian's street that he said, in a voice so quiet Ryan almost didn't hear him over the wind, "I love that."

"What?"

"Everything you just said. I hate to stereotype, but hearing words like that coming from someone like you . . ."

"A big, dumb hockey player?"

Fabian shook his head, but then said, "Maybe. Not dumb, though. Ryan, you are so far from dumb. But you know how I feel about hockey players. About jocks in general. They were always around, invading my life, growing up. My parents placed boys like that—*men* like that—on pedestals. It was so obviously what they wanted me to be, and there was no way I could be that. Ever. As soon as they realized that, they lost interest in me."

"I noticed," Ryan said.

Fabian gave him a sad smile. "I know you did. That's why you were different. You think I had other hockey players showing up at my recitals?"

Ryan's heart skipped at the mention of Fabian's recital. He hadn't realized that Fabian remembered that night.

"Only you," Fabian continued. "I never told you how much that meant to me."

"It was nothing."

"It was definitely not nothing. It was . . ." He laughed humorlessly. "My *family* couldn't be bothered to make time to see me. That was my final recital at the Conservatory, and I was performing a piece that I had *composed*, and even that couldn't compete with a goddamned hockey game. No offense."

"None taken."

"When I saw you there, at the back of that room. It meant everything to me."

They had reached Fabian's apartment building, which was awkward because they were kind of in the middle of a big moment. They stood facing each other at the bottom of the stairs that led to the front door, and Ryan had no idea what to say next.

Thankfully, Fabian spoke first. "I know I was probably rude to you when we lived together."

"You weren't." It wasn't entirely true. Fabian had been blatantly uninterested in Ryan, mostly ignoring him and, when forced to acknowledge him, his words had been clipped and dismissive. But over time he had thawed a bit, and they'd been able to forge a quiet and precarious friendship of sorts.

"I was. I expected you to be like all the others, so I didn't even give you a chance."

"At first, maybe." Ryan gave him a shy smile. "But I think I won you over, right?"

Fabian smiled up at him, just as shyly, and Ryan's breath caught.

Then the rain started. Frigid drops that were on the edge of being ice pellets stung Ryan's face, and Fabian shrieked.

"Come inside!" he called as he dashed up the stairs. He fumbled with the lock. "Fuck this stupid piece of shit door! There." He pushed it open, and Ryan followed him in.

When they were inside the tiny apartment, Fabian hung his coat on a hook by the door, and made a grabby motion for Ryan's. "You may as well stay until the rain stops."

"It might rain all night," Ryan pointed out, but he handed Fabian his coat. Fabian ignored his weather report and walked to the bar fridge that was tucked in one corner, next to a two-burner cooktop and a sink. He opened the fridge and pulled out a bottle of wine.

"I haven't even opened this one yet," he said cheerfully. "Let's warm up. And please make yourself comfortable. You can sit on the bed, or . . . well, just the bed, I guess."

Ryan noted that the desk chair, the only other place to sit in the room, was piled high with discarded clothing. He sat at the very end of the bed, hands in his lap, back straight. He really should say no to the wine. And the bed. And being here at all.

Instead, he said nothing, and took a moment to study Fabian's home. The cluttered desk had what looked like three Catholic prayer candles, but when Ryan leaned forward he could see that the women on them weren't the Virgin Mary, but Dolly Parton, RuPaul, and Beyoncé.

Fabian handed Ryan a goblet that said *Mom's Time to Wine* on it. "It's the second-cheapest pinot grigio they had," he said, before sitting near the head of the bed, resting back against the pillows. His own wine glass said *Bride* on it.

Ryan took a sip of wine, because he didn't know what else to do. "It's good," he said. "The wine, I mean." It could be terrible. It could be actual battery acid. Ryan's brain was in a million pieces right now. Why was he here? Why were they both on Fabian's bed? Was Fabian trying to *seduce* him? Did Ryan *want* him to?

Fabian tapped a socked foot against Ryan's thigh. "You don't have to sit there with your back to me, you know. Relax."

Ryan set his glass on the desk and slipped his boots off. Then he carefully stretched out on the bed, leaning on one elbow. He kept as much distance as possible between their bodies, worried that the slightest invitation might cause him to jump poor Fabian, who was only being nice.

"So," Fabian said breezily, "how's hockey?"

Ryan huffed out a laugh. "Hockey is fine."

"Is it?"

Ryan frowned. "Sure. I don't know. I guess it's been a little . . . tiring. Lately."

Fabian traced the word *Bride* with his fingertip. "Do you ever think about quitting? Or retiring. However you say it."

"Sometimes. I'm only thirty-one, but . . ."

"But?"

"My heart's not really in it anymore."

"Then why do you still do it?"

Ryan shifted on the bed, bending his knees and tucking them in closer to his body. "Because I know how lucky I am. I know how many guys would kill to have a spot on an NHL team. Throwing it away would just be . . . disrespectful."

For a moment, Fabian said nothing, and then he said, "Did you know, after I graduated, I auditioned for the Toronto Symphony?"

"No. But I always imagined that's where you'd end up. I was kind of surprised, to be honest, to learn that you weren't playing with them."

"It was always my dream. So I auditioned. And . . . I was offered a spot."

"Wait. You were a member of the Toronto Symphony?"

"Mmhm. For two whole months."

"What happened?"

"I hated it," Fabian said simply. "I realized, very quickly, that it was not what I wanted to do, musically. I just didn't . . . fit in."

"Oh."

"Now, I realize I could have stayed, and done my own music on the side. But it's very time-consuming, being a part of something that big. That important. It's the big leagues, right?"

"Thank you for dumbing it down for me," Ryan said dryly.

Fabian smiled. "Anyway. I quit. It wasn't an easy decision, and I knew I was torching a very important bridge by doing so, but I've never regretted it. Not even when I am restocking lip balm at the drugstore, or when I am freezing to death in this drafty, shitty apartment. Because this," he waved a hand around, "is all me. I'd rather struggle to do what I love than devote myself to something I hate."

This was a lot for Ryan to take in.

"So, yes. Maybe it was absurd of me to throw away a job that so many musicians would kill for, but wouldn't it be more selfish of me to stay? I figured I should let someone else have that seat." He shrugged. "That's what I tell myself anyway."

"That actually makes a lot of sense," Ryan said slowly.

"And the other thing," Fabian sat up, and stabbed his wine glass in Ryan's direction, "is that someone else might *want* that symphony spot, or a spot on an NHL team, but guess what? They didn't get it. And they didn't get it because they aren't good enough. *We are.* But being good enough does not obligate us to take those jobs. It's okay to use your talent to create happiness rather than wealth. It's okay to not use your talent at all! Fuck anyone who says otherwise."

Ryan grinned at him. "You should be a therapist. Or a motivational speaker."

Fabian snorted, and set his wine glass on his nightstand. "No thank you. My wisdom is for myself, and a select few people who I care about. Same as my makeup skills."

Ryan liked Fabian including him in the select few people he cared about, even if inadvertently. "You don't share your makeup skills?"

Fabian dropped onto an elbow, his face suddenly very close to Ryan's. "I'd share them with *you*."

"*Me?*" Ryan sputtered. "I'd look ridiculous in makeup."

Fabian shook his head. "Not when *I'm* done with you." His gaze dropped to Ryan's mouth, and Ryan wondered if he was trying to decide what shade of lipstick would work best on him. He hoped so, because he couldn't think about the other reason Fabian might be studying his lips.

"I wouldn't look like you," Ryan said hoarsely.

"Have you ever felt beautiful, Ryan?" Was Fabian's face even closer now?

"No." Ryan laughed as if the question were ridiculous. "Of course not. Look at me."

"I am looking at you." Fabian reached out and tucked a strand of Ryan's hair behind his ear. "You don't think you're beautiful?"

"I—" Ryan could only imagine what the two of them, side by side, must look like right now. The stark difference between Fabian's staggering beauty and Ryan's old weathered barn of a body.

Fabian was stroking his hair freely now, his fingertips gliding over Ryan's scalp, then down his cheek into his beard. Ryan wasn't sure when he'd closed his eyes, but when he opened them, Fabian was looking at him like he was something precious.

"Tell me again," Fabian said softly. "About the men you like."

Oh god. "I should go."

"It's pouring out there. Can't you hear it?"

No. I can't hear anything over my blood pounding in my ears.

"Stay. Tell me. Please."

Ryan shuddered when Fabian's fingers traced over his lips. There was no question where this was going now, and he knew he should stop it, but instead he told Fabian what he wanted to know.

"Beautiful, confident men. Men who go against everything we're taught to believe about masculinity in locker rooms. Men who aren't afraid to be themselves." He swallowed, and wished he could stop himself. "Men who aren't afraid to walk away from their dream job if it's making them miserable."

That seemed to be all the invitation Fabian needed. He leaned in and brushed his lips against Ryan's, a sweet and gentle kiss that Ryan was too stunned to return. For a second, at least, and then he was kissing Fabian back. His lips were so soft and lovely, and Ryan allowed himself a moment to savor them before he forced himself to stop.

When he pulled back, Ryan kept his eyes closed and said, "Please don't."

"You don't want to?" The scepticism was strong in Fabian's voice.

"I do. I—you *know* I do. But you don't want this. Trust me." He opened his eyes, and saw Fabian's affronted expression.

"If I didn't want this, I wouldn't be doing it."

Ryan shook his head. "I'm not—"

"Unless the rest of that sentence is *interested in you*, then I don't want to hear it. I want to kiss you, Ryan Price. I wanted to kiss you *then*, and I want to kiss you now. May I?"

Ryan's mouth fell open. "You wanted to kiss me *then*? Like, when we were teenagers?"

"You seem surprised."

"Yeah, I'm surprised."

Fabian flopped onto his back and draped an arm over his eyes. "Ryan. I had a huge teenage crush on you, okay? I'd rather not dwell on it, because it's embarrassing, but yes. I wanted to kiss your adorable mouth when I was seventeen. If I had thought there was even a chance you would have been into that, I would have done it."

Ryan sat up. "*What?*"

"I didn't think you were gay, Ryan. Of course I didn't."

"I would have kissed you."

"Well, yes. I do realize that *now*."

"I wanted to kiss you. Do you remember—"

Fabian lifted his arm enough to peek out from under it. "The ferry. Yes. I've replayed that moment a few times over the years. So it was real, was it?"

Ryan nodded. "It was real."

Fabian covered his eyes again. "Damn. That would have been one hell of a first kiss."

Ryan wanted to walk into Lake Ontario. He could have *kissed him.* It would have been Ryan's first time kissing a boy. Instead it had been a dude he'd met online when his junior team had traveled to Victoriaville the following season.

"Well, no sense crying about it now," Fabian said. He rolled off the bed, onto his feet, and grabbed the wine bottle. "But I still don't see why we can't make up for lost time a little right now." He splashed more wine into Ryan's glass, even though Ryan had barely drank any, and handed it to him. Ryan took a large gulp.

"Maybe this isn't obvious," Ryan said after swallowing, "but I'm a fucking mess."

Fabian rolled his eyes. "God, who isn't?"

Ryan shook his head. He was torn between unloading his entire laundry list of flaws on Fabian right now, or shutting the fuck up and kissing Fabian senseless.

Or leaving. Which is exactly what he was going to do. Right now.

He stood and set his wine glass on the desk. "I'm gonna head out."

"It's still raining." Was Fabian *pouting*?

"I'm waterproof."

Fabian stepped into his space, crowding him against the desk. "I don't understand."

Ryan closed his eyes, because he couldn't possibly say what he needed to if every sense was full of Fabian. "I'm no good for you. It's nice of you to—"

"Don't. You're not a fucking charity case, Ryan. I *want* you. Did you already forget the part about wanting to kiss you since I was seventeen?"

"That's just teenage hormones. It's not—I can't. I can't do this with you. I'm sorry."

He couldn't. If he took this any further with Fabian, he would never forgive himself. More than that, Ryan would never recover from it. He was excited about being friends with Fabian, but he would give it all up rather than risk smothering him. He wanted Fabian too much to just have casual sex with him. He wasn't much for casual sex anyway, but he absolutely couldn't have a one-night stand with Fabian Salah. Ryan knew there were plenty of people who would happily fool around with an attractive friend while waiting for a rainstorm to pass by, but he wasn't one of them. Having sex with Fabian—even kissing Fabian again—would mean too much to Ryan. Much more than it would to Fabian.

"Can I have my coat?"

"Of course," Fabian said. His voice was clipped and angry. He stepped away from Ryan and grabbed his coat off the hook by the door. He thrust it at him. "Here."

"I'm sorry," Ryan said again. He didn't know what else to say.

Fabian held up a hand. "I get it. I feel like an idiot, but I get it."

"You aren't—" Oh god, there were tears in Fabian's eyes.

"Goodbye, Ryan."

Ryan wanted to pull him into a hug. He wanted to kiss his hair and tell him how much he wished he could just *do this* like a regular person. He wanted to tell him *everything*, and hold him until the rain stopped falling and beyond.

This whole evening should never have happened. The kindest thing he could do was leave.

So he left.

CHAPTER THIRTEEN

Goddammit.

God fucking *dammit.*

Stupid fucking hockey players and their stupid fucking *everything.*

The more Fabian replayed the events of the previous evening in his head, the more he could not believe any of it had happened. None of it made sense. Not Fabian basically throwing himself at a hockey player. Not Ryan being so obviously—*openly*—attracted to him, and kissing him every bit as sweetly and tenderly as Fabian had always imagined, and then . . . not. It was like a switch had been flipped inside Ryan and no one else could possibly have flipped it besides Fabian; he'd been the only one there.

What had he done?

Nothing. That's what he kept telling himself. He hadn't done a damn thing except be open and honest about his feelings for Ryan. He'd even told him about the teenage crush he'd had on him, for fuck's sake, which would have been embarrassing enough without Ryan flat out rejecting him.

No. If it had been a flat-out rejection, Fabian could have

understood it. If Fabian had leaned in for a kiss, and Ryan had pulled away and told him that he just wasn't interested. If Ryan hadn't said such beautiful words about Fabian's courage . . .

You don't want this. Trust me.

Oh, fuck you, Ryan Price.

Fabian couldn't possibly work on his music like this. His head was everywhere. He texted Vanessa. Are you at work?

VANESSA:
Not for another hour.

FABIAN:
Coffee?

VANESSA:
Uh-oh.

FABIAN:
Yeah. Meet me in ten?

VANESSA:
k

Fabian had *moods*. He could admit it. And Vanessa knew if Fabian was asking for an emergency coffee meeting, then he was probably going to be agitated and unpleasant. But she was also the one person who was any good at talking him through these moods.

Nine minutes later he was in line at a Starbucks that was halfway between his apartment and Vanessa's work. He ordered a coffee for himself and a latte for Vanessa. She walked in just as he was bringing them to a table.

"Trouble in hockey town?" she asked.

He groaned as he fell into one of the chairs. "What is *wrong* with me?"

"Depends on what we're talking about. What happened?"

Fabian gave her the bullet point version, and waited for her to laugh at him. It would be understandable; this situation was absurd.

But she didn't laugh.

"I wonder . . ." she said. But she didn't finish her sentence, just tapped her fingers against her lips and stared right through Fabian.

"Wonder what?"

"Well, I mean, I don't know him, of course, but do you think he might be dealing with some sort of trauma, maybe?"

"Trauma?" Fabian really had no idea. "I don't know. I think he might have some self-esteem issues. Or, like, anxiety problems. He doesn't exactly talk much, so it's hard to say."

"Now I feel bad for talking about sex toys last night. Fuck, that was really insensitive of me."

Fabian frowned, remembering something. "No, I don't think that bothered him. Maybe surprised him, but we talked a bit more about that stuff when we were walking to my place. And he told me before that he likes sex."

"Oh. Well, that's good, then. So he likes sex, he likes you, but he doesn't like sex with you."

"Yes. Thank you for summarizing that."

She took a sip of latte, her face scrunched in concentration. "He's scared," she decided.

"Scared? Of what? Me?"

"I don't know, but it's the only thing that makes sense. He likes you, and he doesn't want to ruin things."

Okay, that did actually make a lot of sense. The more Fabian thought about it, the more obvious it became. "I wouldn't have pressured him into doing anything he's not comfortable with."

"*I* know that. *He* doesn't. Maybe he's not comfortable with *anything*."

Fabian considered this. "So what should I do? Forget about him? I mean, it was stupid anyway, right?"

She folded her arms. "You want me to tell you it's stupid to like him?"

"Yes please."

"Fabian, that guy is a fucking sweetheart. He's the opposite of all those ding dongs you normally sleep with."

"Yeah, but—"

"You should have seen him when you were on that stage last night. Heart eyes! He was *besotted*. I'll bet he's been pushing himself out of his comfort zone just so he can spend time with you."

What? Really? "We've only hung out like three times."

She held her hands up. "Look, again, I don't know him. But if I had to guess, I would say hanging out with someone three times is a big fucking deal for that guy."

Fabian folded his arms on the table and buried his face in them. "I'm such a fucking asshole."

"No, you're a human being. A good one. And Ryan is too."

"What do I do now? I should just leave him alone, right? Forever?"

"Would that make you happy?"

Fabian didn't even have to think about it. "No."

"Then reach out to him. Be chill about it, and don't go so hard on yourself. He's probably obsessing over everything he thinks he did wrong last night too. Trust me, I've been there. You *know* I have."

That was true. There had been more than a few times where their roles in this type of conversation were reversed. "So, what should I say?"

Vanessa shook her head, and grabbed her bag from the back

of her chair. "Uh-uh. I don't get paid enough for that. If you can't figure out basic conversation with the guy you're doomed anyway."

"I bought you a latte," Fabian pointed out feebly.

"Bye! I love you. Text me later. Tell me how it goes."

She left before he could take up any more of her time, and Fabian pulled out his phone. He stared at Ryan's name in his contacts for a long time.

What exactly did Fabian want? He had happily gone more than thirteen years without having Ryan Price in his life, and he could go right back to being happy without him. These past couple of weeks could just be an awkward road bump, and Fabian could end it right now by deleting Ryan's contact info. Because what was he honestly expecting to happen? That he and Ryan would start *dating*? That he would become the boyfriend of an NHL player?

The thought made him want to erupt into giggles in the middle of the Starbucks. His parents would *love* that.

Holy shit. His parents.

What *would* they think if Fabian started dating not only a hockey player, but one who had lived with them? He was sure they would be shocked that Ryan was gay, for one. That definitely would not compute in their brains. For another, they might think that he and Fabian had fooled around as kids back then, under their roof. Maybe they would think Fabian had been secretly seducing all their precious hockey player boarders.

Gross. As if.

Or maybe they would *like* their son dating a hockey player. Maybe they might finally understand him if they all shared a common interest. Of sorts.

Whoa. Fabian was getting *way* ahead of himself here. He needed to go back to seeing if Ryan even wanted to ever talk to him again, and not worry himself about bringing Ryan home to Mom and Dad.

Okay. He could admit that he *really* didn't want to delete Ryan's info. The idea of never talking to him again was surprisingly painful. Even if Ryan never wanted anything beyond friendship, Fabian would take it. It probably was the best arrangement for them anyway.

After an absurdly long time, Fabian typed out Hi and hit send.

There. Perfect. *Hi*. Completely friendly and nonthreatening.

The game on Tuesday night had felt longer than normal, and it was likely because Ryan had barely slept the night before. He hadn't been able to stop replaying everything that had happened between him and Fabian.

He couldn't stop feeling Fabian's lips on his.

He'd made the right decision, leaving. That was what he had determined after a night of agony. Fabian deserved so much better than him. He couldn't explain why the two of them had such an easy, natural connection, but it didn't matter. As far as he could tell, Fabian had an easy, natural connection with everyone, so it was really only Ryan who was benefiting here.

He rolled these thoughts around as he took an unnecessarily long shower in the locker room after the game. Most of his teammates had been talking excitedly about Kent's upcoming party, and Ryan hadn't wanted to listen to any of it. He was more tempted than ever to just stay home on Friday night.

At least he didn't have to feel bad about not going dancing with Fabian that night anymore. Ryan had done an excellent job destroying any chance that Fabian would still want *that* to happen. It was back to life-as-usual for Ryan: hockey, therapy, reading, and, when he was feeling amorous, porn.

He wrapped a towel around his waist and stepped out of the shower room. The first person he saw was Anders Nilsson, who was stylishly dressed as always. Tonight he was wearing sleek, dark pants, a cobalt button-down shirt, and a crisp, brown trench coat. Did people *iron* their coats? Ryan wasn't sure, but he couldn't spot a wrinkle or flaw on any part of Nilsson's outfit.

Like Ryan, Nilsson had a full beard and he wore his hair a little long. Unlike Ryan, his hair and beard were neat and fashionable, making him look more like a suave European fashion model, and less like a man who had been lost at sea for a month.

"What?"

Ryan blinked. He had been *staring* at Anders. And now Anders was looking at him with irritation, and possibly disgust.

"Sorry. Mind was wandering," Ryan mumbled.

Ryan hurried over to his stall and started to get dressed. He wondered where Nilsson got his hair cut. Should he ask? Ryan's hair and beard situation was definitely out of control; he couldn't remember the last time he'd done more than give his beard a lazy at-home trim.

He wasn't the right guy for Fabian, but, fuck, maybe he could be the right guy for *someone*. He couldn't pinpoint the moment when he'd given up completely on himself, but he missed thinking he might be somebody worth talking to. Worth touching.

Ryan made a decision to look up barbershops in his neighborhood. Maybe he could get an appointment for tomorrow. He was sure it had everything to do with Fabian studying him so closely last night, but he was suddenly so embarrassed about his appearance that he needed to do something about it immediately.

When he put on his coat, he pulled his phone out of the pocket. He'd had it turned off all day, because he hadn't wanted to talk to anyone, and he hadn't wanted to be tempted to text Fabian. But now he wanted to Google barbershops. When he turned the phone on, though, he saw a text message notification. From Fabian.

Hi.

"Hey, Pricey." Wyatt slid into the seat next to him. "What are you doing on Thursday?"

"Playing a hockey game?"

"I *know*. Before that, I mean."

"Uh." Ryan glanced at his phone again. Hi. "I don't know yet."

"Come to the center with me. We're going to play floor hockey. Just for an hour or two in the afternoon, like after school. We'll be out of there way before we have to be at the arena."

Ryan could hear Colleen screaming in his head. *Say yes!* He could picture his therapist's approving smile. "Sure. All right."

"Awesome! I'll pick you up around one. You're going to love these kids."

Ryan *did* like kids. He still wasn't sure why any kids would want to spend time with *him*, but he was certainly willing to help out a good cause any way he could.

Wyatt gave him a friendly arm punch and left. Ryan turned his attention back to his phone. He noticed that Fabian's message had been sent hours ago. Oh god, he probably thought Ryan was ignoring him.

Finally, Ryan wrote back Hi.

He waited a minute. When there was no reply, Ryan went back to his original plan of looking up barbershops in the Village. If he was going to hang out with kids, the least he could do was make himself look slightly less terrifying.

Talking to Vanessa and sending Ryan a text had cleared Fabian's mind enough that he was able to devote himself to music for the rest of the day, and well into the evening. He resented the way his friends would accuse him of going into hermit mode when he was working on his music sometimes, but it was definitely common for him to lose many hours when he was in the zone.

This time, when he finally snapped out of it, Fabian's stomach was growling angrily. He picked up his phone and was surprised to see that it was nearly nine o'clock at night. There was no reply from Ryan.

He cooked up some tortellini and jarred marinara sauce for his dinner. His eyes kept darting to his phone, waiting for a reply. None came.

It wasn't until midnight, when Fabian settled onto his bed with big plans to scroll Instagram for a while, that he saw the reply from Ryan.

Hi.

It had been sent over an hour ago. Oops.

FABIAN:
Hi!

Okay, so he wasn't exactly advancing the plot, but he just needed to make an actual connection. He finally got one a moment later when Ryan wrote, Sorry. Had my phone off all day. Then a game at night.

Game. Right. That's the sort of thing Fabian could have looked up.

FABIAN:
Did you win?

RYAN:
No.

FABIAN:
Next time.

RYAN:
Yup.

Fabian waited for dots to appear, but it seemed that Ryan was done talking. So Fabian wrote, I keep thinking about last night.

He cringed. Was that maybe *too* honest?

But Ryan wrote back, Me too.

Fabian exhaled. Thank god. I don't like how we left things.

RYAN:
Me neither.

Fabian grinned. Can we get together sometime soon? I work tomorrow night.

RYAN:
I have a game the night after that.
Busy both days too.

FABIAN:
And the party is Friday, right?

RYAN:
Yeah. Yours too?

Fabian hadn't *really* expected Ryan to go out dancing with them on Friday night, but he hated knowing that he definitely wouldn't make it. He would love to see what Ryan was like when he loosened up a little.

FABIAN:
Yes. How about Saturday?

RYAN:
Ok.

FABIAN:
LATE Saturday. I'll be hungover.

RYAN:
haha ok.

FABIAN:
Did you score any goals tonight?

RYAN:
No. That only happens when you're watching.

He added a winky face emoji, which Fabian found charming. He liked flirty Ryan and he wanted to see a lot more of him.

FABIAN:
You're just trying to get me to watch hockey. It won't work.

RYAN:
I know.

FABIAN:
Good night, Ryan Price.

RYAN:
Good night.

CHAPTER FOURTEEN

"Holy shit. Who the fuck are you?" Wyatt made a show of whipping off his sunglasses as Ryan climbed into the passenger seat of his Range Rover.

"There's no chance you're not going to make a big deal about this, is there?" Ryan grumbled.

"What? About the fact that you suddenly look like bearded Captain America instead of, like, the dad in *How to Train Your Dragon*?"

Ryan rolled his eyes, but he secretly appreciated the ridiculous compliment. "I got a bit of a trim."

"That's not a bit of a trim. That's like a full-on reality show makeover. You could have warned me!"

"It's just a haircut. Drop it."

Wyatt looked like he had more to say, but he just put his sunglasses back on and pulled away from the curb. Ryan furtively glanced at his reflection in the side mirror and had to admit it: he looked good. The stylist, Guillaume, had talked to him extensively about the importance of product. The small-town boy in Ryan had suspected Guillaume of trying to sell him a bunch of expensive stuff he didn't need, but the part of him who wanted to maybe present himself as a sophisticated, metropolitan man of style decided to take the stylist's advice. All of it.

And thus Ryan had spent more than he'd ever spent in his life on a haircut, and had left the salon with a bag full of hair and beard products. He'd even been talked into buying a new (absurdly priced) hairbrush because apparently there was a difference between hairbrushes. Guillaume did *not* like it when Ryan told him he usually bought brushes at the dollar store.

So now Ryan had a tidy, lightly oiled beard that smelled like hazelnut, and hair that wasn't quite long enough to tie back. His hair also had some fancy cream in it that actually made it look carefully styled rather than plopped on top of his head.

He couldn't help but wonder what Fabian would think.

"You can't stop looking at yourself," Wyatt teased.

Ryan jerked his gaze away from the mirror. "It's just weird, is all. Not used to it yet."

"You got a man you can invite to Kent's party tomorrow night?"

Ryan nearly choked. "Would *you* invite a man to Kent's party? If you were me?"

Wyatt grinned. "If it makes Kent uncomfortable? Fuck yeah, I would."

"That wouldn't be fair to your date, though," Ryan pointed out. He would *never* use someone like that. And even if he had a boyfriend, he wouldn't subject them to Dallas Kent's birthday party. "I'll be going alone. And leaving as soon as possible."

"That's the spirit!"

When they reached the community center, Wyatt hauled a duffle bag out of his trunk and carried it to the building. "Guardians swag," he explained.

They were greeted by an exhausted, and grateful-looking,

woman who was about half Ryan's height with glasses and graying brown hair.

"Hi, Anne," Wyatt said cheerfully. "They giving you hell?"

"I'm just glad you guys are here." She turned to Ryan and extended her hand. "Nice to meet you. I'm Anne."

"With an *E*?" Ryan couldn't help but ask. He'd maybe read *Anne of Green Gables* too many times.

"With an *E*! That's right!" She beamed at him.

"I'm Ryan." He released her hand and waited for instruction.

"I need to make some calls, but you know where to go, Wyatt. It's pretty much a full house today, so good luck."

"That's okay, I brought reinforcement," Wyatt joked, nodding at Ryan. "Let's go meet the kids."

Wyatt led Ryan to a large gymnasium, which seemed to take up most of the building. There were some rough-looking basketball nets at either end, a couple of hockey nets at either end of the short side of the room. There were also about fifteen kids in the room, running in all directions and yelling. A couple of boys were kicking dodge balls as hard as they could without really paying attention to where they were going—or who or what they would hit. It was chaos.

"Hey!" Wyatt yelled. "There are celebrities in the room, so look sharp!"

One girl who looked about twelve scrunched up her face. "Celebrities?"

Wyatt pretended to be affronted, which made her laugh. "Who knows who this guy is?" he asked.

"That's Ryan Price," another girl said shyly.

Wyatt pointed at her. "I knew *you'd* get it, Nicole. That's right, this is Ryan Price. He plays for the Guardians with me."

"He doesn't play with you," one of the boys who had been kicking the dodge balls said with a grin. "*He* plays and *you* sit on the bench."

Ryan laughed. He liked these kids already.

"Uh-huh," Wyatt said flatly. "Well, get ready to be stone-walled by me today, Xander. I will not be going easy on you."

Wyatt very quickly split them into two seemingly random teams and asked one of the older girls to get the floor hockey gear out of a storage room. The gear was a bunch of sticks, a couple of soft rubber balls, and some surprisingly nice road hockey goalie gear. Ryan suspected that Wyatt was responsible for that donation.

Wyatt put one of the sets of gear on, and the girl who had retrieved the equipment put the other set on. Ryan picked up one of the sticks, which were all way too short for him. He noticed there were no gloves. They should really have gloves. Maybe he could buy a bunch of gloves and donate them.

"What team am I on?" Ryan asked.

"Whatever team Xander isn't on," Wyatt said loudly. Xander booed.

They played for about an hour, and Ryan loved every second of it. It took him back to being a kid himself and playing hockey for hours with the other Ross Harbour kids on the backyard rink his father had made. He'd loved the game so much then, and the force of how much that had changed hit Ryan hard as he joked around with these kids.

It was also nice to be the best player in the game for a change.

Ryan switched teams a few times, because it was only fair. He had fun taking shots on Wyatt, who beat him most of the time. Either way, they both laughed a lot.

When it was time to leave, Anne came to help Wyatt distribute the Guardians merchandise he had brought. It was mostly ball caps and pucks, which Ryan and Wyatt both spent some time signing.

"Thank you so much for coming," Anne said to Ryan as he

signed the last of the pucks. "The kids really love having you guys visit."

"I had fun," Ryan said. "I'd be happy to come back. And if there's anything you need . . ."

She laughed. "We need *everything*. But if you want to spread the word about how to donate to us, I'll always appreciate that."

"You ready to go?" Wyatt asked. He was holding the empty, balled-up duffle bag.

"Yeah. Okay."

"Do you think I could come with you again next time?" Ryan asked when they were pulling out of the parking lot.

Wyatt looked delighted. "Absolutely! So you liked the kids? They're great, right?"

Ryan smiled. "I liked them."

Dallas Kent's house was exactly what Ryan had expected it to be: enormous, ostentatious, and stupid. It definitely reflected the personality of its owner.

Ryan had very begrudgingly made the drive out to Kleinburg for Kent's birthday party, hoping the entire way that it would be a laidback sort of affair that would mostly just be his teammates and their partners. He was dismayed to find that, despite the ridiculous size of Kent's mansion, it was uncomfortably crowded with people. Most of the people were young women Ryan didn't recognize. He did not, in fact, see many of his teammates' wives and girlfriends present.

"Kent lives here alone, doesn't he?" Ryan asked. He absently trailed his finger over the keys of a grand piano Kent owned for some reason.

"Well," said Wyatt, "I don't think he spends many nights here *alone*."

Gross.

Ryan wasn't going to pretend he had the best eye for design and decor, but Kent's house looked like it had been decorated by a team of frat boys who had each been given a million dollars and told to spend it on "rich guy things." The result was a hideous mess of giant televisions, marble statues and fountains, framed black-and-white "tasteful" photographs of naked women, leather couches, and, yes, a grand piano. Ryan had only seen a few rooms, but as far as he could tell every light fixture was a chandelier.

"I guess the basement is the real party place," Wyatt said. "Legendary beer pong matches have happened down there. I've heard the stories."

"Great." Ryan took a sip of his beer. "Do some of these girls seem kinda young to you?"

"Everyone seems kind of young to me these days. But yes."

"Where did they come from?"

Wyatt shrugged. "Who knows? Kent always manages to surround himself with women. The guy is obsessed."

Wyatt said it lightly, but Ryan had noticed that Kent seemed to have an unhealthy fixation on women. And on what he could get those women to do. Ryan had played with a lot of guys who talked about women in ways that made Ryan's skin crawl, but Kent was very possibly the worst of them.

"You look like you're expecting the man of your dreams to show up at this party," Wyatt said with a grin.

"*What?*"

"You look stylish. The tight, sexy clothes, I mean. It's a good look on you."

"Whatever," Ryan said, but he felt his cheeks heat. In truth, he had put quite a bit of effort into his appearance tonight. He had used his hair product, and had rubbed oil into his beard, as per Guillaume's instructions. And he'd worn an outfit he had bought with the intention of wearing to a gay club the next time he ever decided to go to one: charcoal jeans that had some stretch in the fabric, so they hugged the significant bulge of his thighs and ass, and a black, short-sleeved button-up shirt that strained around his biceps and across his pecs. The outfit was a lot more revealing than the loose shirts and bootcut jeans he normally wore.

Ryan wasn't sure what had prompted him to dress outside his comfort zone tonight. His teammates had teased him a bit about his makeover when they'd first seen him before the game last night. Now they were back to mostly ignoring him.

"Houde just texted me." Wyatt held up his phone. "There's a poker game starting downstairs. You want in?"

"No thanks. I'm going to stay up here, I think."

"For fuck's sake. This is the Halloween party all over again. You didn't even wear a costume to that!"

"I wore a costume," Ryan protested. "I was a cowboy."

"Yeah, but when your whole costume is a hat, and then you leave that hat on a chair all night, it ain't a costume." Wyatt clapped him on the shoulder. "Don't have too much fun, Pricey."

He pushed his way through the crowd toward the door that led to the basement. Ryan spotted an empty love seat, and moved quickly to sit down. He hadn't even been sitting for a minute when a young woman dropped into the seat next to him.

"Hi." The woman was very pretty. She had wavy blond hair and enormous blue eyes, and Ryan had no idea who she was.

"Hi," he replied. He couldn't think of anything else to say, so he took a sip of beer and glanced away.

She sat there, without speaking, and he wondered if she was expecting him to flirt with her or something. She'd picked the wrong guy. Gay or not, Ryan couldn't flirt with anyone.

Eventually the woman, who he was sure was perfectly nice,

gave up on him and left. Ryan inwardly cringed at how rude he must have seemed. He wished he could just wear a sign that said *I'm sorry. I am terrible at socializing. Please don't take it personally.*

In fact, why was Ryan even here? He didn't want to drink anymore. He didn't want to make conversation with people. He didn't want to gently deflect the poor women who tried to flirt with him. He didn't want to play poker, and he definitely didn't want to see Dallas Kent's legendary party basement.

He wanted to dance with Fabian. He wanted to celebrate Tarek's birthday, who Ryan barely knew. But he *wanted* to know him. He wanted to know all of Fabian's friends.

He glanced at his phone. It was almost eleven thirty. It would probably take Ryan an hour to drive back to the Village, which would probably leave him plenty of time to hang out at the club with people whose company he actually enjoyed. In a place where he could be *himself.*

Or, better yet, be who he *wanted* to be.

CHAPTER FIFTEEN

Fabian didn't feel like dancing.

He'd been looking forward to this night for weeks, and now that he was in the middle of a loud, pulsating nightclub that was packed with beautiful people, he was *bored*.

He and his friends had been at Force for over two hours. Marcus and Tarek were long gone, lost to the throng of bodies on the dance floor. Vanessa had been hanging out with Fabian at the high-top table he'd managed to snag, but she'd gone to the bathroom a while ago and had never come back. Fabian wasn't worried about her; that was classic Vanessa behavior. She had most likely run into someone she knew. Or fifteen people she knew. Vanessa knew everyone.

Fabian used his straw to poke at the mostly melted ice cubes that were left in his gin and tonic glass. He'd already politely declined three different men who had approached him. He wasn't surprised—he was alone and he looked fucking fantastic. He'd worn a white lace tank top, which he'd tucked loosely into his black jeans so it billowed slightly off of his slim torso. He'd splurged on the Anastasia Beverly Hills Moonchild Glow makeup kit, and now his face was a shimmering masterpiece of metallic lavender, pink, and silver.

But who was it all for? Could he admit to himself that there was only one person he truly wanted to dance with? To have admire him. To have touch him.

Oh, Fabian. What have you done to yourself?

He thought about getting another drink, but he didn't really want one. He wanted to leave. Would it be rude if he left? He would text his friends of course. He could say that he had a headache or some such thing. It's not like it was *early*; it was nearly one o'clock.

In his peripheral vision, Fabian saw someone approach the table. He turned, his mouth already forming the beginning of his apologetic dismissal, when he saw who it was.

"Ryan."

"Hey. Good. You're here."

Fabian blinked, dumbfounded. "So are you." God, he looked *incredible*. "You cut your hair."

"Yeah." Ryan ran a hand over it nervously. "I fixed myself up a bit."

"Oh." Fabian knew he should say something more, but his brain was frozen. His gaze ran a circuit from Ryan's stylish new haircut and trimmed beard, down to the open collar of his shirt, and then to the fabric that was pulled tight across his chest and arms. Below that there was the denim that struggled to contain Ryan's enormous thighs. Fabian had never seen such tight jeans on him before, and he was sort of mesmerized by the bulge of his package.

When his gaze made its way back to Ryan's face, he could see how much Ryan appreciated Fabian's outfit as well.

"I didn't think you were coming," Fabian said finally.

"What?"

He leaned in, and Ryan bent down until his ear met Fabian's lips. "I didn't think you were coming."

"Oh." He stood back up. "I changed my mind."

Fabian smiled, unable to conceal his delight. He wanted to know what exactly had changed Ryan's mind, but it was too loud in the club to have that conversation. And besides, there were better things they could be doing right now. "Would you like to dance?"

Ryan grinned back at him and nodded. "Yeah. Let's go."

Fabian took Ryan's hand, then turned and led him to the dance floor. He couldn't remember ever feeling so giddy in his life.

The floor was packed, and Ryan was a substantial size, so they stayed close to one side instead of trying to push to the middle. Fabian also wasn't sure how comfortable Ryan was with people pressing against him. When he found a reasonably spacious spot on the floor, he turned and gave Ryan a reassuring smile.

Ryan smiled back, but he still looked unsure of what to do next. Fabian figured he would be the one leading this dance, so he let his body find the rhythm of the pounding Robyn remix. Ryan tried to move with him, and he was definitely awkward. His eyes darted around, as if searching for people judging him.

Fabian reached up and placed a hand on the side of his face, directing his gaze back down. It was too loud to talk, so he just pointed to his own face. *Focus on me.*

Ryan gave a slight nod, and Fabian let his hand slide off his cheek, down the side of his neck, and onto his chest. It finally landed on Ryan's hip, and Fabian stepped closer until the buckle of Ryan's belt bumped against Fabian's ribs. When he was sure he had Ryan's full attention, Fabian closed his eyes and let himself go.

Dancing had always come naturally to him. Music spoke to him so clearly, and his body knew exactly how to respond. He rolled his hips seductively and lifted his free arm over his head, letting his fingers play with the music. Ryan was stiff against him, so Fabian stepped back a bit to give him a better view.

When he opened his eyes again, Ryan had a wide, delighted smile on his face. He wasn't *dancing* exactly, but his body was moving a bit. Fabian put a hand on Ryan's neck and pulled him down so Fabian could speak in his ear.

"Are you laughing at me?"

Ryan shook his head, then tilted it so he could reply. "No. I just love watching you dance."

His breath tickled Fabian's ear when he spoke, and tingles shot through Fabian's body. He draped one arm lazily over Ryan's shoulder, and returned his other hand to Ryan's hip. Ryan was going to dance *with* him, dammit.

By the middle of the next song, Ryan had finally loosened up enough to follow the movement of Fabian's hips as they dipped and grinded. Fabian was trying not to actively hump him, but it was a challenge because his tree trunk thighs were right *there* and the buttons of his shirt looked like they might pop open at any second.

Inspired by the thought, Fabian trailed a finger up to the top fastened button and deftly opened it. He glanced at Ryan's face to get his reaction. His lips were parted, possibly in shock, but his eyes were pure desire. He gave a barely perceptible nod, and Fabian opened the next button. Then the next.

He was wearing a black tank top underneath his shirt, which Fabian wasn't surprised by, but he was a tad disappointed. The undershirt did nothing to disguise the fact that Ryan was *built*. His pecs were huge and defined, and even through the fabric Fabian could see there was a considerable amount of chest hair coating them.

Ryan's giant hands grasped Fabian around his rib cage, holding him in place until he'd opened every button. When he'd finished, Fabian wrapped his arms around Ryan's shoulders and pushed down on Ryan's open shirt until the sleeves slipped off his shoulders and pinned his arms to his sides.

Fabian leaned in and pressed his mouth—open and wet and hungry—against Ryan's left pec. He realized, after he had left a damp spot on Ryan's shirt, that this might be a bit forward.

Ryan didn't seem to mind. He was watching Fabian with an intensity that made Fabian want to get on his knees in the middle of this crowd. The bulge in Ryan's jeans had grown significantly, and was nudging Fabian's stomach every time Ryan moved his hips in his direction.

Fabian locked eyes with him, trying to match Ryan's intensity. Then he leaned in again and pressed another openmouthed kiss to the distinct peak of Ryan's left nipple.

Ryan's head fell back, and his thumb brushed over the piercing in Fabian's nipple. Fabian sucked in a breath, and gently bit Ryan's chest. It had almost no give under his teeth.

Fabian wanted to see a whole lot more of this ridiculous body, but for now they could just have some fun. As if reading his mind, the DJ transitioned into a remix of Beyoncé's "Get Me Bodied." Fabian jumped up and down in excitement, which made Ryan laugh. He removed his button-up shirt completely, balling it up in his fist as he finally let go and started really dancing.

He was *good at it.* Fabian shouldn't have been surprised—Ryan was an athlete, after all—but it was wonderful to watch. His eyes sparkled with unabashed joy as he watched Fabian dip and twirl in ridiculous, over-the-top moves that were designed to amuse him.

When Ryan lip-synced the opening lines of the chorus, complete with an exaggerated motion of wiping sweat from his brow with his discarded shirt during the *A little sweat ain't never hurt nobody* line, Fabian shrieked with laughter. Ryan beamed back at him, and Fabian wanted him so badly in that moment.

An arm draped across Fabian from behind, and a familiar voice said, "You guys look hot together."

Fabian twisted his head to find Marcus's face right next to his. He grinned and kissed Marcus's cheek. "Where's Tarek?"

"Some lovely gentlemen are buying him birthday shots."

"Uh-oh."

"Mm. Vanessa and I found a table over there." Marcus pointed to a table with actual chairs near the high-top Fabian had been standing at. "Come find us, if you're not too busy." He left with a blatant leer at Ryan.

Fabian and Ryan stayed on the dance floor for another couple of songs, and then Fabian tugged him toward Vanessa and Marcus's table. As soon as Vanessa spotted Ryan, she clasped her hands over her mouth.

"You remember Ryan," Fabian said casually when they sat in the two remaining seats.

"Oh my *god*! You look so *good*! And you're here! I thought you were at another party."

"I left," Ryan said simply.

"Good choice."

"Is my makeup sweating off my face?" Fabian asked. "It's probably a mess, right?"

Marcus shook his head. "You look flawless as always. Stop fishing."

"You do look good," Ryan confirmed. He was wearing that adorable shy smile that Fabian loved. Fabian was glad he was wearing makeup because he was sure he was blushing.

"You guys are so fucking cute," Vanessa said. "Oh! Here's the birthday boy!"

Tarek strolled over, and even from a distance Fabian could

tell that he was quite tipsy. His tight T-shirt was bunched up under his ribs, exposing his stomach, his hair looked like it had been thoroughly disheveled by someone, and Fabian tried to remember if Tarek had been wearing his glasses earlier. He hoped not because they were gone now.

"Heyyyyy," Tarek drawled when he reached them. He slumped over the back of Marcus's chair, letting his arms fall around his shoulders. "Being thirty is awesome."

"Hell yeah it is," Vanessa said.

"Oh hey, it's that guy," Tarek said, nodding toward Ryan. "Are you guys together now?"

Fabian made a face that tried to silently say *Shut the fuck up you sloppy idiot*, but it didn't seem to work because Tarek just kept talking.

"I'm so happy for you guys. Fabian is, like, obsessed with you. What's your name again?"

"Uh, Ryan."

"Ryan. Right. Good for you, man."

Oh god. This was a disaster. Fabian leaned toward Ryan. "I'm so sorry about him."

Ryan waved it away. "It's fine. He's drunk." He covered his mouth with the back of his hand and yawned. "It must be late," he said, blinking.

"Mm."

"I could, um, walk you home. If you're leaving soon?"

"You *could*," Fabian agreed. "Or . . ."

Ryan leaned closer. "Or?"

"*I* could walk *you* home. I believe your place is closer, isn't it?" He kept his gaze locked with Ryan's, making sure he understood him.

"Yeah," Ryan said. "It is. Let's go."

They both stood, and Vanessa of course had something to say about it. "Are you leaving? Both of you? Together?"

Fabian narrowed his eyes at her. "Yes. Very good."

Marcus joined in. "Wait. You're both leaving at the same time? That's weird."

"I swear to fucking god, Marcus . . ."

Fabian expected a comment from Tarek, but he had wandered over to a shirtless man with a giant back tattoo. The man seemed to have his full attention.

Fabian hugged his terrible friends goodbye, then left the club as quickly as possible. After they had retrieved their jackets from the coat check, Ryan and Fabian stood together on the sidewalk. Fabian wasn't sure about Ryan, but he was suddenly overwhelmed by what they seemingly had planned.

"Where was the party you were at?" he asked, wanting to relieve some of the tension.

"Kleinburg."

"Shit. That's far. And rich."

Ryan laughed. "Yep. I drove back here as fast as I could, parked in my garage, and basically jogged to the club."

"Eager," Fabian teased.

"I was," Ryan said, and he wasn't teasing at all. The earnestness in his voice made Fabian's heart stutter.

"Well then," he said breathlessly, "let's make it worth all that effort."

Again, Fabian was torn between wanting to ask what had made Ryan change his mind about engaging in sexy fun, and wanting to keep his questions to himself so he didn't inadvertently destroy the possibility of sexy fun. They walked in silence for a minute and then Ryan put a hand on Fabian's shoulder and gently spun him around. Fabian didn't even have time to be surprised when Ryan crushed their mouths together.

It wasn't anything like the shy kiss they'd shared on Fabian's bed on Monday night. This was hungry and possessive. Ryan was *devouring* him, and Fabian tried to return it but his knees were growing weak and he really didn't need to *increase* their height difference. As it was, Ryan's knees were bent so far he may as well be kneeling on the sidewalk.

Jesus, they were on the sidewalk. Distantly, Fabian could hear people catcalling them, but he didn't care. He didn't care about anything but Ryan's warm, wonderful mouth on his.

"Sorry," Ryan said when they'd broken apart. "I've been wanting to do that since I first saw you tonight."

Fabian was in danger of swooning. Actually swooning. Questions could be asked later. It was definitely time for sexy fun.

"It's okay," he said thickly. "I've been wanting to do a lot of things since I first saw you."

"Oh yeah?"

Fabian sucked lightly on his own bottom lip, savoring the lingering taste of Ryan's kiss. "Mm. Yeah. Take me home, Ryan Price."

CHAPTER SIXTEEN

Ryan opened the door to his apartment. "I haven't really done much with the place."

His nerves had returned during their walk, once he'd gotten the pressing need to kiss Fabian out of the way. Now that they'd made it home, he had no idea what to do next.

"Wow," Fabian said, walking past him into the living room. "I've never been in one of these buildings."

"I couldn't quite afford a unit that faces the CN Tower, but I still have a pretty good view, I think."

Fabian snorted. "My apartment has a view of an alley where raccoons like to fuck. There's a reason why I keep my curtains closed."

Ryan laughed, but he was worried that his apartment was making Fabian uncomfortable. Compared to Dallas Kent's stupid mansion it didn't seem overly ostentatious, but it had still cost him plenty.

Fabian slipped his coat off and draped it over the back of Ryan's sofa. Ryan was oddly touched by how easily Fabian did this, as if he was in his own home.

Ryan hung up his own coat in the closet and slipped off his shoes. Fabian noticed him doing this and looked embarrassed. "Shit. Sorry. I'm super fucking rude." He grabbed his coat off the couch and Ryan took it from him.

"Don't worry about it. Can I get you anything?"

"No. Why don't we just . . . relax?" Fabian went to the couch, dropped onto it, then patted the cushion next to him.

Ryan had thrown his button-up shirt back on before they'd left the club, but Fabian was only wearing the white lace tank top that had been thoroughly distracting Ryan all night. Without sleeves in the way, Ryan could see the muscle definition in Fabian's wiry arms, and he could feast his eyes on the smooth, soft curves of his shoulders. The nipple piercing that Ryan had been curious about for weeks was clearly visible through the dainty fabric of the shirt.

"You're staring," Fabian said.

"Probably."

"You can get a better look over here."

Ryan wasn't sure how far he would be comfortable going tonight, but he decided he would try to let his body, and Fabian, guide him. His brain tended to ruin everything.

He sat in the middle of the sofa, and Fabian immediately crawled into his lap and straddled him. Ryan rested a hand on the side of Fabian's head and let his fingers drift into his silky, dark hair.

"Mm. Play with my hair and I'll let you do *anything*," Fabian purred.

"Anything, eh? Like what?"

"You can . . . kiss me?"

Ryan didn't have to be asked twice. It had been way too fucking long since Ryan had kissed *anyone*, but it wouldn't have mattered if he'd made out with five men that morning, this was

Fabian. It was Fabian's teeth that were nipping at Ryan's bottom lip; Fabian's tongue that was sliding over his own; Fabian's sweet sighs that Ryan was swallowing.

Without even realizing what he was doing, Ryan guided Fabian down onto the couch cushions and covered him. Fabian smiled at him from his new position beneath him, and Ryan took his mouth again.

Ryan knew this was selfish. It was probably the most selfish thing he'd ever done, and he knew he'd feel bad about it later. But that was later. Right now, he was finally kissing Fabian Salah. *Really* kissing him. He was finally making Fabian squirm beneath him by kissing the sensitive skin under his smooth, sharp jaw. God, his neck. Ryan wanted to know every inch of his neck, and his shoulders, and his collarbone.

Fabian arched up so his erection pressed against Ryan's thigh. "What do you want? What do you like? I'm up for just about anything."

Ryan froze, his face hovering above Fabian's. He was suddenly reminded of how bad he was at sex. Kissing was fine, but anything beyond that would definitely leave Fabian disappointed.

"I—we could just . . . kiss?"

Fabian looked confused. "We *could*. Is that all you want?"

"For now. Maybe?"

Fabian stroked his fingers gently over Ryan's beard. "That's okay with me. But is something wrong?"

"No. No, it's just—" Ryan sighed and sat up. His brain had shown up to wreck everything, as usual. "I need you to know, before we do anything, that I'm not . . . normal about this stuff."

"Normal? Who wants normal?" Fabian teased.

Ryan ran a hand through his own hair. He had no idea how

to explain any of this, so he just started talking. "I'm serious. I'm anxious. Like, *clinically anxious*."

"Lots of people are anxious."

"Okay, fine. But I'm also terrible at talking to people. I beat people up for a living and . . . when I'm in the moment—fighting someone, I mean—it's the only time my head is clear. It's like . . . easy. It's so fucked up that I'm *relaxed* when I'm punching someone, but I'm a pile of nerves when I'm ordering in a restaurant." Ryan was babbling now, but he needed to make Fabian understand. "I'm not okay. I see a therapist, I take medication. And I'm terrible at sex. So if that's where this is leading—"

Fabian moved to stand between Ryan's legs. He put his hands on Ryan's shoulders, commanding his attention. "Do you find it hard, talking to me?"

Ryan answered him honestly. "No."

"Do you want to know what I think of you?" Ryan wasn't sure. When he didn't reply, Fabian continued. "I think you're sexy as hell. And you're so fucking sweet. And I don't think you beat people up for a living. I think you *protect* people for a living. Because that's who you are, Ryan. You have a giant heart in that giant chest and . . ." He leaned in, brushing his lips against Ryan's ear. "I'm. Not. Scared of you."

The force of Fabian's words made Ryan gasp, and then, before he could stop himself, he grabbed the front of Fabian's shirt and pulled him forward until Fabian was in his lap again. They kissed wildly, and this time it was Ryan who ended up on his back with Fabian falling on top of him. Fabian straddled Ryan's waist, and Ryan wrapped his hands around his slim, strong biceps. Ryan's cock, which had been half hard since leaving the club, was painfully rigid now, and he could feel Fabian's arousal digging into his leg.

"We can just kiss," Fabian said breathlessly, "but if that's what you want, then I need to change position. Because if we keep up like that I will definitely hump your thigh until I make a mess."

Lord Jesus. "That would be okay. If you want. I don't mind."

Fabian looked amused. "Well, I try to aim a little higher with my sexual partners than doing things they don't *mind*."

Ryan was already fucking this up. "I'm sorry. It's me. Like I said, I'm not good at sex." He closed his eyes and waited for Fabian to politely make his excuses to leave.

"I have no idea what that means," Fabian said. He pushed himself off of Ryan and kneeled between his legs on the couch cushions. "Do you make sure you have your partner's consent?"

"Yes."

"Are you safe? Do you use protection?"

"Always."

"Do you care about your partner's pleasure?"

"Of course."

"Well then." Fabian rested a hand on Ryan's stomach and smiled at him. "I don't see a problem."

Ryan shook his head.

Fabian sighed. "Fine. Tell me the problem. Let's hear it."

The mood was effectively killed anyway, so Ryan decided to go for broke. "I need . . . instruction."

Fabian's eyes widened. "Like . . . domination?"

"No! No. That's not what I mean. I just need a lot of . . ." It took a moment, but Ryan found the right word. "Reassurance. That what I'm doing is good. Because otherwise I just spend the whole time worrying that I'm doing everything wrong."

Fabian seemed to consider this. "Well, that's certainly doable. Is that all?"

"No. I also . . . kind of have body issues. I don't like people looking at me too closely."

"Naked, you mean?"

"Sexually, I guess. Like, I'm naked all the time in the locker room and stuff. It's more about . . . being appraised. Being compared to other people."

Fabian frowned. "You don't think much of yourself, do you?"

Ryan looked away, embarrassed. "Not really. No."

"So let's say we leave the lights off and I give you lots of positive reinforcement. Would that make things easier?"

Ryan truly appreciated how accommodating Fabian was being, and he wished he could just say yes. That it would be enough. But . . .

"I can't . . . I mean, I don't usually, um, come. Even if it feels good and I like what's happening. It's a side effect of the meds I take, but it's also just . . . me. I get trapped in my head sometimes." He blew out a breath. "So, yeah. Sex with me is probably not worth it."

He gathered up his courage and turned his gaze back to Fabian, and was surprised to find him smiling fondly. "We don't have to do anything, if you don't want. But I would like to make you feel good. It doesn't have to involve orgasms. We can even keep our clothes on." He reached for Ryan's hand and brought it to his lips. He kissed his knuckles and said, "I like the way you look at me. And the way you touch me and kiss me."

"I like touching you. And kissing you."

"Then maybe we could start there, and see what happens. No pressure." He turned Ryan's hand over, and began massaging it gently. "But I should warn you . . . I sort of have the opposite problem. In bed, I mean."

Ryan's brow knit. "What? Like, you *don't* have body issues?"

Fabian laughed. "I think we both know I don't. But that's not what I mean. I tend to orgasm way too quickly. So I can't guarantee that it won't happen if we fool around at all."

"Oh."

"I have ways to . . . stave it off. And the good news is that I can usually come at least twice. So it's not, like, *over* after the first time. But I just wanted to warn you. Even if we're just making out, I might go off."

Ryan blinked. "We are not a good match."

"Not at all. Want to make out?"

"Yeah. Bedroom?"

"Yes please."

Fabian fell on top of Ryan's enormous body and kissed him. It was hard to do because he was laughing. And maybe Ryan was laughing too. It felt good to get all of their sexual laundry aired before they started playing around. It was refreshing to be so honest with a new partner.

Ryan had just trusted Fabian with a lot of personal stuff, and Fabian wasn't taking that lightly. He was determined to make this as good as possible for Ryan, who, it seemed, had not had much positive sexual experience.

Fuck that. Fabian happened to be quite good at sex. At least, he assumed he was. He had no reason to believe otherwise.

And Ryan, despite all his warnings to the contrary, was a very good kisser. There was maybe a tad too much beard in the way, even with the trim, but his mouth was heavenly. Warm and soft and welcoming. Fabian squeezed Ryan's hips with his knees and dove in.

Ryan had his enormous hands on Fabian's back, but he kept them on top of his shirt. Fabian wanted to rip the shirt off. He wanted every scrap of fabric between them gone, but more than that, he wanted to respect Ryan's boundaries. So he threaded the fingers of one hand in Ryan's thick hair and planted the other on the mattress. He would let Ryan set the pace.

He could feel Ryan's erection, though. It was . . . difficult to ignore. He didn't like to think of himself as someone who cared about size, but the bulge in Ryan's jeans was certainly intriguing. And encouraging. Ryan couldn't be *entirely* uncomfortable right now.

"You are a fantastic kisser," Fabian murmured, remembering that he was supposed to be providing positive reinforcement.

"Thanks."

"You can touch me, if you want. Under the shirt, I mean." He nipped Ryan's earlobe and whispered, "I'll let you get to second base."

Ryan laughed and gently freed the hem of Fabian's shirt from his pants. He slid his hands under the shirt, gripped Fabian's waist, and curled his thumbs around to rest on his stomach. Ryan's hands were so large on Fabian's slim frame that his fingertips nearly met on Fabian's spine. Fabian wanted those hands everywhere. He squirmed, trying to encourage Ryan to explore, and his ass brushed Ryan's erection.

"Sorry," Fabian said. "Do you want me to move somewhere else? It's kind of hard to avoid that thing." Then he quickly added, "Not that I want to avoid it. But you want me to, right?"

"I, um . . ."

"Anything you want. Tell me."

"Could—could you do that again?"

Fabian could tell the words had cost Ryan something, so he didn't tease him. "Gladly." He rotated his hips, slower this time, as he gave Ryan his best attempt at a lap dance. His ass caressed the substantial length of Ryan's cock, and Ryan shuddered beneath him.

"Oh god."

"Good?"

"Yeah. Fuck. Keep going."

Encouraged, Fabian sat up straighter and kept his hips moving in a slow, grinding pattern as he peeled his shirt off over his head.

"Oh," Ryan breathed. "Wow."

"Touch me," Fabian breathed. "Please."

Ryan's hands slid up his sides and across his chest, pausing to gently rub his nipple piercing. He had worn one of his more ornate ones tonight: a silver filigree clicker with dark blue stones. When Ryan brushed his thumb over it, Fabian lost his rhythm.

"Holy shit," he said, then laughed. "You'd think I'd get used to that."

"I like this," Ryan said. His voice was a low rumble that went straight to Fabian's balls. "It suits you."

"Have at it," Fabian panted.

"Come here. I want to kiss you."

Fabian fell forward, sliding his hands under the hem of Ryan's tank top as he brought their lips together. Ryan held the back of Fabian's head as he kissed him, his thumb caressing the side of his throat. Fabian loved his hands. He wanted those long, thick fingers wrapped around his dick. He wanted them inside him.

"Can I take this off?" Fabian asked, tugging at Ryan's shirt.

"Yeah. Okay. Let me—" He did a crunch and quickly yanked both his shirts off, then lay back on the mattress.

"Look at you. Gorgeous."

Ryan's stomach was flat—not a six-pack, but definitely toned—with a trail of dark red hair leading down from his belly button. His pecs were *spectacular*; huge and solid and blanketed with more red hair. He had no visible tattoos or piercings, but there were several bruises and scars.

Fabian didn't even realize he'd been absently smoothing his palms over Ryan's torso until Ryan stopped him by gently pulling one of his hands to his mouth and kissing the inside of his wrist.

"Do you want me to stop?" Fabian asked.

"No. I'm actually really fucking turned on right now."

Fabian wriggled his ass against Ryan's erection. "I noticed." He bent down whispered into Ryan's ear. "Does he want to come out to play?"

Ryan huffed out a laugh. "I think so."

"Good. Because I know someone who is dying to meet him."

"You're ridiculous."

Fabian winked, then slid down Ryan's body so he could open the button on his jeans. "Tell me if you want to stop. Anytime, okay?"

"Okay. Keep going."

Fabian slowly pulled Ryan's zipper down and peeled open the fly of his jeans to frame the mouth-watering bulge in his briefs. Keeping eye contact with Ryan the whole time, Fabian placed his palm on it. "Fuck, you're huge. Can I take it out?"

"Yeah. It's weird, though," Ryan warned.

"Weird?" Okay, now Fabian *had* to see it. He carefully pulled the waistband of Ryan's underwear down to his thighs, and Ryan's cock thudded against his stomach, huge and solid.

There was absolutely nothing, as far as Fabian could tell, weird about it. It was a beast for sure, long and thick and uncut. The head was an angry red, and his balls were fucking huge, but none of that was anything that Fabian would call weird. *Glorious* was a better word.

"Yeah," Ryan sighed. "Like I said—"

"No! I *love him*!" To prove it, Fabian dipped his head and kissed the underside of his shaft. "There are so many things I want to do to you."

"You don't have to—"

Fabian held up a hand. "Ryan. I am talking to my new friend. Shush."

Ryan laughed, which made Fabian feel a little bit proud. "Sorry. Continue."

"How about we take these pants all the way off?" Fabian suggested.

"Yep. Here. I'll do it. They're tight."

Fabian moved off of him so Ryan could sit up to remove his jeans, underwear, and socks. He could tell, when Ryan was fully naked, that he was starting to feel uncomfortable again. His hands flexed against his duvet, and he couldn't make eye contact with Fabian.

"Would you mind if I joined you?" Fabian asked. "I'm a little worried about ripping these pants, to be honest. The situation is getting dire."

"Sorry. Yeah. Please."

Fabian stood and wriggled out of the rest of his clothing. His rigid cock sprang eagerly out of his underwear the second he began to remove them. He gave it a couple of strokes as a reward for being so patient.

"Oh wow. Can I do that? For you, I mean?" Ryan asked.

"Absolutely." Fabian stood between Ryan's spread thighs and braced himself with one hand on Ryan's muscular shoulder. He plunged the fingers of his other hand into Ryan's hair.

Ryan's hand was dry, but it was so fucking big and warm. Fabian moaned at the contact, and moaned more when Ryan stroked him. God, he'd wanted this. Exactly this: Ryan Price naked with his hand on Fabian's cock. It was perfect.

"You're so fucking sexy," Ryan murmured. "I love your body."

Fabian could only whimper happily in response. He'd meant it when he'd told Ryan that he loved attention. He was addicted to adoration and praise. He'd quit all social media recently, because he'd been addicted to seeing how many likes each of his posts received. Now his label managed his Instagram account for him.

He rarely received the adoration he craved from the men he hooked up with. Not like this. Not like the wonder he saw now in Ryan's eyes, or the reverent way he touched him.

Fabian's toes curled against the fancy carpet in Ryan's bedroom when Ryan teased his slit with the pad of his thumb. Then Ryan leaned in and licked his nipple piercing, and Fabian nearly lost it.

"Fuck! Fuck. Stop. Just for a second, stop."

Ryan released him immediately and looked at him with concern. "You okay?"

"Yeah." He laughed. "I wasn't kidding earlier. About my little problem."

Ryan's expression was puzzled, and then he understood. "It's not a problem. I'd like to make you come now. Can I?"

Fabian nodded, his head foggy with lust. "Okay. Yeah. Do it. Then we can take our time."

Ryan wrapped his fingers around him again, and Fabian's cock twitched excitedly. This wouldn't take long at all. Ryan's other hand gently cupped and caressed Fabian's balls as he stroked this time, and Fabian's eyes rolled back.

"Fuck. Yes. Like that. Just like that. I'm going to—"

As usual, his orgasm detonated before he'd managed to stammer out a warning. But he couldn't be mad about it. Holy fuck, it felt good.

When he opened his eyes again, he saw that his release had landed on Ryan's chest, and was clinging to his chest hair.

"Oops," he said.

Ryan's mouth hung open in an expression of pure astonishment.

"I did tell you—" Fabian started, but Ryan cut him off.

"Your face was so beautiful when you did that. Holy god."

Fabian half crawled, half slumped into Ryan's lap. "Thank you." He rested his head on Ryan's shoulder and closed his eyes. Ryan began stroking his hair, and Fabian was suddenly dangerously comfortable.

"You're sleepy," Ryan observed.

"Nope," Fabian murmured, but he ruined his argument by yawning.

Ryan chuckled, then wrapped his arms tight around him and stood, carrying Fabian like a child and resting him gently on the bed with his head on a pillow. "It's three in the morning. We can call it a night."

"But I was going to show you my trick," Fabian protested. The pillow was a perfect balance of soft and firm. He closed his eyes again.

"It can wait. I'll be right back."

Distantly, Fabian heard Ryan in the bathroom, running water and presumably washing the spunk out of his chest hair. Probably brushing his teeth. Maybe dunking his erection in cold water. A stab of guilt made Fabian open his eyes.

"What about you?" he asked when Ryan returned from the bathroom with a damp cloth.

"What do you mean?" Ryan gently wiped the warm cloth over Fabian's torso, which had gotten sticky when he'd pressed himself against Ryan's messy chest.

"I mean you got me off and I didn't even try to get you off." He noticed, as Ryan stood and tossed the cloth in a laundry hamper, that the other man's erection had flagged almost completely.

"It's fine. I'm probably way too tired anyway." Ryan opened a dresser drawer and pulled out a clean pair of underwear. "Like I said, even at the best of times it's a chore."

"Not a chore," Fabian argued, but it came out as one garbled word as he closed his eyes again.

Ryan got into bed beside him, and Fabian immediately scooted over to be the little spoon. "You're so warm," he murmured happily.

Ryan kissed the top of his head. "Good night. And thank you."

"Anytime." Fabian's last thought before he drifted off was that he knew he meant it.

CHAPTER SEVENTEEN

Waking up with his arms full of Fabian was every bit as wonderful as Ryan had always imagined it would be.

Ryan woke first, and spent a long time lying as still as possible, breathing in Fabian's scent. He didn't want to disturb him, because he was worried that, when Fabian woke and realized where he was, it would all be over. Fabian was relaxed about sex and basic human interaction in a way Ryan never could be. He knew last night hadn't meant as much to Fabian as it did to him. He had been a curiosity to Fabian; one that the other man had been intrigued by for a long time, sure, but Ryan was sure that the itch had been scratched and Fabian would be moving on.

Finally, when he could no longer resist, he nuzzled Fabian's hair, then kissed his temple. Fabian squirmed in his arms and sighed. Ryan could see his lips curl up into a drowsy smile. "This bed rules."

Ryan didn't think he'd ever fully appreciated how great his bed was until last night. He'd slept better than he had in ages. He tightened his arm around Fabian, pulling him closer.

"You ever gonna let me go?" Fabian teased.

"Nope."

Fabian giggled. "I have to pee!"

With an exaggerated sigh, Ryan released him, and Fabian slipped out from under the covers. He was still naked, and looked stunning in the morning light that poured from the windows Ryan had forgotten to draw the curtains on. He scurried off to the bathroom, and a minute later he yelped, "Shit! My makeup!"

He poked his head out of the bathroom, and Ryan could see how badly his makeup had smeared.

"I don't suppose you have any makeup remover? Preferably sulfate-free?"

Ryan laughed. "No. Sorry."

"Well, just a facial cleanser then. Something gentle."

"There's a bar of soap in the shower."

Fabian blinked at him. "I'm sorry. You wash your face with *what now*?"

"Soap. Why?"

He thought Fabian muttered something like "This is a nightmare" as he retreated into the bathroom. A moment later, Ryan heard the sink faucet running. It seemed to take a long time, but eventually Fabian emerged from the bathroom, his face free of makeup and his bangs damp. He darted to the bed, his dick swinging as he ran, which made Ryan laugh.

"Cold!" Fabian complained as he burrowed under the covers and snuggled back up to Ryan. "I can't believe I fell asleep with *makeup on*. God, my skin is going to be a disaster."

Ryan rolled him over so they were face-to-face. "Looks good to me." He loved how Fabian looked in makeup, but he was also a big fan of this version of the man: undecorated and boyish looking, even at thirty-one years old.

"What's on your schedule today?" Fabian asked.

"Nothing."

"I have to work at four. At the drugstore."

"But you're free until then?"

Fabian smiled. "I'm all yours."

God, if only. But for right now, he was. He was in Ryan's arms, in Ryan's bed, so Ryan kissed him. He realized, after they'd started, that he hadn't brushed his teeth yet. Fabian tasted like he'd maybe borrowed some of Ryan's toothpaste for a quick rinse. He broke the kiss. "Sorry. I must be disgusting."

"Hardly."

"I'm going to take a shower. I don't know if you're wanting to, you know, do sex stuff. But I can't unless I clean up a bit."

Fabian kissed his cheek. "You'd better clean up then, because I would very much like to do sex stuff."

Ryan liked the sound of that, and Ryan's dick *really* liked the sound of that. It was nice to be on the same page for once.

"I could use a rinse myself," Fabian said casually. "I noticed your shower is pretty big. Probably enough room for two, even."

"I take up a lot of space."

"I'm sure I could fit myself in *somewhere*."

Ryan flushed. Fabian was so effortlessly sexy. How did he do it? Ryan's best attempt at dirty talk was stammering out suggestions of "sex stuff."

Ryan got the shower started, then took a moment to brush his teeth before joining Fabian under the spray. He had been enthralled by Fabian's body before, but seeing him wet, with water streaming down the smooth, lean lines of his body, was something else. It was so captivating that Ryan didn't have the spare brain power to be self-conscious about his own body.

"If you're not too busy," Fabian said, with a smile that implied that he was very aware of how much Ryan was enjoying the view, "would you mind passing me the shampoo?"

"Oh. Sure."

Fabian frowned at the bottle of Head & Shoulders that Ryan

handed him. With a heavy sigh, he squeezed some out and gave the bottle back to Ryan.

"Can I?" Ryan asked, his hands hovering above Fabian's scalp. It was possible that Fabian had a very specific lathering method, but Ryan hoped his love of having his hair played with would win out.

Fabian nodded and closed his eyes. Ryan dug his fingers in, trying to massage Fabian's scalp as much as clean his hair. Fabian turned and leaned back against Ryan's chest.

"God, that feels incredible," he moaned. "Your hands are so strong."

It felt good to be using his strong hands to care for someone, for a change. He still wasn't sure how he'd gotten lucky enough to have Fabian like this, but he was going to milk it for all it was worth.

He watched as Fabian rinsed the suds out of his hair, and was embarrassed by how quickly his dick reacted. Fabian's cock had chubbed up a little since they'd gotten in the shower, but Ryan was at full mast.

"Your turn," Fabian said and slipped past him so Ryan could take his place under the spray. "I would offer to return the favor, but I'm afraid I can't quite reach."

"It's okay." Ryan grabbed the shampoo. He quickly lathered and rinsed, and when he opened his eyes, he found Fabian kneeling in front of him.

"What—?"

"Found somewhere I can reach," he said with a wicked smile. "May I?"

Ryan didn't let himself overthink it. He couldn't think anyway, not with the way his dick was screaming at him to just say yes. He nodded, and Fabian leaned in.

"Oh fuck," Ryan gasped when Fabian sucked the head of his

cock into his mouth. It had been such a long time since anyone had done this to him. Since he'd been able to let someone do this.

Fabian, it seemed, was an expert. He wasn't taking Ryan all the way in—Ryan would never expect him to—but he knew exactly where to focus his attention. He kept his cheeks hollow, and his tongue busy, and it was fucking incredible.

Ryan shot an arm out to brace himself against the wall. Fabian wrapped one hand around the base of Ryan's cock and began stroking, letting his fist cover the area his mouth couldn't reach. His other hand slid up Ryan's thigh, and then journeyed over to cup Ryan's balls.

Ryan wasn't one for dirty talk. At all. But if he *could* bring himself to talk right now, he'd like to say something encouraging like *Fuck, yes. Play with my balls. Make me come all over your pretty face. Please make me come. Need to come.*

But Ryan stayed silent, other than involuntary grunts and moans and the occasional swear word. Fabian gazed up at him through his long, gorgeous eyelashes, then reached down to give his own cock a couple of strokes. Ryan loved how hard Fabian had gotten while doing this for him.

Ryan felt good. He felt so good that he thought he might actually come. He wasn't quite at the edge, but he could see it on the horizon. The possibility excited him and he threaded his fingers into Fabian's wet hair, trying to encourage him without hurting him or forcing him. Or speaking.

Fabian bobbed his head and sucked him hard and fast. He rolled Ryan's balls in his palm and hummed around his shaft. God, Ryan's orgasm was *right there.* He could do it.

He must have thrust without meaning to because suddenly Fabian was sputtering and coughing. He pulled off and held up a finger. "Sorry. Just give me a second."

"Jesus, did I hurt you?" Ryan asked. "I didn't mean to. I'm sorry. I—"

"It's fine. Just wasn't expecting it." Fabian laughed. "You are *very* big. Not used to that."

Ryan turned off the water and crouched next to him. The orgasm was definitely a lost cause now. "I'm so sorry."

"Don't be! Like I said, I'm fine. Now where were we?"

Ryan put a hand on his shoulder. "It's okay." He stood and offered Fabian his hand. Fabian stared at him, confusion clear on his face, then took his hand and allowed himself to be pulled to standing.

They stepped out of the shower and Ryan quickly found a towel for Fabian. As they were drying off, Fabian asked, "Did it feel good? You seemed to be enjoying yourself."

"I was. A lot. It was really good." Ryan looked away. "Too good, maybe. I kinda got carried away."

"I don't mind trying again," Fabian said gently. Ryan truly appreciated the offer, but he couldn't accept.

"Thanks, but I'm good. Really."

"Or we could just . . . make out? Roll around that amazing bed of yours?"

Ryan smiled. "Sounds like a plan."

Damn. Fabian had gotten Ryan so close. He'd been sure of it.

Failure was never something Fabian had been able to accept easily. He knew he shouldn't view Ryan's orgasm as a challenge, especially after Ryan had explained to him why sex was difficult for him, but he couldn't help it. He really, *really* wanted to make Ryan come.

He wouldn't mind coming himself either. That blowjob had really gotten him worked up, and even his near-death-by-choking-on-a-monster-cock hadn't dampened his arousal much.

He arranged himself coquettishly on top of Ryan's rumpled

bedding, with his legs outstretched and crossed at the ankles, and one arm draped lazily over his head.

"Oh," Ryan said. He stood at the end of the bed, knuckles white from clutching the towel he had wrapped around his waist. His eyes raked over Fabian's body, and Fabian drank it in. He wanted Ryan's undivided attention.

Fabian reached down and gently played with his own erection. "I'll bet," he said slowly, "that you've imagined a few things you would like to do with me."

Ryan's Adam's apple bobbed. "Yeah," he said. It was barely above a whisper, but Fabian heard it loud and clear.

"Why don't you come over here and tell me about them."

Ryan's mouth hung open for a moment, as if his brain had short circuited, and then he said, "I don't know if I can. Tell you, I mean."

"Then show me."

Ryan dropped the towel and crawled onto the bed, covering Fabian's body with his own. He kissed Fabian, hard and deep and possessive, and Fabian's blood sang. *Yes, please. Claim me. Treasure me.*

"Tell me if I do something wrong," Ryan said, then he kissed and sucked at Fabian's neck. Fabian tilted his head back eagerly. He loved having his neck kissed.

"Fuck, that is the opposite of wrong," Fabian said. "Love how your beard feels against my skin."

Ryan grunted in response, which was probably the most Fabian was going to get out of him. He would love Ryan to murmur filthy things to him. God, what would that be like? He tried to imagine sweet, shy Ryan talking dirty in his soft, South Shore accent. The thought made Fabian's dick twitch in his hand.

Good thing Fabian was chatty enough for both of them.

"I want your cock in my mouth again. Whenever you want. Open invitation. I've never had one so big before. I want to work up to deep throating you. I'll bet I could do it."

He was possibly talking total bullshit, but he really did want to try to take Ryan all the way down to the root.

"Think so?" Ryan said, then he captured Fabian's nipple piercing in his teeth. He tugged just hard enough that a sweet jolt of pain and pleasure shot through Fabian's body, down to his toes. He yelped, and Ryan laughed.

"You're obsessed with that thing," Fabian said.

"I've never seen one up close."

"Well I strive to be educational."

Ryan played with the jewelry with his tongue for another minute while Fabian writhed on the bed. He didn't want to push him, but Fabian really wouldn't mind some part of Ryan making contact with Fabian's cock. Soon. He lifted his hips so his erection bumped lightly against Ryan's chest, hoping he would take the hint.

He may have understood, or it may have been a coincidence that Ryan *finally* started to trail kisses down Fabian's stomach, pausing when he reached his cock.

"Can I—?"

"Yes!" Fabian practically yelled. He slapped a hand over his mouth, embarrassed. "I mean, yes. You may. Please."

"It's been a while, so if I don't—"

"Ry-annnn," Fabian whined.

Ryan's brow furrowed as he stared at Fabian's cock, like he was trying to figure out how to approach it. Then, mercifully, he just dove in, wrapping his lips around the head and sliding down.

"Oh fuck yes. Holy shit, Ryan. Just like that."

The truth was, it took almost nothing to get Fabian off, but he could still appreciate Ryan's technique. It wasn't showy, or even practiced, but it was so earnest that Fabian couldn't help but be charmed.

Also, Ryan's beard was tickling his balls, which was pretty excellent.

After what couldn't have been more than three minutes, Fabian warned, "If you don't want me to shoot in your mouth, you'd better pull off."

Ryan did pull off, but then he said, "What?" And then Fabian ejaculated all over his confused face.

"I'm so fucking sorry. Oh my god." Fabian knew his giddy laughter didn't make him sound very sorry. "I was trying to warn you."

Ryan wiped a hand over his beard, removing most of the mess, and then he smiled. "That was okay, then?"

"That was perfect." Fabian covered his own face with a pillow and groaned. Ryan pulled the pillow away.

"It's fine. I liked seeing that. I was just surprised." He stood and started walking toward the bathroom. "I'll be right back."

Was this going well? Fabian wasn't sure. He certainly enjoyed waking up to Ryan, and he got the impression that Ryan was having a reasonably good time, but he had no idea what would happen after he left Ryan's apartment later.

"How about I have another go at making you come?" Fabian suggested when Ryan returned to the bedroom.

Ryan's smile died. "I'm actually really hungry. Aren't you?"

Fabian eyed him warily. "I could eat, I guess."

"I have stuff. I can make breakfast. Or we can go somewhere, if you'd rather."

Fabian sat up. "I'm afraid I have nothing to wear to a restaurant." He gestured to his small pile of gross, sweaty club clothes on the floor.

"Oh. I could wash your clothes for you, so you at least don't have to put dirty clothes on to walk home later."

That actually made a lot of sense, so Fabian accepted. Clean underwear was too tempting to pass up. Ryan rummaged around in his closet and pulled something out.

"I know this isn't really your style, but I bought these for Colleen and she's closer to your size than I am." He handed Fabian a small stack of Toronto Guardians clothes. It appeared to be a hoodie and some pajama pants. "Just until your clothes are clean."

The horror Fabian felt must have been clear on his face, because Ryan laughed and said, "I promise I won't take photos."

Fabian shook his head, disgusted with himself. "I'm being a snob. Sorry. Thank you for the clothes, they look very . . . soft."

"If you like them, you can keep them. Do you like eggs?"

"If they're scrambled, I do."

Ryan kissed his cheek. "Scrambled eggs. Coming right up."

Ryan wasn't at all prepared for what the sight of Fabian wearing official team-licensed clothing would do to him.

He emerged from the bedroom as Ryan was stirring eggs on the stovetop, his slender, bare feet peeking out from the bottoms of the flannel Guardians pajama pants. There was a definite wrongness about Fabian wearing hockey fan gear, but Ryan's heart fluttered anyway. He *liked* seeing Fabian in his colors. In his home.

"How do I look?" Fabian asked sardonically.

"Comfortable."

Fabian shoved his hands in the pocket of the hoodie. "They are quite cozy. I can't lie."

Ryan chewed his lip, and then turned back to the eggs.

"What?" Fabian asked. "I know I look stupid, but—"

"No. I, ah." Ryan's face heated. "I'm a little turned on. Seeing you in those clothes. I know that's awful."

Fabian smiled and sauntered over to him, then wrapped his arms around his waist. "Well, in that case, go team go."

Ryan laughed. "Have a seat." He gestured with the spatula to the high stools that lined the breakfast counter. "You want toast with your eggs?"

Fabian hoisted himself onto one of the stools. "That would be wonderful."

"Coffee? Tea? I'm mostly a tea drinker, but I like coffee in the morning."

"I love tea, but yes. Coffee, please. Would you like me to make it?"

"Nope. You just sit." And before he could stop himself, he added, "If you stand any closer I'll get distracted and burn the eggs."

Fabian laughed at that. Ryan loved the sound of Fabian's musical laughter. He really couldn't believe that Fabian was actually here, in his kitchen, after an incredible night and morning of exploring each other's bodies. It didn't matter that they'd only fooled around a little, or that Ryan hadn't gotten off—it had absolutely been the best thing that had ever happened to him. And he was a Stanley Cup champion.

When the eggs were done and the toast had popped, Ryan split everything between two plates and set them on the counter. He poured them each a coffee, and hoped Fabian didn't take cream in his because Ryan still hadn't bought any. But if Fabian liked cream, Ryan would fill his fridge with it.

"Do you take anything in your coffee?"

"Nope. Black is perfect," Fabian said cheerfully. He waved his nose over the steaming mug. "This smells divine."

Ryan laughed. "It's just Folgers."

"Actual brand-name Folgers? Not the knockoff generic stuff? Okay, moneybags."

Ryan stood at the counter directly opposite Fabian. "Wait'll you see the brand-name dish soap I use to clean up with later."

"Stop. You'll spoil me."

Ryan beamed, then leaned across the counter and kissed him. "You're a better kissing height now."

Fabian smiled back at him, then pushed his plate away. "I'm suddenly full."

"You haven't touched your food. Eat."

Fabian rolled his eyes dramatically as he retrieved his plate. "*Fine.*"

As they ate, Ryan marveled at how comfortable he was in Fabian's company. Even when they'd been teenagers, and even with the terrifying attraction he'd always had for him, Ryan had often felt at ease with him. He knew it hadn't been easy for Fabian to see past his prejudice toward hockey players—a prejudice that Ryan could completely understand because he'd heard countless homophobic slurs during his hockey career. He'd seen the way high school hockey players treated boys who were like Fabian. But Fabian *had* seen Ryan, even back then. Not just another jock, not a threat, but a person worth sharing small parts of himself with.

"What's on your mind?" Fabian asked, because Ryan was probably staring at him with a dreamy expression on his face.

"Nothing." Ryan shoveled the last of his eggs into his mouth.

"I don't believe that for a second."

"I was just thinking about before. Back when we were young."

"I'm *still* young. But if you mean when we were teenagers, I've been thinking a lot about that lately myself."

"I guess our cards are on the table now, so I'll just tell you: I was obsessed with you back then."

Fabian rested his chin in his palm and smiled. "Obsessed?"

"Pretty much. I just thought you were so . . . beautiful."

Fabian waved a hand. "I was a skinny, awkward teenager who was trying way too hard to be edgy."

"No. You were amazing. You're *still* amazing."

Fabian preened a bit, then said, "Well then, Ryan Price, let me tell you what I thought of you."

"Oh, that's all ri—"

"Do you remember when we first met? You had just arrived at our house, and Mom called me into the living room so she could introduce me to the latest hockey player who would be invading my life."

"I remember you didn't shake my hand."

"My nails were wet."

Ryan lit up. "Was that the reason?"

Fabian shrugged. "Yes. I mean, I can't promise I would have been friendlier even if that hadn't been the case, but I honestly *was* concerned about my nails."

Ryan laughed. "I thought you hated me."

"I did. I mean, I didn't know you, but I assumed you'd be an asshole. The other ones were. And you were so tall and my parents were gazing at you like you were a god. Like you were the son they'd always wanted."

Ryan's heart clenched. "No, they—"

"It's fine. They hardly made a secret of it. So I was prepared to hate you, but then you spoke and your voice was so soft. And you had that adorable shy smile. Yes, that one."

Ryan flushed, but he couldn't help but smile more. "I'd never seen anyone who looked like you before."

"Lebanese?" Fabian teased.

"*No.* I mean all sophisticated and glamorous."

Fabian barked out a laugh. "*Glamorous?* Oh my god, you really were sheltered."

"You just . . . looked like someone from Panic! At The Disco or something."

Ryan was worried Fabian was going to fall off his stool. "Stop! Holy fuck," he gasped. "I was a fucking band nerd who was wearing cheap nail polish."

"You had nice hair."

"Well," Fabian said when he'd stopped laughing, "*you* looked like Archie Andrews. But you didn't look at me with disgust, and I couldn't help but find that . . . intriguing."

"I think the last thing I felt when I looked at you was disgust."

"It's a shame you never told me."

Ryan took both of their plates to the sink. "I was still figuring myself out."

"So you'd never kissed anyone before?"

"A girl. Back in Ross Harbour. We were at a party and it seemed like something I should do. I was the star hockey player, so I got a lot of attention from girls back then."

"Were there boys you would have rather been kissing?"

"Not really. Not until—" Ryan stopped himself. Even after everything they'd admitted, this seemed like too much.

Fabian came to stand beside him at the sink. He rested a hand on Ryan's arm. "Not until what?"

Ryan bit his lip, then said, "Not until you."

When Fabian didn't reply, Ryan chanced looking down at him. He was shocked to see tears in Fabian's eyes.

"Oh god. Are you okay?"

Fabian nodded, his lips pressed tight together.

"I'm sorry if—"

"No. I cry easily," Fabian said. "That was just really sweet. I didn't know." He exhaled loudly. "I had never kissed anyone when I'd met you. I told you that already, I guess. But I'd had crushes on friends who . . . couldn't return them. And it made it hard to keep being friends with some of them. But I never expected to have those kinds of feelings for a hockey player. For the *enemy*." He rolled his eyes. "I was such a judgmental prick."

"I understand. Believe me. I've never really fit in with my teammates."

"I'll admit, even now, I'm surprised that I—" He sighed, then looked at the floor.

Ryan could guess the rest of that sentence. *I'm surprised I'm attracted to someone like you*. He wasn't offended because he couldn't believe it either.

"Your clothes must be ready to go in the dryer," Ryan said. "*Can* they go in the dryer?"

Fabian laughed, then sniffled. "My clothes are extremely cheap. They can go in the dryer."

After that was taken care of, Ryan suggested they have more coffee in the living room. Fabian curled up on one end of the sofa, his flannel-clad legs tucked under him. Ryan sat at the other end, but turned toward him.

"I'm sorry about your parents," he said. It was something he had wanted to say when they'd been teenagers.

Fabian traced one of the Guardians logos on his pants with a fingertip. "About what? It's not their fault they didn't get the son they wanted."

"It *is* their fault." Ryan considered what he'd just said, then corrected himself. "I don't mean—I'm just trying to say that they're stupid for not appreciating you the way that you are."

"Well, as I like to say, their loss. But it never feels good to be so disappointing that your parents take to adopting replacement sons. Better ones." Fabian snorted. "Year after year I was introduced to some version of their ideal son. My parents would just be *bursting* with pride whenever their big, jock-y wards would score a goal or be interviewed on TV. I couldn't possibly expect to compete with *that*."

"I'm sorry," Ryan said.

"What on earth for?"

"For being part of the problem."

Fabian crawled across the sofa, then placed a hand on each side of Ryan's face and forced him to hold his gaze. "It has *nothing* to do with you. You are *wonderful*."

Ryan lost himself for a moment in Fabian's dark, beautiful eyes. He resurfaced when Fabian released him with a laugh. "God, listen to me. I'm thirty-one. Why am I still whining about my parents? I'm doing great, they seem to be happy, everything worked out fine."

Ryan wanted to argue, but decided instead to pull Fabian into his lap and kiss him.

"How long until the dryer is done?" Fabian said breathlessly when Ryan finally broke their kiss.

"Thirty minutes, maybe?"

"I have an idea for how to pass the time."

"Oh?"

"Mm. And the good news is it involves you stripping me out of all this fleece."

CHAPTER EIGHTEEN

"There's something different about Fabian," Marcus mused.

"Hmm, new haircut?" Tarek suggested.

"No. Oh! I know! He's just had a mind-blowing sex marathon with an NHL player."

Fabian stuck his tongue out at Marcus. "I did *not*. We talked more than anything. Is there more coffee?"

"I'll make some," Tarek offered. "But then I want to hear *everything*."

"You didn't *just* talk, did you, Fabe?" Vanessa asked. "That would be tragic."

Fabian couldn't stop the smile that tugged at his lips, which made Vanessa shriek. "You totally banged him! Was it amazing?"

"I *didn't* actually. Technically. Depends on how you define such things."

Vanessa set her waffle plate on the coffee table and sat back in her armchair. "You know I don't think sex only counts if there's penetration."

"So we're not being subtle, I guess," Marcus muttered.

"Then by your definition," Fabian said, "yes. We had sex. But . . ."

"Wait! Wait for me!" Tarek said, hustling back from the kitchen to join Marcus and Fabian on the futon. "The kettle is boiling. Spill."

"Okay, so, he's kind of anxious about sex. He has some . . . difficulty . . . getting off."

"Sounds like a challenge," Marcus joked.

Fabian narrowed his eyes at him, even though he had sort of thought the exact same thing.

"It's *not* a challenge," Vanessa scolded. "Lots of people have difficulty with orgasms, for lots of different reasons. Sex doesn't have to be all about coming, you know."

"That's right," Fabian agreed primly. "We had a great time. He was . . . very sweet. He's an incredible kisser. And so strong and sexy." He sighed. "I'm smitten."

Vanessa clapped her hands together. "I love him!"

"I thought you'd bring him to brunch," Tarek said.

"I considered it, but he had a practice or something this morning, and besides. I wanted to gush about him with you guys."

"So are you two a couple now?" Marcus asked. "Are you actually dating an NHL player?"

Fabian's smile faded. "I don't exactly know."

"You didn't talk about it?" Vanessa asked.

"No. But we're going to see each other tomorrow night before he leaves for his road trip."

"Road trip? Boo."

"Yeah, it sucks, but . . ." Fabian shrugged. "I'll be busy. I have an album to finish, a launch to book, and a mini-tour to plan."

"When are you touring?" Vanessa asked.

"There's a middle-of-winter music festival in Kingston that

I've been invited to play. I thought I'd build a little tour around it. I could just take trains instead driving myself around Ontario in February."

"Um, you're not going *alone*," she said.

"I can be careful!"

"Fabian," Tarek warned, "at least find another musician to tour with."

Fabian wanted to argue, but he knew his friends were right to worry. "I'll ask around," he promised. "Maybe my label wants to pair me up with someone."

"Maybe *Ryan* wants to be your roadie," Marcus said.

"Except he'll be playing *hockey* in February. Because that's his *job*."

Marcus threw up his hands. "How the fuck am I supposed to know when hockey is?"

Fabian wanted to roll his eyes, but he couldn't hate how much his friends loved him. Or how much they immediately trusted Ryan. Despite his size, his job, and the fact that he seemingly had nothing in common with them, Fabian's friends had accepted him.

"Thanks," Fabian said. "I'll bring him to brunch soon. If he wants to come, I mean." *If we're actually dating, or whatever.*

"Awesome," Tarek said. "Now can we talk about literally anyone besides Fabian for a change?"

When Ryan arrived at the practice facility on Sunday, he was surprised to find most of his teammates gathered around the television in the lounge.

"What's going on?" he asked Wyatt.

"Shane Hollander and Ilya Rozanov are hosting a press conference. They just announced this new charity thing they are starting."

"What, *together*?"

Wyatt laughed. "Wild, right? I guess anyone can put their differences aside if those two can."

Hollander and Rozanov were famously bitter rivals and had been for years. They were two of the biggest stars in the league—Hollander for Montreal, and Rozanov for Boston before he signed with Ottawa over the summer—and, as far as Ryan or anyone else knew, were not friendly off the ice.

"I guess they're friends or something," Wyatt said. "That's what Hollander said today anyway. That's going to blow some minds."

"Yeah."

They watched as Rozanov shared some heartfelt words about his mother losing her battle with depression.

"God, I didn't know his mother killed herself," Wyatt said bluntly.

"I don't think anyone did." Ryan had played with him for an entire season and he'd had no idea.

"Except Hollander, I guess. I wonder how long they've been friends."

Ryan couldn't even begin to guess. When would they even have spent time together off the ice?

It was none of his business, really, so he stopped trying to figure it out. Besides, he was too busy floating on the memories of the past twenty-four hours. His brain was basically useless. He didn't even have the mental capacity to panic about having to get on a plane on Tuesday.

"They're probably fucking," Troy Barrett sneered, which made the group around him laugh.

"Gross," said Dallas Kent. "Rozanov would never. But I'll bet Hollander is a fucking homo."

That launched a debate about Shane Hollander's sexuality that Ryan walked away from. He could remind them that *he* was a "fucking homo," but he just didn't have the energy.

Wyatt found him in the dressing room. "I told those guys to grow the fuck up," he said. "Just so you know."

"You didn't have to do that."

"Uh, yes I did. I'm not putting up with that shit and you shouldn't either."

Ryan knew that. He should be doing what he could to shut down that sort of bullshit, but he'd spent so many years just trying to escape everyone's attention, to not cause problems, that the idea of confronting his teammates was intimidating. Which was ridiculous because his *job* was fighting. But there was a huge difference between dropping the gloves and trading punches on the ice—that was rarely personal—and getting in your teammate's face in the locker room.

He should say something. He *would* say something. He waited until everyone was in the dressing room, then he swallowed his nerves and said, "Hey, Kent."

The room went *silent*. It was weird. Ryan supposed that's what happens when someone who doesn't talk much finally uses his voice.

"What?" Kent asked. Ryan could tell he was trying not to look nervous. Ryan had seen *that* look on a lot of guys' faces on the ice.

He rolled his shoulders back and raised his chin so every inch of his height was on display. "Just so you know, I'm gay."

For a moment, no one said anything. Ryan didn't think anyone in the room even *breathed*. And then Kent said, "Okay."

"Keep that in mind," Ryan said. Judging by the way Kent's eyes widened, he hadn't missed the threat in Ryan's tone. Not that Ryan would ever beat up a teammate, but Kent didn't know that.

Kent put his hands up. "Whatever, man. That's your business. I don't have a problem with you."

"I have a problem with you saying homophobic shit about

anyone. I don't want to hear it again." Ryan felt oddly calm. Almost like he did when he was fighting during a game.

Someone behind Ryan whispered, "Holy shit."

Kent looked around the room for support, but everyone looked away. "Sure. Fine. I'll watch what I say, all right?" he finally said.

"Glad to hear it." Ryan gave him one last hard look, then turned away and sat back down in his stall. The rest of the team went back to whatever they'd been doing before, and the room filled with chatter.

Wyatt elbowed Ryan. "I wish I had a video of that."

"Should have done that a long time ago." Ryan's heart was racing now, but he felt good. It was more like adrenaline and less like fear or panic.

"That shit isn't going to fly for much longer in this league. Not when one of the biggest stars in the game is out."

It was true that Scott Hunter coming out the same season he had won the Stanley Cup, the Conn Smythe Trophy for playoff MVP, and the Hart Trophy for regular season MVP had taken a lot of the wind out of the sails of the argument that hockey was a sport for straight men only. But obviously there was still work to be done.

It was time for Ryan to step up and do some of it.

CHAPTER NINETEEN

"Wow."

Ryan stared in amazement at Fabian's apartment. Not only was it tidier than Ryan had ever seen it, it looked like some sort of fantasy sex den. The room was mood lit with a combination of dim lamps, candles, and white fairy lights, which made the red walls seem extra sultry. The candles must have been scented because there was an intoxicating sweet and spicy aroma filling the small space.

Also, there were sex toys on the bed.

And if all that wasn't enough, Fabian was wearing a sleeveless black jumpsuit with flared legs and a plunging V-neck, as well as smoky black eye makeup and dark red lipstick.

Even Ryan's *wildest* sexual fantasies weren't this good.

"Just in case you weren't clear about what I want tonight," Fabian said, reaching up to drape his arms around Ryan's neck, "I thought I'd spell it out."

He pulled Ryan down for a kiss. Dimly, Ryan worried about ruining his lipstick, but then he stopped caring because Fabian's mouth was hot and urgent on his.

"Mm," Fabian murmured happily when he pulled away. "I've been looking forward to that."

Miraculously, Fabian's lipstick hadn't been ruined. It must be some sort of invincible lipstick. That was good news because Ryan hoped to do a lot more kissing tonight.

"You look incredible," he said.

"You like?" Fabian released him, then did a little twirl. "A friend made it for me. I'm afraid it will have to come off for what I have planned."

"I'm okay with that. But can I kiss you some more first?"

"Oh yes."

This time Ryan hoisted Fabian up, and Fabian wrapped his legs around Ryan's waist. Ryan pinned him against a wall and kissed him the way he'd been wanting to for days. He dipped his head so he could work on Fabian's gorgeous neck, which made Fabian gasp and squirm in his arms.

"God, you're good at that," Fabian panted. "Missed you."

Ryan chuckled. "It's only been a couple of days."

"You missed me too. Admit it."

Ryan licked his Adam's apple. "I missed you."

Fabian sighed happily and said, "I am so excited to play with you."

Ryan loved the way Fabian talked about sex. *Playing.* That's what it was. Just fun and games. Nothing to worry about.

When Ryan let Fabian get his feet back on the floor, Ryan could see the very prominent outline of Fabian's erection pressing against the tight fabric of his jumpsuit. Fabian's hair was disheveled but his makeup remained flawless, and Ryan had never seen anything sexier in his life.

"Are you sure you have to take that off?" Ryan asked, trailing a finger along the V of the plunging neckline.

"I think you'll like what's underneath."

Fabian turned so Ryan could unzip him. "I have some wine, if you want," Fabian offered.

"Not thirsty." Ryan pinched the zipper's narrow tab between his thick fingers and slowly pulled it down, fascinated by the reveal of Fabian's skin as he went. He was expecting Fabian to be naked underneath, but when the fabric slipped off Fabian's shoulders and pooled at his feet Ryan could see that he was wearing . . .

"Holy shit."

Fabian glanced back over his shoulder. "It was a risk, I know. But I thought you might like it."

"Yeah." Ryan swallowed hard. "I like it." He'd never seen a man wearing lace underwear in person before. Panties, Ryan supposed was the best word. It was hot as fuck.

He smoothed his palm over the delicate black lace that stretched over the perfect globes of Fabian's ass. Without even thinking about it, he ran his thumb down the seam that dipped into Fabian's crack, and Fabian moaned his approval.

"I love wearing lace," Fabian said. He reached back and covered Ryan's hands with his own, guiding him. Ryan stepped closer so the bulge in his jeans pressed against Fabian's ass.

"I wouldn't mind if you wore it all the time," Ryan growled.

Fabian tipped his head back. "How about you take your shirt off? I want to see that gorgeous chest."

Ryan stepped back so he could pull his T-shirt off. Fabian turned to face him, and now Ryan could see Fabian's erection straining against the lace.

"Oh fuck," Ryan said. He gripped himself through his jeans as a powerful jolt of arousal shot through him.

Fabian's lips curved into a devilish smile as he fingered his sparkling, heart-shaped nipple piercing. "What do you want, Ryan? We have all night."

Ryan dropped to his knees. He was overwhelmed by the desire to get his mouth on the lace that was pulled tight against Fabian's cock. He started by nuzzling him there, then rubbing his face and beard against his dick as Fabian moaned. "God, you *do* love it."

Ryan opened his mouth and pressed it against Fabian's rigid shaft. He felt *wild* with lust. Some fucked-up part of him wished his teammates could see him now, on his knees for a man wearing lace underwear and makeup. They'd never understand. This wasn't for them to understand. This had nothing to do with them, and Ryan couldn't be happier about it.

He licked and kissed until Fabian gasped, "Stop. Fuck. I don't want to come yet."

Ryan liked the idea of Fabian coming while still wearing the underwear, but he obeyed and pulled back. Fabian caressed Ryan's cheek with the back of his hand. "You're too good to be true, Ryan Price."

Ryan turned his head and caught Fabian's thumb between his teeth. His mind was so wonderfully focused right now. He wasn't nervous or unsure of himself. He wanted to make Fabian feel good. He wanted to *fuck*.

"Can I just say, jeans and no shirt is a *very* good look for you." Fabian almost sounded drunk, but Ryan doubted he'd had a drop of alcohol. He grinned and stood up so Fabian could get a good look.

"Oh yes," Fabian purred. He stepped forward and ran his hands over Ryan's chest. "I love all this hair."

"Yeah? I thought about waxing it."

"Don't you dare." Fabian rested his fingers on Ryan's belt buckle. "May I?"

Ryan nodded. He couldn't deny Fabian anything right now. Not when he was gazing up at him through those long lashes, his eyelids shimmering with black shadow. Ryan dipped his head to kiss Fabian again. He liked that Fabian made him feel attractive. Made him feel . . . sexy.

Fabian worked open Ryan's belt while they kissed, then popped open the top two buttons of Ryan's fly. He stepped back to admire his work as Ryan stood panting, unable to feel even a little self-conscious.

"Let me just commit this to memory," Fabian said. "Because you look absolutely perfect right now."

Ryan laughed, and then he may have flexed his ab muscles a bit.

"Oof. Okay," Fabian said. "Let's have some fun."

Fabian went to the bed and lay on his side. Ryan remained standing at the end of the bed because he couldn't get enough of this image of Fabian sprawled out in a decadent offering. It was the very picture of hedonism, and Ryan still couldn't believe any of this was really happening to him.

"So," Fabian said, his fingers walking playfully across the mattress toward the large, purple dildo, "this is the one I promised to review."

"Should we, uh, start with that, then?"

Fabian held it up and turned it over. "It's awfully *big*. Maybe you could get me ready for it?"

Oh hell yes. Ryan was definitely into that. He wanted to get Fabian all loose and open and begging to be filled with that thing. And then maybe with Ryan's cock.

"And it doesn't necessarily have to be *me* on the receiving end," Fabian said. "I love it all."

Oh. Ryan had always topped, in the past. It was probably because of his size, but his partners had always wanted him to fuck them.

"Only if you want," Fabian said quickly. "I'm happy either way. Or we can do both. Like I said, we've got all night."

Ryan decided to try saying what he wanted, without worrying about how embarrassing it might sound. "I want to see you with that dildo in you. I want to watch you take it."

Fabian's eyes widened. "My goodness, Ryan. Come over here and tell me more of your good ideas."

Ryan shucked his pants and socks but left his briefs on, then covered Fabian's body with his own, kissing him hungrily. He rolled his hips so his own erection ground against Fabian's, letting Fabian know how turned on he was.

"Oh god," Fabian gasped. "Tell me what you want to do to me. Tell me."

Ryan couldn't come up with words, so he just kept kissing him everywhere. Down his neck, across his chest to his nipple piercing, then down to his belly button. He licked a long stripe up the length of Fabian's cock, still trapped by the lace underwear, then returned to Fabian's mouth.

Fabian gripped Ryan's cock outside his briefs and squeezed, and Ryan thrust involuntarily into his hand. "Fuck yes. Touch me."

Fabian shoved his hand inside Ryan's briefs and wrapped his slim fingers around his rock-hard dick. "Keep talking," Fabian murmured into his ear.

Dirty talk was extremely far outside of Ryan's comfort zone, but he *wanted* to be able to do it for Fabian. It was such a small, simple thing, putting the desires that were filling his head into words. He could try. He was safe here.

"I want to stay in this room forever and make you come over and over again. You're so fucking beautiful."

"*Ryan*," Fabian whimpered. "More please."

"I want your red lips around my dick." Ryan *did* flush after he said that. He couldn't help it. But Fabian's only reaction was to plant both hands on Ryan's chest and tip him onto the mattress.

"My pleasure," he said, then wriggled down Ryan's body and tugged his briefs down to his thighs. Ryan's cock thudded against his stomach, and then Fabian wrapped his fingers around the base and took the head into his mouth.

"Oh god. Fuck." If Ryan didn't get off tonight, then there was a very real possibility that he might never achieve orgasm ever again in his life. He would never be in a situation this hot again, he was sure of it.

He watched Fabian suck him off as pleasure built but never threatened to spill over into orgasm. It was perfect. He wanted to ride this feeling for as long as possible. But he also really did want to see how many times Fabian could come.

He stopped Fabian by resting a gentle hand on his cheek. "That felt amazing. Thank you."

Fabian pulled off with a parting lick, and then kissed the inside of Ryan's thigh. "I certainly don't mind doing that for a whole lot longer, if you like."

"I want to try this on you." Ryan turned his head and grabbed the dildo. It was large, and sort of complicated looking. It had a curvy part at the bottom and a springy part at the top. Ryan studied the toy, brow furrowed, and Fabian laughed. "I'll talk you through it. It will be fun, I promise."

He made a shooing gesture with his hands at Ryan. "Get up for a second. I have to put a towel down. This comforter needs two dryer cycles and I'm not made of money."

Ryan stood and decided he may as well take his underwear all the way off. Fabian quickly set things up the way he wanted on the bed, plopping a pillow in the middle of the mattress and layering a couple towels on top. "Sorry," he said. "I know this isn't super sexy."

Ryan was pretty sure Fabian could unclog a drain and be sexy if he was wearing lace underwear and makeup. "Don't worry. I'm plenty turned on."

Fabian smiled over his shoulder. "Good." He finished his work, then stood in front of Ryan. "Now then." He tucked his thumbs into the waistband of his lace underwear and slid them down over his slim hips. Ryan would have been dismayed, except without the underwear he could see that Fabian was wearing a black ring around the base of his cock and behind his balls.

"Holy hell," Ryan said. Fabian was like one of those presents that you just keep unwrapping. What would Ryan find under the cock ring? A tattoo of his own name?

"It helps with endurance," Fabian explained. He glanced down. "I also like how it makes my balls look."

"Yeah," Ryan said hoarsely. "Looks good."

Fabian grabbed the bottle of lube that had been on the mattress next to the dildo and handed it to Ryan. "Use plenty. I've got more." He lay on his back with his ass positioned on the pillow. "Start with your fingers," Fabian instructed. "Have you done this part before?"

"Uh, yeah. Been a while, but yes." Ryan poured lube on his fingers and Fabian spread his legs. Fabian's slender, curved cock was like steel, and his balls looked ready to burst, choked by the silicone ring. Ryan couldn't stop himself from brushing a fingertip over them.

"Ahh." Fabian trembled, and his balls twitched under Ryan's touch. God, they were so tight. He trailed his fingers down to Fabian's hole, and began tracing light circles. He was going to take such good care of him. He would worship him the way he deserved, and then he would let him take whatever he wanted.

Fabian was having a fantastic time.

"Just tease me with the tip for a bit," he suggested. "Get me loose."

Ryan gently nudged his hole with the lubricated tip of the dildo, not quite pushing it inside. He was so obedient and sweet. Fabian wanted to do this for Ryan sometime. He wanted to show him how incredible toys could be, how good it felt to have a vibrator or beads inside you. For now he would have to lead by example.

"I think the top button makes it vibrate a little. Turn it on," Fabian instructed. Ryan frowned at the base of the vibrator for a moment, then pressed the correct button. The toy began buzzing gently against Fabian's hole. "Mm. That's perfect. Keep it like that for a bit."

Fabian stretched his arms over his head and sighed, loving the feeling of utter relaxation that washed over him. After a couple of minutes he said, "You could try a finger now. Lots of lube, okay?"

"Yeah." Ryan's voice sounded strangled, which Fabian loved. He watched with interest as Ryan inserted the tip of one of his strong, thick fingers inside.

"God, those fingers. That's so good, Ryan. Open me up."

Ryan rolled the vibrating head of the dildo along Fabian's balls and shaft as he worked him open. Christ, Fabian hadn't even thought to ask for that. He moaned his approval.

Fabian had been with lovers who would be telling him how hot and tight his ass was right now, but Ryan only seemed to be able to stare in speechless wonder. Which was perfectly charming in its own way.

"Want more," Fabian murmured. "Give me the toy. Turn it off first."

He let out a long breath as Ryan gently guided the head of the dildo into Fabian's ass. Oof. No matter how many times he did this, that first moment of penetration was always exhilarating.

"Good?" Ryan asked.

"Divine. Now you can get creative. Turn it, wiggle it, pull it back out. You decide."

Ryan's brows pinched in an expression of deep concentration as he slowly rotated the toy, and then popped the head back out.

"Oh! Yes. Deeper this time."

Ryan did as told, but first he gripped one of Fabian's thighs in his hand and carefully pushed it back to better expose Fabian's hole. Fuck, those hands. So strong.

"More. Deeper." When the dildo was all the way in, Fabian's eyes rolled back. "Oh Jesus. That's good. Is the bendy part that sticks out touching my perineum?"

"That's, like, your taint, right?"

"Yes, cutie."

"Yup. It's there."

"Okay. So, I read the manual before you came over. It vibrates at five different speeds, and it also thrusts at three different speeds. So let's start by going through the vibrator settings, and then we'll get to thrusting."

Ryan pressed the vibration button, and a very low-grade buzz tickled Fabian's ass. "Okay. Go higher. That feels like nothing."

"How about now?"

"Did you press the button?"

"Yes."

"Press it again. Feels the same." Fabian drummed his fingers on the mattress, waiting. "Ryan?"

"I pressed it."

Fabian let out an exasperated sigh. "This sucks. Press it again. And I swear to god if—aaah!" Fabian arched off the bed as the toy suddenly rattled like a busted washing machine inside him. "Turn it off! What the fuck! Turn it off!"

Ryan turned it off, and Fabian could see that he was trying not to laugh.

Fabian glared at him. "Next time I'm going to stick weird toys in *your* ass, Giggles."

"Seems to go from zero to a hundred in a hurry, huh?"

He huffed. "I'm almost scared to suggest this, but I suppose we should *try* the thrusting feature."

"You sure?"

"Yes. But lowest setting only!"

Ryan nodded, still biting his lip to hold back laughter, and pressed the bottom button.

"Ow! Fuck! Stop! Take it out!"

Ryan removed the toy as fast as he could without hurting Fabian. "What did it do?"

"God, it was, like, *pinching* the inside of my ass. It was not a good feeling."

Ryan frowned at the toy as if he was thinking about punching it, which made Fabian laugh. "Just throw it in the sink."

Ryan darted to the bathroom, where he presumably dropped the terrible toy into the sink, and returned to the bed. "So it's not getting a good review?"

They both cracked up, laughing until they became tangled in each other on the bed. "Oh god," Fabian wheezed, "this was supposed to be such a sexy evening."

"It's still sexy," Ryan assured him, and kissed Fabian's hair. "Sorry that toy didn't work right, because I loved watching you take it."

"*Did* you?"

"Mmhm." Ryan shifted them so Fabian was flat on his back, Ryan covering him, and kissed him breathless. Ryan's cock had probably flagged a bit during the sex toy disaster and the laughing fit that followed, but it was like steel now. Fabian pressed his own erection against Ryan's stomach, letting him know that he was very much still interested in more.

"I have condoms. If you'd like to fuck me."

Ryan froze. "Could I?"

"No sense in wasting all that prep work," Fabian said with a wry smile. Then he kissed Ryan's cheek and whispered. "I have been dying to have that cock in me. So, yes, Ryan. You can fuck me. *Please* fuck me."

Ryan growled and wrapped one of his giant hands around Fabian's aching cock. When he stroked, Fabian cried out like he'd been electrocuted.

"God, you're so hard with that thing on," Ryan said, one finger tracing the ring of silicone that was wrapped snug around Fabian's cock and balls. "Can I suck you?"

"Oh, I suppose," Fabian said with an exaggerated sigh.

Ryan's lips twitched up in a bit of a smile, and then he slid down to take Fabian into his mouth. It was heavenly, and even more so when Ryan thrust two fingers inside him.

"Oh, Ryan. Yes. Just like that."

Ryan pulled off and said, "Want you to come."

"I definitely will. Especially if—aah." Fabian shuddered when Ryan sucked his tight ball sac into his mouth. "Oh, I love that. Keep going." Fabian put a hand around his own cock and stroked, loving the triple sensation of having his ass, balls, and cock stimulated.

"I'm close. Fuck." God, it was embarrassing how easily Fabian came undone, even with a cock ring, but there was nothing to be done about it. His whole body was trembling with the need for release.

"Do it," Ryan commanded, then gave Fabian's balls another lick. "Let it out."

Fabian only had time to whimper before he erupted. His release sprang from his cock in ribbons and landed on his chest and stomach.

After it was over, he closed his eyes and sank into the pillows. "That was incredible," he sighed.

"Are you done?" Ryan asked. He was kneeling between Fabian's limp thighs, holding his own throbbing erection. "It's okay if you want to go to sleep."

"Oh god no," Fabian assured him. "I *really* want your cock in me." He blew out a breath. "Soon, I mean. Give me a second."

"We don't have to if—"

Fabian sat up and grabbed Ryan's face with both hands. "I want to. I've possibly never wanted anything more, all right?"

Ryan smiled. "Okay."

Fabian wedged a finger between the silicone ring and his softening cock. "I'm taking this off, though." He carefully eased it off, then took it to the bathroom to join the dildo in the sink, and gave his chest and stomach a quick wipe.

"You good?" he asked when he returned to the bedroom.

"I'm great. Fuck, that was hot." Ryan was stroking himself, which Fabian liked. He really hoped Ryan could come tonight. He opened the nightstand drawer and pulled out a strip of condoms.

"So," he asked, "how do you want me?"

Ryan didn't even know how he wanted Fabian. Every way at once, if he was being honest.

"I want to see you," he said. "Maybe . . . could you be on top?"

Fabian smiled. "I can *definitely* be on top. You just made a very wise decision."

Ryan kissed him, grateful that Fabian made this so *easy*. He settled himself on the mattress and waited for Fabian to make the next move.

But Fabian didn't budge from where he was kneeling at the end of the bed. "Do you have any idea how hot you are?" Fabian asked.

Ryan shook his head, which made Fabian glare at him. "I would like to *live* between these thighs. They are spectacular." He crawled up the bed until his face was between them. "Right here. This is where I want to build a home."

Ryan laughed. "You can thank hockey for that."

"Ugh. I guess it's good for something. Does hockey give you huge, gorgeous balls too?"

"No," Ryan gasped as Fabian took one of his balls into his mouth. "That's just me."

Fabian hummed his approval, which made Ryan moan. Fabian sucked his balls and then his cock for a while, and then kissed his way up to Ryan's mouth.

Ryan was so ready. He was buzzing everywhere, desperate for release. He was *sure* he could do it tonight.

Fabian retrieved the strip of condoms from somewhere on the bed and tore one packet off. He opened it and raised an eyebrow. "Shall I get you dressed?"

Ryan grinned. "Sure."

Fabian slipped the condom over the head of Ryan's cock and rolled it down the shaft, then grabbed the lube and got to work slicking him up. "When was the last time you came?" Fabian's tone was casual, as if asking about the weather.

God, when was it? Ryan had successfully gotten himself off in the shower one morning, but that seemed like ages ago now. "I don't know. Two weeks? Maybe a little longer?"

Fabian looked at him with sympathy. "Oh, sweetheart. Let's see what we can do about that."

Ryan just nodded. *Please, yes. Let's do that.*

Fabian lined himself up, then sank down on Ryan's cock. They both moaned at the same time as Ryan slipped in with very little resistance.

"Oh, I *like* this toy," Fabian purred when Ryan was fully

inside him. "You're so fucking big. It feels amazing." Ryan noticed that Fabian was almost fully hard again. Unreal.

He let Fabian take the lead at first, staying as still as possible as Fabian fucked himself on his cock. He didn't want to hurt him, and he also really enjoyed watching Fabian work himself on him.

It felt incredible, but if he was going to come, he was going to have to start thrusting.

"Can I move? Are you okay?" he asked.

"Yeah, I'm good. Fuck me."

Ryan did. He held Fabian's hips and pounded up into him as Fabian threw his head back and groaned. Ryan was mesmerized by his beauty. How could anything so stunning be on top of him right now? How could Ryan be *inside* him?

Oh fuck. Ryan was getting wonderfully close. "Can I—can you get on your back? I think that could work."

Fabian's face lit up. "Hell yes. Let's get you off."

They switched so Fabian was on his back, and he wrapped his legs around Ryan when Ryan entered him again. "Can you come again?" Ryan grunted.

Fabian began stroking his own cock. "I think so. Keep going."

Ryan adjusted his angle, hoping he was skilled enough to target Fabian's prostate with his thrusts.

"Right there," Fabian gasped. "That's perfect, darling."

Ryan smiled, pleased with himself. When was the last time he had *smiled* during sex? Fabian noticed, and he grinned right back at him.

"Kiss me," Fabian whispered. "Please."

Ryan slowed his thrusts, then brought his mouth down on Fabian's. He expected Fabian to greet him with a wild, passionate kiss, but instead it was slow and sweet. Ryan sank into it, his head swimming.

"You," Fabian breathed against his lips, "are incredible."

Ryan kissed him again, trying to match Fabian's tenderness. Trying to show him how much all of this meant to him. When he couldn't hold off any longer, he began to roll his hips, sliding in and out of Fabian in long, slow thrusts.

"Mm. Don't stop," Fabian murmured. "Feels so good."

Ryan didn't want to stop. Every thrust was sending waves of pleasure through him, driving him toward release. Finally, he could feel that pressure at the base of his spine and in his balls that was usually so elusive. "Fuck, I think I might come."

"Really? Come on. I'm close too."

Ryan lost all semblance of rhythm as he chased his orgasm. It was *right there*.

"Can you pull out?" Fabian asked. "I want to see it. I want it all over me."

Oh *fuck*. That did it. Ryan pulled out and ripped the condom off just as he felt the first wondrous pulse of his release. He gasped with relief as strand after strand of come burst out of him, falling all over Fabian's chest and neck. A second later, Fabian cried out, and an impressive amount of come joined Ryan's, considering it was Fabian's second orgasm.

"Holy fucking god," Ryan panted as he flopped onto the bed next to Fabian. "Thank you. Fuck, I needed that."

Fabian turned his head and smiled at him. "I knew we'd figure it out. That was lovely to watch."

They stayed on the bed until their chests stopped heaving, and then they took turns getting cleaned up. When Ryan came out of the bathroom, Fabian patted the mattress beside him. "Come snuggle."

Fabian made himself comfortable with his head on Ryan's chest, then took Ryan's hand and tangled their fingers together.

"Thank you," Ryan said. "For everything tonight. No one has ever put this much effort into . . ."

"Seducing you?"

Ryan huffed. "Yeah. I guess."

"Stick with me," Fabian murmured sleepily, "and you'll be bewitched, bothered, and bewildered."

"Bothered?" Ryan teased, but he was mentally stuck on Fabian's suggestion of sticking with him.

"Oh, I can be very annoying," Fabian said. "Fair warning."

Ryan hugged him tighter. "Noted."

Ryan realized, as he drifted off to sleep, that he hadn't thought about his flight in the morning once all evening.

CHAPTER TWENTY

"Are you *smiling* on an airplane, Pricey?"

Ryan covered his mouth with his hand, pretending to be smoothing his beard. "Nope."

Wyatt batted his hand away. "You *are*! What's going on?"

Ryan's gaze darted around the plane. None of his teammates seemed to be paying any attention to them as they waited for the plane to take off. "Nothing. Just in a good mood."

Wyatt eyed him skeptically. "What were you up to last night?"

Ryan knew his cheeks were heating, but he tried to act cool. "Not much. Hanging out with a . . . friend." Damn. He probably shouldn't have hesitated before saying friend.

Wyatt beamed. "Holy shit. Did you get lucky, Pricey?"

Yeah. Really fucking lucky. But all he said was, "Maybe."

"And he cured your fear of flying."

Ryan snorted. "I'm still terrified. Don't worry."

"Nothing to worry about. We're going to get through this road trip and get you home safe and sound to your new man."

Even the thought of having Fabian to come home to sent a rush of happiness through Ryan.

"Look at you!" Wyatt said, elbowing him. "You're glowing! You really like this guy."

Ryan shrugged, but he was still smiling. "I do. I like him a lot."

An absurd amount, probably, given their short time together. But Ryan couldn't help his feelings. It was like he'd just been going through the motions of living for the past thirteen years, dragging himself from city to city. Waking up alone in hotel rooms and barely furnished apartments, watching videos of hockey fights, and trying to hide the fact that he was just barely holding himself together at any given moment.

Now it was like the lights had been turned on and Ryan's world was full of color and possibility. It was terrifying in its own way, but now that he'd gotten a taste of what his life *could* be he would do whatever he could to push the darkness away.

He checked his phone and saw there was a text from Fabian.

FABIAN:
What are you doing Sunday morning?

RYAN:
Nothing. Why?

FABIAN:
My friends get together every Sunday for brunch. It's just Vanessa, Marcus, Tarek, and me. Do you want to join us?

RYAN:
Really?

FABIAN:

Yes. It's not fancy. We put things on frozen waffles. And drink cheap Baby Duck mimosas.

RYAN:

Do you toast the waffles?

FABIAN:

Yes! We're not monsters!

RYAN:

Sounds good then.

FABIAN:

The rule is everyone has to bring one waffle topping.

RYAN:

Like what? Syrup?

FABIAN:

No. Like something creative. Use your imagination.

Ryan frowned and typed, I'm not sure I have an imagination.

FABIAN:

Of course you do. You were very creative last night.

This text was accompanied by one of those winky face emojis that Ryan always found so thrilling.

"You're texting him right now, aren't you?" Wyatt teased.

"What makes you say that?"

"Your face is bright red and you have a giant dopey grin."

Ryan read over the text conversation, excited that Fabian had invited him to hang out with his friends. That had to mean something, right? He knew Fabian was generally friendly and social, but still. This seemed like a step in the right direction.

He wrote back, I can't wait to see you again, which he hoped sounded more romantic than desperate.

When Fabian wrote back, Counting the minutes, darling, Ryan beamed.

"Geez," Wyatt laughed. "I hope he likes you as much as you like him!"

Ryan tucked his phone into the seat pocket, nestling it against his *Anne of Green Gables* book. "Me too."

"I want everyone on their best behavior." Fabian shot a hard look at each of his friends. "Be nice to him."

Marcus gave him his best innocent face. "I have no idea what you're talking about."

"We're not going to scare off your big strong boyfriend," Tarek said.

"He's not my—" Fabian huffed, and continued. "I'm serious. No grilling him with questions. No oversharing about sex." He gave Vanessa a particularly pointed look for that one. "No teasing. No implying that I'm in love with him. Just. Be. Cool."

Vanessa put her hand over her heart. "I promise I won't do at least some of those things."

The buzzer downstairs sounded, and Fabian darted to the door.

"Oh my god, he's so excited! I love this so much," Marcus said.

Fabian glared at him over his shoulder before he opened the door and ran downstairs. Of course he was excited; Ryan had been away since Tuesday morning, and he'd only gotten back late last night. Fabian was dying to see him again. When he opened the door that led to the street, he found Ryan wearing a black wool coat, a gray toque, and an adorable smile.

"Hi," Ryan said.

"Hi."

For a moment, Fabian just stared at him. He realized they were, with Fabian standing on a stair above him, at perfect kissing height. So he kissed him. He would have leapt into his arms, except Ryan was carrying two large grocery bags, and they both appeared to be quite full.

"What on earth is all this?" Fabian asked.

"I wasn't sure what to bring, so I bought a bunch of stuff," Ryan said sheepishly. "Hopefully some of it is good."

"I should have explained that we are extremely easy to please."

He led Ryan up the stairs and into the apartment. All three of Fabian's friends were staring unabashedly at the door.

"So you remember Tarek, Vanessa, and Marcus. They all live here."

"Hi," Ryan said. "Thanks for having me."

Fabian heard Marcus mutter, "God, I *wish*," and he narrowed his eyes at him in warning.

"You brought groceries," Vanessa said, taking the bags from Ryan. She peeked inside one. "Is this *real champagne*?"

Everyone gathered around Vanessa as she pulled out a bottle of Moet from one of the bags.

"Ryan, what the fuck?" Fabian said. "I said bring, like, Nutella. Not hundred-dollar champagne."

"Someone gave it to me as a gift," Ryan said. "I was never going to drink it. I thought it might be appreciated here."

"Oh, it's appreciated," Tarek said happily. "I'll just get this on ice." As he went to the kitchen he called back, "I love your boyfriend, Fabian!"

Holy fucking hell. Fabian's friends were garbage.

Overall, though, brunch went pretty well. Ryan mentioned the community center he'd visited, and Tarek got excited because he was familiar with the place. As the two of them discussed all the great things the center did and the improvements it could benefit from, Fabian's heart swelled. Since the moment he'd become aware that his feelings for Ryan went beyond curiosity, he'd worried about how he could possibly fit into Fabian's life. Or how Fabian could fit into his. Fabian still wasn't sure about that last thing, but watching Ryan with his friends now—infiltrating their sacred Bargain Brunch tradition, even—left him with no doubts that Ryan could fit in just fine.

Fabian didn't like to think about Ryan's *other* life too much, or how Fabian could belong there. Maybe he was getting too far ahead of himself, but the idea of being asked to go to hockey games, to attend team parties, to be around other hockey players and hockey fans, wasn't something Fabian could quite stomach. He'd like to say that he wanted to try, but he really didn't. What he wanted, and he knew it was horribly selfish of him, was for Ryan to walk away from hockey.

He told himself that it wasn't *just* for himself that he wanted Ryan to quit; hockey wasn't good for Ryan. Fabian didn't have to follow the sport to see that. But suggesting that Ryan change his whole life after having known him for a few weeks seemed a bit extra, even for Fabian.

Fabian decided right then, as Ryan laughed at a joke that Marcus made, that he would get over himself and take an interest in Ryan's career. He wasn't sure where things were headed between them, but if their relationship was entirely about Ryan supporting and being a part of Fabian's life and Fabian giving nothing back, it couldn't possibly last.

Ryan hit play on the eighth video in a row of Duncan Harvey fighting. Fabian was asleep beside him, peaceful and beautiful. It was late, and Ryan should be trying to sleep, but his body hummed with anxiety. So instead he was sitting on his bed in his underwear, his laptop balanced on his thighs.

Ryan had enjoyed hanging out with Fabian's friends that morning, but he couldn't shake the certainty that he didn't belong. They'd all been talking about music and art and things their friends were doing, and Ryan couldn't contribute. And he couldn't help but wonder, as he had been since Friday night, what exactly he and Fabian were doing. If this was just sex for Fabian, Ryan would prefer to know now because it would save him a lot of pain later.

And if it wasn't just sex, then what was it? Were he and Fabian *dating*? The idea seemed preposterous, and it had seemed more preposterous when Ryan had been trying not to make a fool of himself at brunch that morning.

Preparing for the inevitable fight with Harvey was at least something productive Ryan could do to distract himself from all of his stupid, horrible thoughts. Although one of those horrible thoughts was how things like Ryan having to study videos of hockey fights were exactly why he didn't deserve Fabian.

But he *did* have to study, because the alternative was getting brutally beaten by Harvey. Ryan didn't lose many fights. Between his size advantage, his years of experience, and the boxing basics his dad had taught him, Ryan had the upper hand in almost every fight he'd ever been in.

Still. Duncan Harvey was terrifying.

Harvey didn't fight with the skill that Ryan did. He fought like he had nothing to lose, and that both scared and saddened Ryan. He knew that Harvey had had troubles with addiction in the past, and that he'd been forced into rehab by the league a couple of times. Ryan wasn't sure if Harvey was still having problems—he really didn't know him well at all—but he didn't seem like a guy who had straightened his life out.

The fans loved it when Ryan and Harvey fought each other. There were plenty of videos of the two of them going toe-to-toe, but Ryan avoided those ones. He didn't like to watch himself fight. The few times he had watched a video of one of his own fights, he'd felt something akin to vertigo. It was a weird sensation, watching himself do something that he *could* remember doing, but being unable to believe he had actually done it. He looked *scary* when he was fighting, like his body had been temporarily possessed by a demon. But Ryan knew that wasn't the case. When he dropped the gloves, he pulled a dark part of himself forward. It was, strangely, one of the only times he ever felt truly calm.

But preparing for a fight. The anticipation of fighting. That was different.

He watched Duncan Harvey land a punch, and Ryan winced as his opponent fell to the ice. Brutal. He knew that Harvey tended to wait and let his opponents get a few futile swings in before dropping them quickly with a merciless right hook. It was like watching a predator toying with its prey, giving it false hope.

"What are you watching?"

Ryan's head whipped around so fast he nearly injured himself. Fabian's head was still nestled into the pillow, but his eyes were open.

"Oh. Uh, nothing. Just hockey stuff."

"Fights?"

"Maybe." Ryan closed his laptop.

Fabian raised himself on an elbow. "Are there really videos of just the fights from hockey games online?" He scoffed. "What am I talking about? Of course there are."

"Yeah. I sometimes watch them before games. Of the guy I'm expecting to fight."

Fabian's brow furrowed. "The fights are planned in advance?"

"No, no, not like that. But if we're going to be playing a team with another enforcer, chances are pretty good that I'll have to fight him."

"Because you . . . hate each other?"

Ryan sighed and set the laptop on his nightstand. "No. I don't have a problem with Duncan Harvey or anyone else."

"So why would you fight him?"

"It's part of the game."

Fabian made a face. "I don't understand why you would punch someone for no reason. I won't pretend to be an expert, but aren't hockey fights an in-the-heat-of-the-moment thing?"

"That's usually it. Sometimes our star player gets attacked somehow, and then I have to fight the guy who did it. Or maybe I have to fight that team's enforcer. It's like . . ." Ryan tried to think of the word. "It's like we're proxies, maybe?"

Fabian's mouth quirked up. "You're like knights. You fight on behalf of your king's honor."

"I guess. Except my king at the moment is a fucking asshole."

"Kings usually are." Fabian rested his head on Ryan's thigh and gazed up at him. "So tomorrow night, you are going to beat up a man you have no problem with to protect a man you hate?"

Ryan threaded his fingers through Fabian's hair, which made him sigh happily. "You make it sound stupid."

"It's *very* stupid."

He stroked Fabian's hair in silence for a while. The soothing, repeating motion was making Ryan feel drowsy, which was a welcome sensation.

"I don't like thinking about you fighting."

Ryan's fingers paused for a moment, then resumed their stroking. "Me neither."

CHAPTER TWENTY-ONE

"Hey. Duncan."

Duncan Harvey glanced up at Ryan from where he was stretching on the ice near the center line. Ryan wasn't *technically* supposed to be talking to his opponents during warm-ups, but he was hoping he could maybe stop a pointless fight before it happened.

Duncan spat on the ice and said, "What?"

Ryan bent at the waist so he was closer to the other man's face. Duncan had noticeable bags under his eyes. "I just wanted to say, we don't have to fight tonight."

Duncan shifted so he was up on one knee. "The fuck are you talking about?"

Their faces were inches apart, and Ryan was sure it was getting the attention of the crowd, so he backed off a bit. "Just saying. We don't have to."

"You'd like that, wouldn't you?"

Yes, Ryan *would* like that. That was sort of his point. But he skated away without replying.

"How's your buddy Duncan?" Wyatt asked when Ryan got

down on the ice next to him to stretch. "Does he like your new haircut?"

"I think he wants to fight."

"Well, that doesn't sound like him."

Ryan grunted as he deepened his hamstring stretch. "He doesn't look good. He's sweaty and the game hasn't even started."

"Just worry about yourself." Wyatt's tone was uncharacteristically serious. "I'm not kidding, Pricey. If he wants to fight, end it as fast as possible. Did you see that last fight, against what's-his-name in Calgary?"

Ryan *had* watched that fight, and he had also noticed how wild Harvey's swings had been. How hard he'd hit. How damaged his opponent's face had been after. "Yeah. I know."

In the second period, Harvey shoved Ryan. Nothing had happened between them up to that point, but Harvey must have decided it was time for them to fight.

"Fuck off, Harvey," Ryan said tiredly.

But Harvey shoved him again. "Let's go, fucker."

Ryan turned to face him. The Pay the Price chant had already started. "I'm not gonna fight you."

Harvey's eyes bugged out. He looked *feral.* "The fuck you aren't." He threw his gloves off and Ryan watched them skid across the ice.

"Let's go," Harvey snarled.

"No."

Harvey tried to grab his jersey, but Ryan skated backward and Harvey ended up grabbing air and almost losing his balance. "Fight me, you coward!"

Ryan didn't want to. He was a *good* defenseman. He could contribute to a team without having to do this.

And besides, Harvey wasn't well.

Harvey launched himself at Ryan, this time taking a wild swing. Ryan grabbed both of Harvey's wrists and wrestled his arms out to his sides. Harvey lost it. He was full-on screaming in Ryan's face, demanding that he drop the gloves. Ryan just shook his head.

And then Harvey *headbutted* him.

The front of his helmet smashed into Ryan's mouth and chin, and it hurt like a motherfucker. Ryan staggered back, completely in shock that Harvey would do something so dirty, and then his mouth filled with blood.

Ryan's brain went quiet, and it was all he could do to stop himself from knocking Harvey to the ice. But he didn't. Instead, he dropped Harvey's wrists and skated away. Behind him, he could hear Harvey's hysterical screaming.

"Where the fuck are you going? You're a fucking joke, Price! Come back and fight me, you asshole!"

Ryan ignored him. When he got to the bench, his teammates were quiet. There were no sticks being knocked against the boards like there always was after a fight, and no congratulatory words. Just uncomfortable silence, and a disapproving glare from his coach.

"Go to the dressing room," Coach Cooper barked. "Get your mouth cleaned up. And stay there until intermission."

"Yes, Coach," Ryan mumbled. As he made his way down the hallway, he hoped he hadn't just thrown his career away.

Fabian felt sick.

He'd thought it was time he tried to watch one of Ryan's games. He'd met Tarek at a pub in the Village that showed Guardians games on their big screen televisions, and had been doing his best to follow the action. Ryan didn't get shown up close very often, so the game was pretty boring.

Until it wasn't.

There was a player who was almost as big as Ryan who kept shoving him. Fabian held his breath when Ryan turned to face the other man, sure that he was going to have to watch his sweet possible-boyfriend punch someone. Fabian covered his mouth with his hand, but forced himself to watch the screen.

So he saw what happened next.

"Holy shit!" Tarek said. "I don't know shit about hockey, but I am pretty sure you're not allowed to do that."

Fabian knew enough about hockey to know that head-butting was not a normal part of the game. He knew enough about pain to know that Ryan must be in a lot of it right now. For a second, Ryan's face changed into something Fabian didn't recognize. It was dark and intense and terrifying.

"Oh my god," Fabian said hoarsely. "Ryan, don't."

As if Ryan could hear him, his face immediately softened, and he skated away as the other man was dragged off the ice by some of the officials.

"Are you okay?" Tarek asked gently.

"I don't know. Why does he do this? Why would anyone do this for a job? Why does anyone like *watching* this?"

"I have no idea."

"It's awful. He's too good for this."

"He didn't fight him," Tarek pointed out. "You could tell he was trying to talk the guy out of it."

Fabian pressed his lips together. His eyes were stinging. It was true, Ryan hadn't fought him. *Why* hadn't he fought him? Not for Fabian's sake, surely.

"Come on," Tarek said, covering one of Fabian's hands with his own. "Let's get out of here, huh? I think there's karaoke happening tonight at the Lighthouse. I could see if Vanessa—"

"Thanks," Fabian said. "But I think I'd like to go home."

Tarek nodded, then stood. "Then let's go."

★ ★ ★

Ryan had left his apartment the moment he'd gotten the message.

FABIAN:

Please come over. I know it's late. I know we said tomorrow. But I need to see you.

It had been a long fucking day, and Ryan's mouth was swollen and sore, but if Fabian wanted to see him, Ryan was there.

Fabian was standing outside his building when Ryan arrived, which he didn't like seeing at all. "What are you doing out here? You shouldn't be—"

But Fabian cut him off by engulfing him in a fierce hug.

Ryan didn't understand what was happening, so he just wrapped his arms around Fabian and held him tight. It wasn't until he heard Fabian sniffing that he finally asked, "What's wrong?"

Fabian's reply was so muffled, Ryan couldn't make it out. Fabian's fingers dug into Ryan's back, and Ryan was getting scared. He'd never seen him so upset.

"Hey," he said softly, "it's okay. I'm here. What is it?"

Fabian finally loosened his hold and looked up at him with damp eyes. "I watched the game." He reached up and brushed his fingers very gently against Ryan's split and swollen lip. "I saw what happened."

Ryan swallowed. His throat felt like sandpaper. "I wish you hadn't."

"You didn't fight him."

"No."

"Why not? Isn't that what you do?"

Ryan cradled Fabian's face with one palm. "I didn't want

to." He stroked Fabian's cheek with his thumb. "I don't think I want to fight anymore."

Fabian covered Ryan's hand with his own. "Then don't."

"I don't know if I'll have a choice. Coach was pretty pissed with me." What Coach Cooper had said was that he had plenty of decent fourth-line defensemen he could call up from the farm team, and all of them were younger and faster than Ryan. If Ryan didn't want to do his job anymore, he could be easily replaced. But Ryan didn't need to tell Fabian any of that.

"Are you all right? God, your mouth must hurt."

"It doesn't feel great, but nothing is broken or anything." Ryan attempted a smile. "Didn't lose any teeth."

Fabian squeezed him again. "That was so fucking scary. I hated it. I don't want to watch hockey. I'm sorry."

"It's okay. You don't have to." Ryan actually didn't like the idea of Fabian watching him play. And he especially didn't like the idea of him watching him fight. Ryan wanted to take care of him, for them to take care of each other. Fabian would make him laugh and try new things, and Ryan would make him feel safe and loved. Because those were things that Ryan could *do*. Effortlessly.

If Fabian wanted that.

"We should go inside," Ryan suggested. Fabian nodded against his chest, then pulled away with another sniffle.

When they were inside the apartment, Fabian said, "I can't watch you get hurt. How do all those hockey wives do it?"

"They're tough. I think the season is harder on them than the players, honestly."

Fabian smiled at that. "Can you imagine me sitting with the wives at the games?"

No. For lots of reasons, Ryan couldn't imagine that at all. "I would never expect you to do that."

"I know. Of course not. And," Fabian's cheeks colored, "I'm

not comparing myself to your teammates' *wives*. I'm not that delusional. We're not even—" Fabian crossed his arms, hugging himself tightly, and pursed his lips as if to stop his words from escaping. "Do you think—?"

Ryan sat on the end of the bed so they could be closer to eye-level with each other. "Think what?"

Fabian reached for Ryan's hands and held them. "Would I be out of line if I asked if I could be your boyfriend?"

Ryan's heart bounced excitedly. "You want to be my boyfriend?"

Fabian stared down at their joined hands. "I know that our schedules are very hectic, but yes. I'd like to explore this. If you're willing."

"Fabian. Look at me." That was probably a mistake because Ryan forgot how awful his mouth looked. He noticed Fabian's flinch when he turned his eyes up. Ryan tugged him closer. "My life is a fucking mess, but the one thing I know for sure is that I like being with you. And I would like to be with you as much as possible."

Fabian squeezed Ryan's hands, and his lips curved up into an adorable smile. Ryan decided to say the rest.

"I'm *happy* when I'm with you. This probably sounds ridiculous, but I haven't felt happy in so long. I can't even remember. So . . . yeah. I want to be your boyfriend." He huffed an embarrassed little laugh. "I can't believe I finally got to say that out loud after all these years."

He held his breath and waited for Fabian to respond. For a long moment, Fabian didn't say anything, and Ryan was worried he had come on too strong. Maybe he was putting too much pressure on him.

Then Fabian said, "I wish I could kiss you right now."

Ryan's heart soared. "Me too."

As a compromise, Fabian retrieved one of his hands from

Ryan's, kissed the tips of his fingers, and pressed them gently to Ryan's lips. It was one of the sweetest kisses Ryan had ever received.

They ended up spooned together in bed, snuggled under the blankets. Ryan thought Fabian had fallen asleep until he heard him say, "There's always been something about you. I've always been drawn to you. Is that weird?"

Ryan considered it. "I don't know. But I feel the same way."

"When you walked into the store where I work, I was shocked. And then . . ." Fabian turned in Ryan's arms to face him. "I had this overwhelming feeling of *relief*. Like this was what I'd been waiting for. This was what was missing. You."

Ryan stared at what he could see of Fabian in the dark, completely speechless.

"Sorry. That probably sounds nuts."

"That's how I felt," he said quietly. "Like I'd finally found you. I didn't know I'd been looking but . . . I found you."

Fabian smiled so brightly that Ryan could see it even in the darkness. "Then we'd better stick together."

CHAPTER TWENTY-TWO

Ryan groaned as a ball sailed over his leg and into the back of the net behind him.

"Not as easy as it looks, is it?" Wyatt said gleefully.

Ryan stood up with some effort. He wasn't used to having giant goaltender pads on his legs. Around him, the kids were laughing and cheering—it had been their idea for Ryan and Wyatt to switch roles for today's floor hockey match. Ryan had let in about a million goals.

"All right," Ryan grumbled. "I think I'm done."

"You're like the worst goalie I've ever seen," Xander said.

"Yeah, well." It was the best comeback Ryan could come up with. In truth, he had expected to be better at goaltending. He was a defenseman, after all. It wasn't *that* different.

He removed the glove and blocker, and then the mask. His hair was embarrassingly sweaty for a friendly floor hockey game against a bunch of kids.

"What do we do at the end of the game, kids?" Wyatt said loudly.

"Hug the goalie!" the kids all yelled back. And then Ryan was nearly knocked over by a tidal wave of young people hugging anywhere they could reach. Wyatt piled on at the very end. It was ridiculous, and Ryan loved every second of it.

"All right, we've gotta get going," Wyatt announced when Ryan had finally been released. "Ryan has to ice his fractured ego."

Ryan snorted and shook his head.

"What are you actually doing tonight?" Wyatt asked as they were walking to his car.

"I, uh." Ryan couldn't fight his dopey grin. "I have a date."

Wyatt looked delighted. "Yeah? With that same guy?"

"Yeah." They got to the car and Ryan said, "His name is Fabian."

"Fabian, eh? What's he do?"

"He's a musician."

"What, like, in a band?"

Ryan shook his head and opened the car door. When they were both seated he said, "He's a solo musician. His music is really good. You can buy it online."

Wyatt backed out of the parking space, then said, "How did you meet him?"

Ryan chewed his lip, unsure of how Wyatt would react to this. "He was actually the son of the family I billeted with. Back in Halifax."

"No shit? And you just started dating now?"

"We reunited in October. Here in Toronto."

"That's cool." Wyatt pulled out of the parking lot onto the street. "I still talk to my billet family from junior. I lived there for four years, so we got pretty close."

"I only lived with the Salahs for one season. Then I was traded."

"Jesus, Pricey. Have you ever played anywhere for more than one season?"

Ryan huffed a laugh. "A couple of places."

"So where's your date?"

"Just dinner somewhere. Maybe go for a walk."

"Well, I hope love can keep you warm. It's supposed to be freezing tonight."

Ryan's stomach flopped. *Love.* "I'll wear a hat."

"You gonna bring him flowers?" Wyatt asked. "Do guys do that?"

Ryan hadn't thought about it. *Should* he bring flowers? "We can do that," he said. "Men can like flowers."

Wyatt seemed to consider this. "Y'know? I would love to get flowers. Why don't men ever get flowers?"

"Because the world is stupid."

"No kidding. Hey, let's stop at a flower shop and we'll both impress our sweethearts, huh?"

Ryan smiled. "Okay."

Fabian sat cross-legged on his bed, staring at his laptop screen. The blinking cursor in the YouTube search box dared him to type the words he had promised himself he wouldn't.

Nothing good can come from this, he told himself. Then he shook his head and typed Ryan Price fight.

God, there were so many results.

Price Destroys Comeau.
Ryan Price Top Fifteen Fights.
Ryan Price Most Devastating Fights.
Ryan Price Gets Revenge.
Price vs Harvey... BRUTAL!

Fabian looked away. He couldn't click on any of them. He didn't want to know this side of Ryan.

But it *was* a side of Ryan. A big side. The only side that most of the world knew, apparently. Shouldn't Fabian face it?

He took a shaky breath, and clicked on the *Top Fifteen Fights* video.

It opened with Ryan wearing a red jersey—Fabian wasn't sure which team it was—and circling another player in a white jersey who was several inches shorter. Both players had their gloves off, and the shorter guy was removing his helmet. He gestured to Ryan to do the same, and Ryan smiled at the guy before removing his own helmet and letting it fall to the ice. It wasn't a warm smile, and it wasn't the sweet, shy smile that Fabian loved. It was a cold, mocking smile that looked all wrong on Ryan's face.

In the video, Ryan kept circling the other man, waiting and watching, fists raised like a boxer's in front of his face. The other player finally lunged at him, and Ryan hit him hard with three quick punches to the side of his face. The other man was swinging wildly, but almost nothing landed. A second later, he was on his back, and Ryan was on top of him. Then the refs came and broke it up.

Cut to the next clip where Ryan was wearing an orange jersey. He was glaring at his opponent, his face showing real anger. There was no fanfare before this fight; Ryan just grabbed the front of the other guy's jersey and started punching the guy's face. When it was over, the camera showed a close-up of the defeated man's bloody face, and then Ryan's bloody hand as he skated to the penalty box.

Fabian closed the window. He couldn't watch any more of this.

But he had to, didn't he? He couldn't pretend this part of Ryan's life didn't exist. He couldn't tuck himself against Ryan's strong body at night, and kiss his sweet smiles, and shiver under the caress of his enormous hands, without accepting that those hands, and that body, were also used for . . . this.

He couldn't be with a man if he only allowed himself to see the best parts of him. It wouldn't be fair to Ryan or to himself. If he was serious about this relationship—and he was—he had to be brave enough to take the rose-colored glasses off.

He tried to psych himself up. He could do this. Maybe he could even try to find it . . . sexy? He had friends who were very hot for professional wrestling and MMA fighting. This wasn't any different, was it?

He was about to reopen the browser and watch another video when his phone lit up with a text. Fabian realized his eyes were wet when he tried to read the blurry message. He quickly wiped them.

RYAN:

Hey. I'm here. Early. Sorry.

He checked the time and saw that Ryan was almost an hour early for their date. Fabian wasn't ready at all.

FABIAN:

You're outside?

RYAN:

Yes.

Fabian closed his laptop and rushed to the door. He probably looked like shit—no makeup, eyes red, and he was wearing pajama pants and an oversized white T-shirt. When he opened the front door and found Ryan standing outside, holding a bouquet of flowers, he didn't care. He cupped a hand over his mouth and felt fresh tears stinging his eyes. This *couldn't* be the same person he'd just watched in that video.

"Hi," Ryan said shyly. "I thought you might like these."

Fabian threw himself into his strong arms, careful not to crush the flowers.

Ryan chuckled. "Miss me?"

Fabian's reply was a slow nod against the wool fabric of Ryan's coat. Ryan kissed the top of his head and said, "Everything okay?"

"I just really needed to see you. I'm glad you're here."

"I'm glad I'm here too."

Fabian stepped back, and took the flowers—a luxurious bouquet of lilies and roses that, like his apartment, was a bold mix of reds and purples. "They're beautiful. Thank you. Come inside."

When they were inside the apartment, Fabian asked, "How was your trip?"

"Not bad. We won both games."

"Congratulations." Fabian glanced furtively at Ryan's hands as he was hanging his coat on a hook by the door. They didn't seem to have any recent bruises on them. He couldn't shake the image of how bloody his hand had been in the video after he'd punched another man's face in.

When Ryan shot him a puzzled look, Fabian realized he'd been standing, frozen, holding the flowers. He snapped out of it. "I have a vase I can put these in." He laughed, and he could hear how forced it sounded. "It will be excited to be of use again. It's been a while since anyone has given me flowers."

"Fabian?"

"Where did I put it?" Fabian's voice was trembling. He swallowed. "Oh, here it is." He reached up and pulled it off a shelf over his sink.

"Did something happen?"

"Nope. No, I'm fine. I—" The vase fell to the floor with a spectacular crash. "Shit!"

Ryan was there, pulling Fabian away from the broken glass. "Sit on the bed," he instructed.

"I have to clean it up. Fuck, I can't believe how clumsy I am."

"You're not." Ryan wrapped a hand gently around Fabian's wrist and lifted his hand. "Look, you're shaking."

"I'm just cold. It's always freezing in here."

"Sit down." Ryan's voice was firm and steady. Fabian sat. "I'll clean that up. And then you'll tell me what's wrong, okay?"

Fabian wasn't used to Ryan taking control of a situation, and Ryan acting out of character was doing nothing to help how rattled he felt. He watched as Ryan cleaned up the glass, hoping to god that Ryan didn't cut himself because Fabian didn't think he could take the sight of blood on those hands right now.

When the mess was cleaned up, Ryan crouched on the floor in front of him. "What's wrong?"

Fabian didn't know what to say. Should he admit that he'd been purposely watching videos of Ryan's fights? He knew Ryan wouldn't like that. And if he did tell him, and Ryan learned that the reason for Fabian's anguish was that he was horrified by what he'd seen—by what Ryan did on a regular basis—how would that make Ryan feel? Like a monster, probably.

Ryan wasn't a monster. No matter what Fabian had felt when he'd watched those fights, he knew that for certain.

So he didn't tell him. Instead, he sank to the floor, into Ryan's lap, and nuzzled his neck. "I want you," he murmured.

It was cowardly of him, but Fabian needed to erase the images of Ryan fighting from his brain. He needed to replace them with Ryan's kisses and sighs, and the reverent way Ryan touched him.

"Fabian—" Ryan's protest was cut off when Fabian kissed him. It only took a moment before Ryan was kissing him back, and then Fabian was unbuckling Ryan's belt. Ryan sucked in a breath, and suddenly Fabian was being lifted off the floor as

Ryan stood, still holding him. Ryan set him gently on the bed, and Fabian scooted back until he was lying against the pillows, grinning up at Ryan as he covered him. Ryan still looked apprehensive, so Fabian helped by removing his own shirt.

"Are you sure you're—?"

Fabian slid his hands up the sides of Ryan's broad torso, pushing his T-shirt up. "The only thing that's wrong with me is that you're not kissing me."

It was almost the truth; Fabian was feeling remarkably better now that he had Ryan's huge body pressed against him. And then Ryan fixed the remaining problem by kissing him exactly the way Fabian wanted to be kissed—slow and adoring. Fabian sighed happily as the tension left his body, replaced by the wonderful feelings of comfort and affection that always warmed him when he was with Ryan.

They made out for a long time, trading soft kisses on each other's cheeks and necks and sharing deep, tender kisses when their mouths found their way back together. It didn't feel like foreplay; instead of becoming aroused, Fabian felt loose and gooey with bliss.

He rolled Ryan onto his back and snuggled against him, resting his head on Ryan's solid chest. Ryan wrapped an arm around him, and Fabian couldn't remember ever feeling so safe and comfortable.

"Do anything fun today?" Ryan asked.

"I wrote a new song." Fabian bit his lip, trying to decide how much to reveal. "It's a bit . . . sappier than my usual style."

"Oh?"

"Something inspired me to write a love song. Can't imagine what."

For a long moment, Ryan was silent. Fabian raised his head and bravely glanced at his face. Ryan was smiling at the ceiling.

"I don't think I've ever inspired anyone to do anything before."

"I didn't say it was *you*," Fabian teased. Ryan's smile faded. "Oh my god! *Of course* it's you!" Fabian climbed on top of him, sprawled out on his stomach with his chin propped on his folded hands. "I don't want to alarm you, but I'm quite fond of you, Ryan Price."

Ryan shook his head. His face was pure wonder. "I used to listen to you practice. I'd be in my room in the basement, and when I heard your violin I would just lay on my bed and listen."

Fabian's heart fluttered. "Did you?"

"Yeah. All the time. It . . . helped."

"Helped?"

Ryan sighed. "That wasn't a great year for me. I was away from home for the first time—and Ross Harbour has less than two thousand people, so even being in a city was an adjustment—and your family was really nice, but it was still, y'know, not my home."

Fabian had never really considered things from the hockey player's view when he'd been forced to cohabit with them. As far as he'd been concerned at the time, the world had been their fucking oyster, and they probably saw it as their right as an elite hockey player to take over someone's home. "That must have been stressful for you."

"It was. I was at a new school, trying to graduate while also playing hockey and dealing with . . . stuff."

Ugh. Fabian was an asshole for ever assuming that he had been the only person suffering in that house. "Hockey stuff, or . . . ?"

"I was trying to fit into my new team, and having a hard time. Plus I was suddenly playing in front of ten thousand people instead of, like, fifty."

"Yikes. Yeah."

Ryan began absently stroking Fabian's hair. "Plus there was the being gay thing. That was a whole other problem."

Right. Fabian obviously hadn't known at the time that Ryan had been dealing with that, but now that he knew . . . "Jesus. That must have sucked."

"It was a lot to hide at once. The fact that I was attracted to men, that I was scared, that I was homesick, that I . . . hated fighting. And some of my teammates." His lips twitched up a bit. "Didn't help that I also had to hide the crush I had on you."

God, why wasn't time travel real? Fabian wanted nothing more than to go back thirteen and a half years, walk into Ryan's bedroom, and tell him how much he liked him. To lie on his bed beside him and hold his hand. Or maybe tell his younger self to do that. That would make more sense. Time travel was confusing.

He took Ryan's hand now, first rolling off the man to lie beside him. "I wish you hadn't," he said. "Hidden your crush, I mean. We could have had a lot of fun in that basement."

Ryan huffed. "I think I would have been pretty awkward. *More* awkward than I am now, if you can imagine."

"Do you really think I would have been a skilled and adventurous lover at seventeen?"

Ryan turned his head and smiled at him. "Probably. It wouldn't have surprised me."

Fabian laughed, and then kissed him. He decided, right then, to forget about the video he'd watched. It didn't matter. Ryan had said he was going to stop fighting, so why even think about it anymore? The man in the video didn't matter. The man who bought Fabian flowers and used to secretly pine for him while he listened to his violin practice; that was the man who was here now. That was the man who mattered.

"What would you have done?" Fabian asked. "If I had gone down to your room and come on to you?"

"I probably wouldn't have even known that's what you were doing. I would never have let myself believe it."

Fabian traced a finger around Ryan's belly button and up to his chest. "But if I made it *very* obvious, let's say."

"Like what?"

"Well . . ." Fabian was suddenly giddy imagining the scenario. "What if I'd closed the door behind me and . . . taken off my shirt?"

"Oh geez. I definitely would have thought I was dreaming."

"What if I'd told you I couldn't live another day without telling you how much I wanted you? How badly I needed to touch you?"

Ryan seemed to be seriously considering his answer. "I still wouldn't have believed you."

"Let's skip ahead to the part where you believe me."

He blew out a breath. "Okay. I guess I would have . . . kissed you?"

"Would you have?"

He shook his head. "No. I would have waited for you to kiss me."

"And when I did?"

"I would have liked it?"

Fabian pressed his lips together to keep from laughing. He would put role-playing on the list of things to work on with Ryan.

When the urge to laugh had passed, he kissed Ryan and said, "I would have liked it too."

"Are we still going on this date, or should we just stay in?"

Fabian got to his feet and went to the closet. "Oh, we are going *out*. I am going to romance the hell out of you, Ryan Price."

CHAPTER TWENTY-THREE

For the rest of December, things were as close to perfect as they'd ever been for Ryan. Coach had been riding Ryan to fight more, but he couldn't argue with the effort Ryan had been putting in on the blue line. Ryan felt he was playing the best hockey of his career for Toronto right now. And maybe that wasn't saying *much*, but he was still proud.

Nilsson had been out for the past few games with a minor injury, so Wyatt had gotten to take over starting goaltender duties, which made games more entertaining for Ryan. Wyatt had also been on fire, winning three of the past four games, and even getting a shutout in the last game. Ryan had earned himself three assists in the past week. For the first time in a long time, hockey was *fun*.

Ryan and Wyatt had also visited the community center a couple more times together, and that had only bolstered Ryan's renewed love of the game. The kids were fantastic, and the center had greatly appreciated Ryan's donation of a bunch of pairs of brand new hockey gloves.

The rest of Ryan's days and nights were full of Fabian. They split nights between Fabian's apartment and Ryan's. Although

Ryan's was much bigger and newer, he preferred the hominess of Fabian's place. Ryan went to Bargain Brunch whenever possible, and went out with Fabian and his friends to interesting performances and talks and art exhibits. He loved all of it, and was even starting to feel less like an outsider when they all hung out together. He felt at home for the first time since he'd left Ross Harbour as a teenager. Toronto's Village was something else; it was easy for Ryan to believe, if he stayed within in its boundaries, that the entire world was gay. It was exciting.

Almost as exciting as his relationship with Fabian. When Ryan went to his shows, he could never quite believe that he'd be going home with the gorgeous man onstage. The man who had an entire club full of people entranced and in love with him, but who had chosen Ryan. It was unreal. It was, in fact, so hard for Ryan to believe, that he was often shy about approaching Fabian after he got off stage. Ryan would linger off to the side, waiting patiently as Fabian talked and laughed with the many people who wanted time with him.

But then Fabian would smile at Ryan, beckon him over, and go up on his tiptoes to give Ryan a slow, toe-curling kiss in plain view of anyone who happened to be watching. Ryan couldn't believe how lucky he was.

He still had to get on planes and leave Fabian behind, but even that was easier to bear when he had a wonderful boyfriend to call from the road. His therapist had noticed the change in him, and was very encouraging and excited.

So of course something had to go wrong.

"Traded?" Ryan asked miserably. "Where?"

"Ottawa," Wyatt said. "They need a goalie, and they like what they've been seeing from me lately."

Ryan swallowed hard, and was glad they were having this conversation over the phone. He was embarrassingly close to crying. "When do you leave?"

"Today." He exhaled loudly. "I'm sorry, Pricey. I wanted to call you so you'd hear it from me first."

"Thanks." Ryan really did appreciate it. He couldn't imagine how devastating it would have been to find out by seeing a headline online, or hearing it second hand.

"At least I won't be too far away, right?"

"Right." Fucking hell. Wyatt was the first teammate Ryan had ever had that he could truly call a friend. But, "This will be good for you," he conceded.

"I know. I'm excited about it. And Lisa already has a lead on a job at a hospital in Ottawa, so that should work out too."

"Good." Ryan got out of bed and started pacing. "That's good."

"I'll miss you, big guy. You'll keep going to the center, right?"

God, *would he?* Ryan didn't like the idea of going alone. "Sure," he said. "I can do that."

"You definitely should. Those kids are nuts about you."

Ryan smiled at that. "I can't believe you're going to Ottawa."

"I know. The enemy, right?"

"You'll get to play with Rozanov. You still have a crush on him?"

Wyatt laughed. "Maybe I can get to the bottom of this mystery friendship he has with Shane Hollander."

"Don't be nosy."

"Never. I've gotta finish packing and get to the airport. I'll see you soon, though, all right? And have a good Christmas."

"Yeah. You too. And, uh, thanks." Ryan cringed, but he really needed to say this. "You made a difference this year. To me, I mean. Sorry if that's a weird thing to say, but . . . thanks."

There was silence, and then Wyatt said, "You're one of the good ones, Pricey. Remember that."

They said their goodbyes, and Ryan sat back down on his

bed. In all his years of playing, this was the first time he'd been upset about someone *else* being traded. The thought of being in that locker room—of being on a *plane*—without Wyatt there was depressing.

Three days later, Fabian flew home for Christmas, and Ryan was completely alone. On Christmas morning he enjoyed a long video call with his parents and Colleen. They'd seemed surprisingly cheerful despite his not being there. Ryan was glad they weren't upset about it, but he couldn't help but feel that he'd disappointed them so many times now that they were beyond caring.

He'd considered going home this year. He really had. The possibility of flying to Halifax with Fabian had been enticing, but Ryan wasn't sure he wanted Fabian to see what he was like on a plane.

Returning to Ross Harbour could also be overwhelming, sometimes. He was the hero of his small town, and the attention he got whenever he went home made him uncomfortable. Jetting home for two days for Christmas wouldn't give the townsfolk much time to bother him, but still. Spending the holiday safe and alone in his apartment rather than dealing with planes and travel and over-interested neighbors was a much more appealing option.

He did miss Fabian, though.

He'd bought him a gift, which he would give him when he got back. He wasn't sure how Fabian would react, but when Ryan had seen it at the mall he'd been killing time at in Dallas, he hadn't been able to resist.

Ryan was ready to enjoy a quiet afternoon of reading, and then maybe finding a good restaurant that was open on Christmas Day, when disaster struck. He bent to pick up a pair of socks he'd dropped and he threw his back out completely.

"Son of a—" Ryan cursed, then howled, "Fuuuuuck!"

He'd been through this enough times to know that nothing was going to help except patience and caution. He hobbled around his apartment, piling the pillows from his bed onto the couch, then wincing as he had to reach for the heating pad he kept on the top shelf of his closet. It was a stupid place to keep it.

He got himself settled on the couch, with the heating pad tucked under his lower back, and at least was able to read as he'd planned. He turned on the television he'd finally bought and played the fireplace channel as he read. He'd taken some muscle relaxers, and they were making him feel a bit floaty.

He wasn't sure when he'd fallen asleep, but he woke to his phone ringing. The noise startled him, which caused him to cry out in pain. He fumbled blindly for his phone, keeping his eyes squeezed shut against the agony that was coursing through him. "Hello?"

"Merry Christmas," purred his favorite voice.

"Fabian. Hi." Ryan could hear the strain in his own voice. Fabian didn't miss it.

"Are you all right?"

Ryan blew out a breath as the worst of the pain subsided. "No. I threw my back out."

"Oh no! When did that happen?"

"This afternoon. It's been a pretty excellent Christmas."

"I'm sorry. I wish I was there to help you."

"I'll manage." Ryan grimaced at how grumpy he sounded, and added, "I do wish you were here, though. I miss you."

"I miss you too, darling. I have had more than enough family."

"How are they?"

"Oh, fine. Sonia's husband, *Paul*, is a former hockey player, of course. He works in marketing or something now. He is the absolute worst." He sighed. "He makes Sonia happy, though. And everyone is excited about the pregnancy."

"How'd your show go?"

Fabian brightened. "It was great! I haven't played in Halifax in so long, it was a really appreciative crowd. It was nice to see some old friends too." He laughed. "Amy snuck in with a fake ID."

"I still can't believe she's eighteen."

"You'll have to see her. She was asking about you."

Ryan nearly sat up in surprise, until he remembered his back. "She was? What do you mean? Did you tell her about . . . us?"

"I told my family that we'd reconnected, and we've been hanging out. I think my parents were mystified enough by that. I didn't feel like adding to it by telling them that I'm . . . well anyway. I didn't tell them. But Amy figured it out."

Ryan's stomach knotted up. "What did she say?"

"She's thrilled. She remembers you very fondly. You used to pretend to be a dinosaur and let her ride on your back."

Ryan chuckled. "That was fun. She was a great kid."

"I have hope for her. I might just have a friend in my family after all."

They talked for a while longer, and Ryan tried not to over-think the fact that Fabian hadn't told his parents they were together. It wasn't that he was disappointed Fabian was keeping their relationship a secret from them, it was more that he understood all the reasons why. Reasons that reinforced his fear that this thing he had with Fabian couldn't possibly last. They were simply too different. They didn't make *sense*.

"I'll see you in a couple of days," Fabian said. "Rest that back. I'll be there to soothe and comfort you before you know it."

"Looking forward to it."

"Me too. Good night, Ryan."

"Good night. Merry Christmas."

Ryan set his phone on the coffee table and picked up the

remote. He flipped around until he found *The Shop Around the Corner* on Turner Classic Movies. He ordered some Chinese food and forced himself to walk around the apartment a bit, because he knew it would be better for his back if he moved around.

The thing was, even with the injured back, this wasn't Ryan's most depressing Christmas ever. At least this year he had a boyfriend who was concerned about him and called him darling. A boyfriend who missed him, and who would be back in his arms in a couple of days.

Which was why Ryan *really* needed his back to heal.

Fabian could not believe how much he missed Ryan. It was *staggering*. Even though they had spent plenty of time apart in the weeks since they'd first hooked up, he'd never felt Ryan's absence as acutely as he did now. It probably had a lot to do with Fabian being back in the house where they'd first met, all those years ago.

His old bedroom was unrecognizable. The band posters that had covered the walls were gone. There were no books, no knickknacks, no *color*. It was a drab and generic guest bedroom. It actually reminded Fabian a lot of Ryan's apartment.

Except Ryan's apartment would have Ryan in it, which would make it infinitely better.

Fabian ate dinner with his family for the last time for what he was sure would be months, if not a year or more. They had ordered Lebanese food from a restaurant that was owned by a family friend because neither of Fabian's parents had any interest in cooking. Fabian had grown up eating a lot of takeout and heat-from-frozen convenience food.

"Where did you say you ran into Ryan Price again?" Dad asked.

Fabian chewed and swallowed his mouthful of falafel as

fast as he could without choking, and said, "At work. The drugstore."

His mother made a sound that Fabian interpreted as, *The drugstore is no place for a man of thirty-one to be working.* He ignored it.

"Did he recognize you right away?" Amy asked.

"Yeah. We recognized each other."

"That's cute."

Dad made a sound that Fabian interpreted as, *Men don't do things that are "cute."* He ignored that too.

"So what sorts of things have you been doing together?" Mom asked.

Fabian was glad he didn't blush easily. "Just stuff. He comes to my shows. He's hung out with my friends. He's nice. We get along."

"Have you been to any games?" Sonia asked. "If you can get free Guardians tickets and you're not taking them, I'm going to scream."

"I've never asked," Fabian said truthfully. He felt suddenly guilty about that. *Should* he feel guilty about that?

Sonia made a noise that Fabian interpreted as *God, my brother is such a fucking weirdo.* He couldn't ignore that one.

"*What*, Sonia?"

"Nothing. I just can't believe he's friends with you. It doesn't make any sense."

"Well," Mom said. "He's always been a little odd, hasn't he?"

"He definitely has a history of strange behavior," Dad agreed. "And there was that thing that happened last year."

Fabian couldn't stop himself. "What thing?"

Sonia laughed. "Oh my god. You don't even know, do you? He had a total fucking meltdown."

"During a game!" her stupid husband, Paul, added. "On the bench. He just . . . freaked out and had to leave the game. I heard he stripped naked and was screaming about bugs living in his brain or something."

"Could be drugs," Mom said. "Some players just can't handle the pressure. They become addicts."

None of that sounded right to Fabian. He frowned at his plate, no longer hungry. Under the table, Amy put a hand on his knee and squeezed. "I'm sure it was all exaggerated," she said.

"I don't know," Dad said. "He didn't play much for the rest of that season. And then Buffalo traded him to Toronto."

"Surprised Toronto wanted him," said stupid Paul. "I guess he's still scary as hell. Maybe being crazy makes him scarier."

"He's *not* crazy," Fabian said.

"It's a shame, whatever it is," Mom said. "He was a good kid when he lived with us. Very polite."

Fabian excused himself and went to his room, exactly the same way he'd done countless times when he'd been a teenager. His stomach hurt and his eyes were stinging. Had Ryan really had a public meltdown? If so, what had caused it? And how hard was it for him to keep playing hockey after it happened? After knowing everyone in the hockey world thought he was . . . broken? An addict? A joke?

God, Ryan.

Fabian sent him a single red heart emoji, and then got into bed. It would seem like a silly gesture, but it was the best representation of how Fabian was feeling right now. He wanted to give Ryan his heart.

But who was he kidding? Ryan already had it.

CHAPTER TWENTY-FOUR

Fabian could tell Ryan was still in pain when he met him in the lobby of Ryan's building. He wanted to leap into his arms, wrap his legs around his waist, and kiss him breathless. But he settled for gently resting a hand on each of Ryan's biceps.

"Hi."

"Hi."

"How are you feeling?"

Ryan grimaced. "Still sore."

Fabian took Ryan's hand and tugged him toward the elevator. "It just so happens that I am in the mood for a day of doing absolutely nothing but loafing around with my adorable boyfriend."

"You're in luck," Ryan chuckled.

When they got into the apartment, Fabian tried to steer Ryan toward the bedroom. "You need to rest," he said.

"I know. But first . . ." Ryan pointed at the kitchen stools, and Fabian quickly got the message and climbed up to sit on one. From this height, Ryan could kiss him without bending or having to lift Fabian.

"I missed you," Ryan said when they broke apart.

"Me too. I'm sorry about your back."

"I think it's getting better."

"Good." Fabian was dying to ask Ryan about his supposed meltdown last season, but he knew now wasn't the time. Instead he said, "Let's get you lying down, and then I'll give you your present."

"Uh, I can't do anything, you know. So if your plan is to—"

"No," Fabian said, and kissed him again. "As much as I'd love to get my mouth on every inch of your body right now, that's not what I meant. Go lie down. I'll just grab my bag."

Ryan pulled a slim, festively wrapped box from the top drawer of his dresser and waited nervously for Fabian to return. While he waited he gently twisted and stretched his back. Fuck, it hurt.

"It's just a little thing," Fabian said when he entered the bedroom. "I saw it at the farmer's market in Halifax and I thought you might like it."

He handed Ryan a soft package that looked like it had been hastily wrapped in red paper with green Christmas trees all over it. Ryan set the slim box he'd been holding on top of the dresser, and opened the present.

"It's hand woven," Fabian said excitedly. "The man who made it was a sweetheart, and I love the colors."

It was a long, wool scarf that was made up of a splashy blend of jewel tones. Ryan immediately wrapped it around his neck and smiled at his reflection in the mirror. He didn't normally wear bright colors, and he liked how it transformed him.

"I love it," he said honestly. "It reminds me of you."

"A bit of color never hurt anybody." Fabian smiled, then went up on his toes to kiss Ryan's jaw. "It suits you."

"Thank you. I have something for you too. I hope it's not

too much. I don't have a lot of experience buying gifts for men I'm dating."

"Well, let's see how you did," Fabian teased as he took the box. When he opened it, he gasped. "Ryan, are these *Mikimoto pearls*?"

"Maybe? I forget the name."

"Holy fuck. Ryan, are you serious here?"

"If you don't like it I can—"

"Like it? Ryan, it's *gorgeous*." He carefully pulled the long, white-gold chain from the box. The necklace was dotted with black pearls and tiny diamonds.

"I thought it would look good with that black jumpsuit you have."

"God, it *will*. I can't believe this. Is this really for me? I own this now?"

Ryan laughed. "It's yours. The lady at the store was really excited about it. She assured me my 'wife' would love it."

"She *does* love it. I want to put it on, but it won't go with this sweater."

"You could take the sweater off," Ryan suggested. "And . . . everything else?"

Fabian smiled seductively at him. "You're supposed to be resting."

"My eyes still work."

"Lie down, darling. Let me model this for you."

Fabian stripped off his clothes and Ryan got as comfortable as he could on the bed. When he was fully naked, Fabian slipped the chain over his head, then groaned orgasmically. "I feel like a mermaid. *Real* jewelry! I've never owned real jewelry." He admired himself in the mirror. "Oh, Ryan, it's *stunning*. You have exquisite taste."

Ryan beamed at him. "I'm glad you like it."

"I'm never taking it off."

Ryan would be okay with that. The sight of the pearls and diamonds glinting off Fabian's gorgeous skin, trailing down to his belly button, made Ryan's mouth water.

"Oh," Fabian said, noticing the tent that had suddenly appeared in Ryan's sweatpants. With his back injury making it hard to dress himself, Ryan hadn't bothered with underwear. "Do you have another gift for me?" He crawled onto the bed like a cat, diamonds and pearls dangling from his neck.

"I can't do much," Ryan reminded him hoarsely.

"You don't have to do a thing, darling. There are so many things I could do for you in that position."

Ryan swallowed. He really shouldn't do anything. If he came, which was admittedly unlikely, the spasms would be agony. But at the moment he was horny as hell, so he said, "Could I watch you?"

Fabian seemed to like that idea. "Would you like me to remove your pants first? You can't be comfortable like that."

"Okay. Yeah. Thanks." He carefully lifted his hips so Fabian could slide his waistband down. He removed his own shirt because he felt silly wearing only a shirt.

"Oh, I've missed him," Fabian sighed as Ryan's cock sprang out of his sweatpants. "He looks happy to see me."

"Definitely."

Fabian kneeled between Ryan's legs and took his own cock in his hand. "Do you want to hear the fantasy I cooked up when I was getting myself off last night?"

Oh fuck. "Where? In your old bedroom?"

Fabian bit his lip, then said, "That's right. Reminded me of being a teenager, jerking off in secret in my room." He smiled. "Thinking of you."

Ryan's mouth dropped open. He knew, of course, that Fabian had had a crush on him when they'd been teenagers. He still couldn't quite believe it, but he did know. Still, he hadn't yet considered the idea of young Fabian pleasuring himself to thoughts of Ryan. "You did that?" he asked. "When we lived together?"

"Frequently. Were you doing the same?"

"Yeah. Like, all the time."

Fabian closed his eyes and smiled. "God, that's hot."

"What were you thinking about last night?" Ryan asked, not wanting to lose the opportunity to hear all about it.

"Okay," Fabian said, keeping his eyes closed. "So I imagined you banging on my door. Maybe I'm home in my apartment in this scenario. I'm on my bed, playing with myself. Just getting started. And then there's this loud pounding on my door. And somehow I know it's you. Like I've been waiting for this."

"Yeah?" Ryan rasped. "Do you let me in?"

"Patience," Fabian scolded. He trailed his fingers over the chain, pausing to roll each pearl between his thumb and forefinger. "So I get up to go to the door, and when I open it, you're standing there and you look *wild*. Your eyes are blazing, and your shirt is hanging open like you didn't even have time to dress properly. Your chest is heaving, like you *ran* all the way to me. I can see how hard you are through your jeans. Like you're going to burst right out of them." He opened his eyes. "Just as hard as you are right now."

Ryan cursed and wrapped his hand around his dick, just to give it a squeeze. It wasn't enough. "What do I want?"

Fabian licked his bottom lip, then closed his eyes again. "You tell me that you need to come. That you've been edging yourself all day but you can't quite get there on your own. That you need me. Need my ass."

"Oh. Fuck." Ryan started stroking himself, quickly losing his ability to care about his back.

"You tell me that you got so close so many times, but you

couldn't find release. You *need* that release. You have so much come for me and you need me to take it from you."

Fabian was stroking himself faster now, and his voice got higher and breathier. "I tell you I've been waiting for you. That I'm ready. I show you the plug I have in, and you growl and yank it out. You shove me on the bed, face first. You're rough, but I'm not scared. I love it. I love how badly you need this. And you don't even wait, you just . . . *aah* . . . you just slam into me, shoving that giant cock inside, and it's so good. It's so fucking good, Ryan. You hold me down with those giant hands and fuck me so goddamned hard."

"You like that?" Ryan panted. God, he might actually come for real.

"Fuck yeah I do. Love feeling how strong you are. Love you losing control like that."

"I'll fuck you like that," Ryan grunted. "When I'm healed up, I'll fuck you as hard as you want."

"Yes please. God, I'm close."

"Tell me the rest." Ryan sounded like he was begging. "Please, *fuck*. How does it end?"

"You ask me if I want your come. And of course I say yes. I'm dying for it. And you warn me that it will be a lot, and I tell you to do it. To give it all to me."

Ryan whimpered. His pleasure was mixing with the pain from his back as his muscles tensed.

"And you do. You let out this gorgeous howl of relief and unload in me. It's so much that you pull out and still—oh *fuck*—you spurt more on my back. And then I come too, and, oh god. I really am going to come."

"Fuck. Do it."

With a tiny noise of surprise, Fabian hunched forward and shot all over Ryan's thigh. Then he fell forward and took Ryan's dick in his mouth, and Ryan's eyes rolled back.

"Goddamn you, Fabian. This is going to hurt. Fuck, don't stop. I'm so close."

Fabian was merciless, and in seconds Ryan was coming hard into his mouth, and screaming against the pain even as it was eclipsed by pleasure. He didn't even care if he never walked again.

"Ow," he said as the aftershocks subsided.

Fabian wiped his mouth with the back of his hand, and laughed. "You actually *could* have warned me that it was going to be a lot. Holy smokes."

"Sorry. It's been a while."

"I'm aware." Even though they were regularly enjoying amazing sex together, it was still a rare event for Ryan to actually orgasm.

"That was amazing, though," Ryan said. "You have a good imagination."

"If stories are what you need to get off, I'm sure I can dream up some more." Fabian curled up against him on the bed, resting his chin on Ryan's chest. "Are you all right? That was irresponsible of me."

"I'll be fine. I've been in more pain for worse reasons, that's for sure."

Fabian leaned forward and kissed him. Ryan could taste himself in Fabian's mouth, and he savored it. He wrapped an arm around Fabian and pulled him tighter, the pearls on the necklace getting caught between their bodies and pressing hard into Ryan's chest. He was thrilled by how much Fabian had loved his gift. He wanted to *cover* Fabian in jewels. He wanted to decorate his body with all the beautiful things he deserved.

"I just confirmed the album release show," Fabian said. "I'll wear the necklace that night."

"I think I'm going to like seeing that."

"Are you?" Fabian rolled onto his back beside Ryan and

fingered the necklace. “I didn’t think you were the possessive type, Ryan Price.”

“I’m not.” He considered his next words carefully. “Sometimes I just need a reminder that we’re really together. Especially when you’re onstage. Because it’s pretty hard to believe.”

For a long moment, Fabian didn’t say anything, which made Ryan worry. Then he said, “I hope you don’t think you’re getting the better end of this deal, Ryan, because I have never been with anyone who makes me as happy as you do.”

Ryan smiled at the ceiling. He was dangerously close to telling Fabian *exactly* how he felt about him, but instead he just kissed the top of Fabian’s head, and silently resolved to always make him happy.

CHAPTER TWENTY-FIVE

"Can I ask you something?"

Ryan had been watching, somewhat mesmerized, as Fabian tried on different shirts while getting ready to go out. Because of this, he was slow to respond to Fabian's question. "Sure. What?"

Fabian pulled the latest shirt off over his head, then turned to where Ryan was reclining on the bed. Ryan tried to focus on his face and not on the sexy curve of his hip where it dipped into his tight pants. "Did something . . . happen. With your last team?"

"Uh."

"I just—okay. When I was home my family was talking about how you . . . well. They said you had a meltdown."

Ryan didn't say anything for a moment. *Meltdown*. He cleared his throat. "I guess that's one way of putting it."

Fabian kneeled beside the bed and took Ryan's hand in his. "Tell me?"

Ryan really didn't want to talk about this. Ever. He'd gone through it with his therapist and that had been plenty. But Fabian looked so concerned, Ryan sighed and decided to give him at least the gist of what had happened.

"I was on the bench. And the crowd was chanting, because—oh. There's a chant. When the crowd wants me to fight."

"A chant?"

"Yeah. It's, um, 'Pay the Price.' Like my name, and like I'm going to make them pay, right?"

Fabian's brows pinched together. "Gross."

Ryan nodded. "Yep. So the crowd was chanting because, well, a hockey thing happened. I won't bore you."

Fabian didn't smile. "Ryan."

They'd showered together before Fabian had gotten dressed, and Fabian's damp hair fell in his eyes. Ryan reached out and brushed it aside. "I don't know what it was about this time, because it wasn't different from any other time, but I guess it was my breaking point. This was before I'd seen a therapist or tried medication. I was lonely, miserable. I don't know. Anyway."

"What happened?"

Ryan closed his eyes and remembered how he couldn't get his heart to stop racing, and how he couldn't get enough air into his lungs. His gear had been too hot, too tight, and when he'd looked down at his skates and tried to take a breath, it was like his throat had closed. His chest had *hurt*, lungs burning from lack of oxygen, and his damn heart had felt like it was going to explode.

"I thought I was having a heart attack. No joke. So I just . . . walked out." He opened his eyes.

"Of the building?" Fabian looked very confused.

"Off the bench, in the middle of a game. And as soon as I was in the hall I just started tearing off my gear. Total panic. I didn't even know what I was doing, I just knew I had to take my gear off or I was going to die. And people were yelling at me, and I didn't even know where I was or what was happening."

"Jesus."

"I guess I ended up on the floor. Or on my knees or something. People were surrounding me and I was trying to push them away."

"Panic attack, right?"

Ryan nodded. "Turns out, yeah. They got an ambulance to take me to the hospital because I kept saying I was having a heart attack. The hospital said it wasn't my heart. Just a panic attack, they said." He laughed humorlessly. "I was so embarrassed about it."

"That's ridiculous," Fabian said angrily. "It wasn't *just* anything. A panic attack is nothing to be embarrassed about."

"I get that now. I started seeing a therapist after that. I took a little break, to sort myself out a bit. I don't think my teammates or my coaches ever looked at me the same way again, though." He shrugged. "Then I got traded over the summer to Toronto."

Fabian smiled. "Well, that part worked out okay."

Ryan returned his smile. "Yeah. I guess it did."

Fabian kissed Ryan's hand. "Do you still have panic attacks?"

"I haven't had another one that bad, but . . . yeah. Sometimes. And I can feel them lurking, y'know?"

"I'm glad you told me. If I can do anything to help, let me know."

Ryan rested a palm on Fabian's cheek. "You *are* helping."

Fabian kissed him quickly, then resumed getting dressed. When his back was turned to him, Ryan allowed himself to wince from the back pain that had been torturing him all day. He'd told Fabian that his back was healed because he didn't want him to be upset about the fact that Ryan had been practicing and playing hockey all week.

The fact was, his back still felt pretty terrible. He'd been getting physio for it, and massages, so it was loosening up a bit, but the team doctor had also been supplying him with painkillers that made it easier to play. Fabian didn't need to know any of this.

Just like Fabian hadn't needed to know about that panic attack. Ryan wished no one had told him; it would only strengthen his belief that Ryan should quit hockey. He didn't outright say it, but Ryan knew it was how he felt.

But Ryan was managing both the anxiety and the back pain just fine. He couldn't expect Fabian to understand the demands of professional hockey.

Fabian wasn't stupid.

He knew Ryan's back was still bothering him. It was possibly worse now than it had been at Christmas. He saw how Ryan was trying to hide it, with slow, careful movements and with transparent reasons not to do things. Fabian had no idea how he was able to play hockey in his condition.

Which was exactly what Fabian intended to find out by watching this game.

Ryan was out of town, playing against Philadelphia. Fabian was at the same sports bar he'd been at with Tarek last time, but tonight he was accompanied by Marcus.

"So, that's your boyfriend," Marcus said. He and Fabian were both watching the giant television screen, where Ryan had done something in front of the net that seemed to require many slow-motion replays.

"Yes," Fabian said.

"That guy. On the television. Playing hockey. He's your boyfriend."

Fabian sighed. "Are we still not over this?"

"Just making sure." Marcus grinned and took a sip of his gin and tonic.

The game had not been particularly interesting, except for the fact that Ryan seemed to be much more physically comfortable playing a very rough sport on *skates* than he was when

Fabian watched him, for example, take a carton of milk out of the fridge.

Whenever Ryan wasn't on the ice, Fabian and Marcus chatted. He hadn't hung out with just Marcus in a while. Whenever Ryan *was* on the ice, Fabian watched him like a hawk.

"He looks healthy," Marcus remarked. "I definitely wouldn't guess he's in pain."

"It doesn't make sense. I know he's hiding it from me. I can see him wincing when he thinks I'm not watching when we're together."

"God, he's huge," Marcus sighed. "I'm so fucking jealous."

"The pads make him look bigger," Fabian said weakly.

It was weird, watching Ryan use his size to intimidate. There was a scuffle behind the net after the play stopped and Ryan was looming over a player on the opposing team. He couldn't see Ryan's face, but he could see the fear in the other player's eyes, even as he bumped up against Ryan and yelled something at him.

"Are they going to fight?" Marcus asked. He seemed a little too excited about the idea.

God, Fabian hoped not. "I hate this," he said.

"What? Ryan lying?"

"Yes. And him looking like *that*." He gestured toward the television, where the new camera angle showed Ryan glaring menacingly at his opponent. Fabian sighed. "And Ryan playing hockey, if I'm being honest."

Marcus frowned at him. "Maybe you shouldn't be dating a hockey player, then?"

Fabian watched as Ryan—thankfully—skated back to his bench instead of fighting. "He's not just a hockey player."

"But he *is* a hockey player."

"Yes, I know that, thanks," Fabian snapped. He sighed. "Sorry."

"You can't ask him to quit, Fabian. That's not fair."

"I *know*. And I would never do that except . . ." Marcus raised his eyebrows. Fabian looked at the table. "It's not just that I hate hockey. Obviously I can't ask Ryan to give up hockey because I don't like it. I'm not that selfish. But I don't think Ryan likes it either. I mean, he's basically *told* me that. And it's destroying his body, and it makes him miserable. He's so sweet and he deserves so much better than this."

"But *he* needs to make that decision. Not you," Marcus argued.

Fabian nodded. "I know. It's just hard, seeing him in pain and not letting himself heal. It's . . . scary."

Marcus looked at him sympathetically. "You can tell him how you feel, but you need to be careful, okay? No ultimatums."

"Of course not." Fabian wondered if he *could* bring any of this up with Ryan.

He wondered if he could stay with Ryan if he didn't.

Three days later, Fabian sat on Ryan's bed, holding a well-loved copy of *Anne of Green Gables*. "Do you always bring this with you?"

"Whenever I fly somewhere, yeah."

"Why?"

Ryan shrugged and pulled some rumpled-looking clothing out of his travel bag. "For comfort. Mom used to read that book to Colleen when we were kids, and I would always listen in. Then I read it to Colleen myself. It's always kinda been our thing."

"So it's like an anchor? Something you can focus on when you're scared?"

"I guess."

Fabian handed it to Ryan, who placed it back in the bag. "How's your back?"

"Fine. Why?"

"Is it?"

Ryan looked confused. "I told you it's better, didn't I?"

"Yes," Fabian said pointedly. "You did."

"What's wrong?"

Fabian stood. "You've been lying to me."

Ryan's eyebrows shot up. "Lying?"

"You can't be serious."

"Serious about what?"

"About thinking I don't know! It's obvious your back hasn't healed."

"It's not that bad," Ryan grumbled.

Fabian felt like he might explode. "Don't play tomorrow night."

Ryan stared at him like he had no idea what Fabian could possibly be concerned about. "Of course I'm playing. I have to."

"Your back is still completely fucked!"

"My back is always fucked. It's just more fucked than usual right now."

"You can't play hockey like this."

Ryan snorted. "You're the expert."

Fabian rounded the bed and stood in front of him, fists clenched at his sides. "Really? That's how you're going to play this? Your sissy boyfriend doesn't know anything about sports, so he's stupid to be concerned about your health?"

Ryan narrowed his eyes at him. "Don't call yourself that."

"Don't play hockey when you're *hurt*."

Ryan's face softened, which only made Fabian madder because now it looked like Ryan was amused by how stupid he was being. "It will be fine. It's *been* fine. The doctor gives me something for the pain."

Excuse me? "Gives you something? Gives you what?"

"Toradol," Ryan mumbled.

"Great. So you'll just swallow some pills and go get knocked around the ice for a couple of hours?"

Ryan looked away. "It's not a pill. It's a shot."

Fabian threw his hands up. "Great! Awesome! So your doctor shoots you up full of drugs. And then what? What happens when the shot wears off?"

"They give me some pills."

Fabian's jaw dropped. "Jesus Christ. You don't see a problem with that?"

"I'm careful. I'm not going to develop a problem, or whatever you're thinking."

"Why can't you just let yourself heal? Why is that so terrible?"

"It's just not what we do, okay? If there's any chance I can play, I play."

"And if you play, you fight, I guess," Fabian said, glancing at Ryan's freshly bruised knuckles.

Ryan's jaw clenched. "Yeah, I fight."

"I thought you were done fighting."

"I can't just stop fighting, Fabian."

"It's not your choice?"

Ryan huffed. "I'm a hockey player. Nothing is my choice."

Fabian's heart broke a little at those words. His throat was tight when he said, "Why do you even play hockey still? It makes no sense."

Ryan turned away. "This is stupid." He left the room, and Fabian stormed after him. When he caught up to him, Ryan turned and said, "I figured this was coming. I was waiting for it. You want me to quit so you don't have to date a hockey player, right?"

Fabian's jaw dropped. "This has nothing to do with me. Hockey is *destroying you*, Ryan. Can't you see that?"

"Hockey is all I am!" Ryan shouted back. It was the loudest Fabian had ever heard him speak, and it startled him.

"No," he said gently. "You're so much more. Please don't say that."

"Why not? It's true. I'm not walking away from an NHL career, Fabian. I'm not that stupid."

"I told you about the symphony," Fabian argued.

Fabian hated how bitter Ryan's answering laugh was. "Yeah. But guess what? I can't quit the NHL and become an independent hockey player. So I'm glad you got to do music your way, but I don't have that option."

"You could do something else."

"Like *what*? What the fuck am I supposed to do?"

"Anything you want!" Fabian practically screamed.

Ryan rolled his eyes and sucked his teeth for a moment, then exhaled and said, "You don't understand."

And that was it, wasn't it? Fabian didn't understand hockey. Didn't understand why Ryan would let it ruin his life if he seemingly got no joy out of it. Didn't understand why he'd ever thought this relationship could work. "I guess I don't." Fabian pushed past him and headed for the door.

"Where are you going?" Ryan asked as Fabian shoved his feet into his sneakers.

"Home."

"Why are you being like this? You know what my job is. You knew who I was when we got together."

Fabian swallowed the lump in his throat. "Yes, I did know. I knew exactly how sweet and wonderful you are."

Ryan's shoulders slumped, and his voice got quiet. "I don't know why you do that. You seem to think I'm better than I actually am. I can't be the person you have in your head."

"You *are* the person I have in my head. In my *heart*." Fabian was crying now. Damn it. "That's why I can't watch you hurt yourself. Or anyone else."

One of Ryan's giant hands landed on Fabian's shoulder.

Hands that would be used to punch someone later that week, no doubt. "I'm sorry."

It wasn't what Fabian wanted to hear. He could tell it was the kind of apology that meant *I'm sorry I can't be better*, not *I'm sorry, I'll try to do better.* If Fabian stayed, nothing would change. Walking out the door right now might break his heart, but not as much as watching Ryan destroying himself would.

"I can't do this," he said in a tiny voice. "I thought I could, but I can't. You're right, I don't understand." He let out a shuddering breath. "I just don't. I never will."

"Don't." Ryan was crying now too, which Fabian couldn't stand to see. He turned toward the door. "Please."

Fabian turned back. He really wanted to wrap Ryan in his arms and tell him he was sorry. That he would stay. That he could overlook everything and be his boyfriend. But he couldn't. It wouldn't be fair to either of them.

So he said, "Take care of yourself, Ryan Price." And then he left.

CHAPTER TWENTY-SIX

The next two weeks were total misery for Ryan.

The flights, which would have been difficult anyway without Wyatt, were absolutely harrowing. It was all Ryan could do to force himself to board each plane. When he was on board, he sat alone near the back and hyperventilated. By the third flight, he asked the team doctor to give him something extra to help him calm down. The pills didn't cure his anxiety, but they made him drowsy and downgraded his panic to a manageable level.

Despite what he had promised Fabian during their fight, Ryan could feel himself developing a dependence on drugs. He was in so much pain all the time, and the relief that came from a Toradol shot was heady. The pills he took after the game helped keep the excruciation of the aftermath of playing with an injury to a minimum.

He'd also started asking for sleeping pills. Every second he wasn't focused on his back pain, he was overcome by the agony of his shattered heart.

The hardest part was knowing that Fabian had been absolutely right. Every word had been the truth. And because of that, Ryan knew he shouldn't try to contact him. Just as Ryan had always believed, Fabian deserved so much better than him.

He knew Fabian was playing shows. He knew his album release show was coming up next week, but Ryan wouldn't dare go. The best thing either of them could do was forget this entire stupid relationship.

Like all NHL teams, the Guardians had a week off either before or after the NHL All-Star weekend. This year the Guardians had theirs the week before. Ryan tried not to think about how wonderful it would have been to spend it with Fabian. Instead, he holed up in his apartment and focused on healing his back.

On Wednesday, Ryan was woken by a phone call from Wyatt.

"Hey, Pricey. How's vacation?"

"It's okay. Quiet." Ryan's head felt a little thick. He'd taken a sleeping pill late last night and the effects hadn't quite worn off.

"I'm just calling because I wanted you to hear this from a friend before you heard it somewhere else."

Ryan blinked. "Did you get traded again?"

"No. It's about Duncan Harvey."

"Harvey? What about him?"

He heard Wyatt exhale and then say, "He died. They found him yesterday. At home. It looks like suicide by overdose."

Ryan sat up. "*What?*"

"I know. It's awful. It'll be all over the news today."

Ryan was stunned. He didn't know what to say. "Is there a funeral?"

"No details yet, but I imagine it will be in his hometown. He's an Ontario farmboy, but I forget the town. I'm in the Bahamas with Lisa right now, otherwise I'd try to go."

"Yeah." Ryan wished he could will away the effects of that pill. He couldn't quite wrap his head around any of this.

"I'm sorry to have to give you this news. Will you be okay? Is your, um, boyfriend—?"

"I'm fine," Ryan said quickly, not wanting Wyatt to mention Fabian even in vague terms. "Thanks for calling. I appreciate it."

"Are you sure you're all right?"

Ryan was so far from all right it wasn't funny. "Yeah. I'll look into the funeral. Have fun on the beach, okay?"

"Sure. But, y'know, call me if you need to."

God, Ryan missed Wyatt. "I will. Thanks."

They said their goodbyes and Ryan hauled himself out of bed and stumbled to the bathroom, where he immediately turned on the shower as hot as he could stand it.

Okay. He would find out when and where the funeral would be held, and he would drive there. That was something he could do. It was the *least* that he could do. Hopefully a lot of NHL players would do the same.

He couldn't help but replay their last fight—or, more accurately, their non-fight—as he showered. Was Ryan partially to blame for what had happened to Duncan? Had his refusal to fight him pushed him closer to the edge?

He couldn't let himself think these things.

When he stepped out of the shower, his head felt clearer and he realized his back wasn't bothering him as much. It seemed that actually taking the time to rest and heal was indeed effective.

"You were right, Fabian," Ryan said to the empty room.

"Feel free to take that off the shelf, if you want a closer look."

Fabian blinked, and realized, as his eyes focused, that he'd been staring at a stainless steel anal bead wand with what must have been an expression of deepest longing. But the truth was he'd only been thinking about Ryan. Again.

"I can give you the staff discount on one if you want," Vanessa continued. "It's the least I can do after I made you test out that garbage vibrator."

"No, sorry. I wasn't even looking at it. I'm just . . . scattered."

Vanessa turned away from the shelf of lube bottles she'd been straightening and rested a hand on Fabian's arm. "You could reach out to him, you know."

Fabian shook his head slowly, and forced a laugh that sounded hideous. "The whole idea of us was absurd. We don't make sense."

"But you miss him."

"God, so much."

Vanessa gave an exasperated sigh, then went back to straightening the lube shelf.

"What?" Fabian asked.

"I don't know. It's like you went into this thing with Ryan determined to prove that it couldn't work or something. Yeah, I never would have expected you to fall for a professional hockey player, but you did. And then as soon as the hockey stuff got real, you bolted."

"That's not fair," Fabian argued. "He was lying to me. Hurting himself. He's . . . self-destructive."

She jabbed a bottle of lube in his direction. "Sounds like he could use some love and support."

Fabian didn't have anything to say to that. He knew it was true, and it was the reason he'd felt like complete shit for the past two weeks. He wasn't strong enough to be Ryan's boyfriend. He wasn't able to overcome his own hatred and fear of everything hockey was. Everything it did to people.

"I saw Claude last night," he said quietly, changing the subject.

The disappointment was clear on Vanessa's face. "Oh, Fabian. No. You didn't, did you?"

"No. No, I promise. Nothing happened. I ran into him at Greta's art opening. We talked. Shared a joint outside." He looked away. "I mean, he did *try* to kiss me. But I told him I couldn't."

"Oh. Good. Why are you telling me, then?"

"Because seeing Claude just made it all so much clearer. I don't want him or anyone like him. I think I might be ruined for anyone other than the one person I really shouldn't be with."

"Which brings me back to my first suggestion: reach out to him." A customer walked in the door then, and Vanessa gave Fabian an apologetic smile. "We'll talk later, okay?"

"Sure," he said, but Vanessa had already left to help the customer. Fabian shouldn't have been bothering his friend at work anyway. He left the shop with a wave and an abysmal attempt at a smile in Vanessa's direction, and walked out into a light snowfall.

As soon as the hockey stuff got real, you bolted. Oh god, that was exactly what Fabian had done, wasn't it? He could handle dating a hockey player as long as he didn't have to see any real evidence of it.

But maybe that wasn't unreasonable of him. His whole life, Fabian had only known hockey to be a horrible, toxic thing that celebrated homophobic bullies and trained boys to believe there was only one acceptable way to be a man. Hockey was the wall that separated Fabian from his own family, the blueprint for masculinity that prevented his parents from understanding their only son. Fabian knew himself, and he knew he would never be a fan of the game, or the culture that surrounded it. So wouldn't it be unfair of him to pretend he could overlook all of that?

He liked Ryan a lot—he always had—and he wished he could be the strong, supportive cheerleader Ryan deserved. All he could do was worry about Ryan while refusing to even watch his games. That was a terrible foundation for a relationship.

But still, Fabian *wanted* to be with him. So maybe he could meet Ryan in the middle somewhere. If Ryan would just take time to let his fucking injuries heal, it would be *something*. If he could tell his coaches that he didn't want to fight anymore. If he could . . .

Fabian sighed. He knew enough about what hockey was like to know that Ryan couldn't do either of those things without risking his entire career. Ryan wasn't a superstar; he was in no position to make demands. He was replaceable.

But not to Fabian, obviously. With each passing day it was becoming clearer that Ryan had completely claimed Fabian's heart. Fabian had no doubt he could find an attractive man to replace Ryan—tonight, probably, if he wanted—but the man wouldn't have Ryan's sweetness. His giant heart. His courage.

Because Ryan was the bravest person Fabian had ever met. Ryan might not believe it, but Fabian knew it was true. He faced his fears every day—flying, fighting, socializing—and how many people could say that? Fabian was the coward. Ryan's career terrified him, so he'd run away.

Fabian wanted to fix this problem desperately. He had no answers right now, and he really needed to focus on the album release show, which was only days away. Maybe after that show he could devote some time to this. Maybe a healthy relationship with Ryan was impossible, but if there was even a chance, he had to try.

Ryan entered the small funeral parlor that sat across the street from the Tim Hortons in Duncan Harvey's hometown. His back was a little stiff after driving for three hours, but overall wasn't bad.

Ryan wasn't sure what he'd been expecting, but there were a lot of empty seats in the room where the service would be held. He didn't see any NHL players among the crowd. He recognized some of Harvey's coaches, but none of his teammates. Chicago's team captain, Clarke, wasn't even there.

But, of course, today was Friday. And Clarke would be at All-Star Weekend in St. Louis.

Ryan found a seat in the back row and tried to swallow his anger. It was like Harvey had never existed. He'd given everything he had to hockey, and when there was nothing left, hockey had abandoned him. He didn't even seem to have many friends or family here, and maybe that was what happened when you were a miserable addict everyone feared.

Someone sat next to Ryan. Not at the end of the same row, but *right next* to Ryan. He glanced over and was surprised to see who it was.

"Hey, Price."

"Rozanov. Shouldn't you be at the All-Star game?"

Ilya shrugged. "There will be others."

Did Ilya even know Duncan Harvey? He'd never played with him. It seemed bizarre that he was here.

The service was short and impersonal. Harvey, it turned out, didn't have much family. His parents had died years ago, and although a sister was listed in the obituary, she didn't seem to be there.

Was Ryan looking at his own future? He didn't like to think so. Despite everything, his family still loved and supported him. He was still confident he wasn't addicted to painkillers or anything else, but he was starting to understand how easily he *could* become addicted. There was no question that he had preferred how he felt when he was high these past few horrible weeks.

When it was over, Ilya stood and said, "Walk with me?"

"Sure. Okay."

When they got outside, they trudged across the snowy parking lot. Ilya stopped walking when they reached a large, leafless tree at the far end. He pulled a pack of cigarettes out of his coat pocket, tilting it first toward Ryan in offering. Ryan declined.

Ilya pulled one out for himself and lit it. He leaned back against the tree's trunk as he took his first drag. He was a very attractive man: almost as tall as Ryan, with sparking hazel eyes and curly, golden-brown hair that fell lazily around his face in a manner that matched his unbothered personality.

"Was nice of you to come," Ilya said after he exhaled.

"Figured it was the least I could do."

"Yes. Well. Least you could do was too much for most players, it seems."

"Yeah, I noticed that."

Ilya blew out more smoke and said, "This game can be really fucking terrible."

Ryan shoved his hands in his pockets and nodded. "I know."

A moment of silence passed, and then Ryan couldn't help but ask, "Why are *you* here anyway? Did you know Harvey?"

"No. Not really. But . . . his death. Suicide. It matters to me."

"Oh." Right. Ilya's mother. The whole reason he had started a charity with Shane Hollander.

"We don't talk about it enough in this sport. Depression. Addiction. Mental health." Ilya glanced at him. "*You* know about it."

Ilya had never had a problem with being direct. "Yeah. I know about it."

"How are you doing?"

"Some days are better than others. But I see a therapist. It's, like, on Skype, but it still works. And I take meds. I should probably talk about it more, but . . ."

"You are a private person. I understand that."

He had to smile. "Do you?"

There was a funny little twist to Ilya's lips. "We all have secrets."

Ryan nodded. Of course Ilya had secrets. He wondered if Ilya was possibly as lonely as he was.

"Do you like playing hockey?" Ilya asked suddenly.

Ryan almost answered "Of course" without thinking, but he stopped himself and instead considered Ilya's question.

"No. I don't think I have for a long time."

"It doesn't make you happy?"

The last thing hockey did was make Ryan happy. "I think it makes me miserable, to be honest."

"That's a problem," Ilya said.

"I know."

Ilya finished his cigarette. "Wyatt Hayes is a good guy."

"He is. I miss him."

"He said you help out at a place with kids? Play hockey with them?"

"Oh." Ryan looked at the ground, embarrassed that Wyatt had been talking about him to Ilya Rozanov. "Yeah. When I can. Which isn't often."

"You like it?"

"I do. I like kids."

Ilya nodded. "What are you doing this summer?"

Ryan was having a hard time keeping up with Ilya. "I don't know. Might go back home to Nova Scotia. Why?"

Ilya fished his phone out of his pocket and handed it to him. "Give me your number. We are organizing these camps for our charity. Me and Shane. Hollander, I mean." He looked oddly embarrassed for a moment. "They are hockey camps for kids. They will be in Ottawa and Montreal this summer. We could use help."

"What, *me*?" Ryan truly couldn't fathom being a coach at the same camp where kids would be learning from stars like Shane Hollander and Ilya Rozanov.

"I don't want to teach kids how to fight," Ryan said, just to make it clear.

Rozanov looked at him like he was stupid. "No. You are a defenseman. You will teach them how to stand still and not score goals. Defenseman things."

Ryan laughed. "Asshole."

"Also, it is going to be for everyone, you know? Like . . ." Ilya seemed to wrestle with how to say the next part, but then just bluntly asked, "You are gay, yes?"

Ryan snorted, surprised by another subject change. "Yes."

"Good. That's what I mean. The camps will be for that too. I mean we will teach, um . . ."

"Tolerance?"

Ilya smiled. "Yes. Try to change things, right?"

"You should ask Scott Hunter then."

He made a face. "Maybe."

They walked back to their vehicles in silence. As Ilya was unlocking his Mercedes SUV, he said, "Find something that makes you happy, Price. Hold on to it."

Ryan nodded, and his throat suddenly felt tight. He'd had someone who'd made him happy, and he'd let him go. And for what? A life of nothing but pain and misery that he felt obligated to endure. There was money, sure, but Ryan didn't even enjoy spending it. He could live without an NHL salary. He just needed to find something he truly enjoyed doing.

During his drive back to Toronto, he considered the fact that he had quite a bit of money saved. He could sell his ridiculously expensive apartment and live quite comfortably for a long time while he figured out the rest of his life. He was only thirty-one. Outside of the hockey world, he was still a relatively young man.

He could quit. He could *just quit.* His heart started racing at the realization of how possible this was. There was literally nothing stopping him. Sure, he would piss some people off, and probably get yelled at, but would anyone really care? His coach had been threatening to replace him for two months now.

Let him do it. Let someone else live the NHL dream. Ryan was done.

CHAPTER TWENTY-SEVEN

"Can you believe how many people are out there?" Vanessa said as she bounced into the green room. Fabian had not, in fact, looked to see how many people were in the club. It was one of the largest venues he had ever played; he was impressed that his label had booked it for his album release.

In truth, there was only one person he wanted to see in the crowd. And there was no chance of that.

"You look incredible," Vanessa said. "I love that jumpsuit."

Fabian had worn the black jumpsuit that he now thought of as Ryan's. He had paired it with the exquisite necklace that was indisputably Ryan's. He'd stopped short of wearing the lace underwear.

His stomach churned. He'd never had stage fright once in his entire life, but he was a ball of nerves tonight. He'd been horribly fragile since he'd walked out on Ryan.

God, he hoped Ryan was all right. Fabian should have been more patient with him. Leaving him the way he had couldn't have been helpful, and he had been worried for weeks that Ryan may have spiraled as a result. Fabian had considered reaching out to him before this show, but he hadn't been able to make himself do it. Some part of him still thought their relationship was impossible, no matter how he felt about Ryan. So now Fabian had no choice but to haul his broken heart onto the stage.

The manager of the club entered the room. "You ready?" she asked.

Fabian nodded and stood. He took some deep breaths to try to calm his stomach, then turned and hugged Vanessa. "Thank you," he said. "I love you."

"I love you too. Knock 'em dead, all right?"

He straightened, and attempted a smile. "Of course."

He walked onstage to a wall of enthusiastic applause and whistles. He smiled at his audience—as enormous as Vanessa had described—and waved as he walked to the middle of the stage. When he reached the center, he lifted his violin and bow from its case, stood in front of the mic, and closed his eyes. He took two more slow breaths, centering himself. This was where he came alive. He *loved* this.

He opened his eyes and brought his violin to his chin. He took one more long breath, and started to play. He let the music wrap around him, reverberating off the walls of the club and returning to him. He let it feed him, filling all the places inside him that had been empty for weeks. He needed this energy so he could give it right back to his audience. Later, when there was nothing left of him, Fabian could drag his husk of a body back home and fall apart, but right now his audience deserved him at his best.

He put on the show of his life. He played his heart out, and he knew his own anguish was very present in every melancholy note he sang.

He didn't play the song he'd written about Ryan.

When he finished his set, he smiled, then bowed as the audience went wild with applause. Sweat beaded along his hairline from the exertion of playing, and he flicked his bangs aside with the tip of his bow.

He'd worked so fucking hard for this moment. Ten years almost since he'd quit the Symphony to make exactly *this* happen. His eyes burned with tears and he let them fall. He covered his mouth with his hand, trying to stop himself from full-on sobbing in front of this audience. Because they weren't just happy tears. He regretted how this night *could* have been, if he'd still had Ryan.

He wiped at his eyes, making a mess, he was sure, of his makeup. He blinked to clear his vision and took another moment to remember this audience. To really soak it all in before he left the stage. His gaze traveled over the crowd until it landed on a flash of red hair in the very back, standing head and shoulders above everyone else.

Ryan?

It was definitely Ryan. There was no mistaking him. And when Fabian's gaze stayed on him, Ryan smiled sheepishly and gave a little thumbs-up.

Fabian gasped. His heart beat for what felt like the first time in weeks. Without thinking, he lowered himself down from the stage, into the crowd. People were touching him, patting him on the back, grabbing his arms, but he ignored them. He just kept walking, forcing people to step aside because he would walk right over them if they didn't.

It took forever to reach the back of the club, and for a moment Fabian worried that he had hallucinated the whole thing. But then he saw him. Huge and gorgeous and real. And wearing the scarf Fabian had given him for Christmas.

"Hi," Ryan said.

Fabian didn't say anything. He just wrapped his arms around

him and held on as tight as he could. A second later, Ryan returned the hug, wrapping his strong arms around him and pulling him close.

"Good show," Ryan said.

"You came," Fabian sniffed.

"Yeah. Is that okay?"

Fabian nodded against his wonderful, solid chest. "It's okay."

"You got plans after this?"

"Not anymore."

Ryan laughed. "I was hoping we could talk."

"Yes." Fabian pulled back and smiled up at him through wet eyes. "Don't leave, all right? I need to stick around for a bit but . . . stay. In fact, stay right by my side. I don't want to lose you." *Not again. Not ever again.*

"Okay."

They took a cab back to Fabian's apartment. It was twenty below zero outside, and the club was outside of the Village.

Ryan had been uncertain about going to Fabian's show, but he knew he had to at least try. He literally had nothing left to lose. When he saw Fabian onstage, wearing his necklace, Ryan's heart had lifted. Fabian couldn't completely be done with him if he was wearing his present to such an important show.

He'd been planning what he would say, if given the opportunity, for days. It seemed his opportunity had arrived.

He followed Fabian into his apartment, and was overcome with relief. He thought he'd never see this room again.

Fabian was still wearing his stage outfit. He was also still wearing his makeup, though the black liner around his eyes had smudged quite a bit.

"Give me a moment?" Fabian asked. "I want to clean myself up before we talk."

"Of course."

Ryan sat on the end of the bed and waited while Fabian did whatever he needed to do in the bathroom. Fifteen minutes later, Fabian emerged in a black satin dressing gown with a freshly scrubbed face and wet hair. He was still wearing the necklace.

Ryan laughed. "Do you ever take that off?"

Fabian smiled, and walked to the stove. "When I have to." He took the kettle that was on one of the burners and filled it with water, then returned it to the stove. "Truthfully, this is the first time I've worn it since . . . well. You know."

Ryan knew. "I'm glad you wore it tonight."

"I'm glad you were there to see it." He pulled two mugs out of a cupboard above the fridge and set them on the tiny counter. "Is mint tea okay?"

"That sounds perfect."

Fabian prepared their tea while Ryan watched in silence. There seemed to be an unspoken agreement between them that they would wait until the tea was ready to really get into things.

By the time Fabian handed him a steaming mug of mint tea, Ryan's nerves were up again. He had planned to speak first, but maybe that wasn't the best idea. Fabian sat in the chair that was free of discarded clothing tonight, facing Ryan and the end of the bed. His bare toes nearly touched the ends of Ryan's socked ones.

"I quit hockey," Ryan blurted out.

Fabian's eyes widened.

"I mean, I am quitting. I'm in the process of quitting. But I won't be playing any more games. I'm done."

"Wow. That . . . wasn't what I was expecting."

"I don't know what I'm going to do next, but I have money, so I can take some time to figure that out. And . . . heal."

"How's your back?"

"A lot better. I had some days off and I rested it."

"I'm glad."

Ryan could tell Fabian was being cautious. He didn't blame him.

"I haven't taken a painkiller in over a week. Not even an Advil. Nothing."

Fabian chewed his lip, then said, "I'm such an idiot. I don't know the first thing about hockey, or chronic pain, or medicine, and I should have trusted you."

"Maybe. But I'm not always sure I can trust myself. I've always done what's best for the team, and you're right, sometimes that meant taking a stupid amount of painkillers instead of letting myself heal. Hockey is selfish that way."

Fabian cupped his hands around his mug. "Even if you were developing an addiction, it was heartless of me to walk away like that. You needed help and support. Not . . . that."

"You were scared."

"I was *terrified*," Fabian corrected. "But I want you to know . . . you don't have to quit hockey. For me, I mean. If that's why you did it—"

"It's not the only reason. What you said was true—hockey isn't good for me."

Fabian looked relieved. "All right. But if you think quitting is the only way I'll be with you, it isn't true. I was being selfish and that was a ridiculous thing to demand of you."

Ryan's heart flipped. "You want to be with me?"

Fabian's lips quirked up. "You caught that, did you?"

Ryan grinned stupidly at him, then snapped out of it and remembered what he'd wanted to say. "Okay. I've been thinking a lot about what I want to say. And I practiced it. So I want to say it."

"You practiced it?"

"Yes."

"Well by all means, let's hear it."

Ryan stood and set his mug on Fabian's desk. "The thing is—" He paused, already lost. "These past few months—" Damn it. "I know we haven't—" He sighed, and then cursed under his breath.

"Ryan." Fabian stood and placed a hand on his arm. "You don't have to say anything."

Ryan shook his head. "I'm in love with you." He swallowed. "I had to say that. Just that."

Fabian pressed his lips together, and his eyes glistened. He let out one long shuddering breath, and said, "I think it might be possible that I've always been in love with you. I know how absurd that sounds, but it's the truth."

Ryan smiled so wide it hurt. "Can I kiss you, then?"

"Yes. One moment." Fabian climbed onto the chair he'd been sitting in, standing on it this time. He stood a couple of inches taller than Ryan now, which made Ryan laugh.

And then he tilted his head up to kiss the man he loved. Fabian wrapped his arms around Ryan's neck, and Ryan hooked an arm under Fabian's ass and hauled him off the chair so he could carry him to the bed.

"Your back really *is* better," Fabian said happily.

"Yeah. Let me show you what else it can do."

Fabian's eyebrows shot up. "My goodness!"

Ryan laughed and dropped him on the mattress. "You look so sexy in that thing."

"What?" Fabian asked, gliding a hand over the silky material of his dressing gown. "This? I'm glad you like it because I'm *freezing*. It's not at all appropriate for frigid midwinter nights."

"I'll warm you up."

"Of course you will. Get your clothes off."

* * *

"Ryan," Fabian murmured later, when they were tangled up in bed together, sleepy and sated, "I have a very important question about your thighs."

"What's that?"

"What happens to them after you stop playing hockey?"

Ryan paused a moment from stroking Fabian's hair. "They'll probably turn into regular thighs."

"That's what I was afraid of."

"Quitting hockey doesn't sound so great now, does it?" Ryan teased.

"Hm. I suppose I'll have to learn to live with only your towering height, your gorgeous face, and your enormous cock."

"And my fun personality."

Fabian slapped his arm lightly. "You're plenty of fun." He rolled on top of Ryan and gazed down at him. "And you're sweet. And I love you."

"I love you too."

"I'm playing some shows out of town later this month. Would you like to join me?"

"Flying?"

Fabian laughed. "You greatly overestimate the travel budget of an indie musician. No, I'll be driving or taking the train."

"Oh." Ryan grinned. "Yeah. Okay. I'll go with you. We can take my car."

"My label is planning a Canadian tour for me this summer. If spending the summer driving for hours between Canadian cities with a rising star appeals to you, you could come along."

For a long moment, Ryan didn't say anything. It sounded perfect, driving across the country with the man he loved. Being there to watch Fabian dazzle audiences in different cities. Being there to kiss Fabian after his shows, and then taking him back to their hotel room and showing him exactly how proud he was to be his boyfriend.

"But this isn't all about me," Fabian added, breaking Ryan's giddy fantasy. "We're going to figure out what you need. What makes you happy, Ryan?"

At the moment, Ryan couldn't imagine needing more than the man he had in his arms, but he said, "I don't know. But I can't wait to find out."

EPILOGUE

FABIAN:
When are you done for the day?

RYAN:
Just wrapping up. You at the hotel?

FABIAN:
I'm at a café.

He sent Ryan a photo of a cappuccino sitting next to a plate with a half-eaten pain au chocolat.

FABIAN:
I love Montreal.

Ryan smiled. He'd just finished his first day of coaching at Rozanov and Hollander's charity hockey camp, and it had gone surprisingly well. He'd felt a little awkward standing next to some of the superstars that had agreed to help out, but at least Wyatt was there.

Although, Wyatt was practically a superstar himself these

days. Since being traded to Ottawa, he'd played extremely well for the struggling team. Ryan was happy for him.

The first day of camp had been a little chaotic, with everyone trying to figure out how exactly this was going to work, but it had been fun. The kids were great, and Ryan liked that the camp welcomed all genders. He'd ended the day by working one-on-one with a thirteen-year-old girl on improving her pivoting. It was awesome being able to share actual hockey skills with someone. It was awesome to be reminded that he *had* actual hockey skills.

"Nice work today, Pricey." Wyatt came up behind him, and clapped him on the shoulder. "Is that Fabian you're texting?"

"Yeah. He's eating pastry somewhere."

"Jesus, and he's sending you photos of it? That seems cruel. Listen, do you know where Roz or Hollander are? I got Owen's mom to sign the incident report and now I don't know what to do with it."

"Incident report? What happened?"

"Aw, nothing much really. Some shoving in the locker room. I think he's got some old beef with that Harper kid."

"Oh." Ryan couldn't imagine what kind of beef two twelve-year-olds could have. "I can take that for you. I'll give it to them."

"Thanks, buddy. Lisa is waiting for me, so I'll see you tomorrow, all right?" He handed Ryan the paper and jogged away.

Ryan glanced down one end of the hallway he was standing in, and then the other. He was pretty sure there was some sort of office somewhere that Rozanov and Hollander were using. Maybe one of them was in there.

He chose a direction and started walking. He was glad he had decided to accept Rozanov's offer and coach this camp. It had taken a lot of convincing on Ilya's part, but after Ryan had some long conversations with Fabian, his parents, Colleen, and his therapist, he had decided that this would be a good way to see if hockey had anything left to offer him.

He was thinking seriously about getting into some sort of childhood education program. Or maybe a physical fitness education program. He liked working with kids, and he liked being active. He *really* liked the idea of making hockey a positive and inclusive thing for everyone. It was a cause he could be passionate about.

He heard Rozanov's unmistakable voice—a heavily accented teasing drawl—coming from a room down the hall. He headed toward the sound, and then stopped when he heard a second, angrier voice. It sounded like Hollander.

He moved a little closer and could confirm that it was Shane Hollander, and he seemed to be arguing with Rozanov. Well, that wasn't really a surprise. Ryan still wasn't over the fact that they liked each other at all.

The arguing stopped, so Ryan went to the door. He should have knocked before nudging it open because the next thing he saw was Ilya pinning Shane against the wall.

With his mouth on Shane's.

Shane saw him first, and immediately shoved Ilya away from him. Ilya turned to see who the intruder was, not looking nearly as panicked as Shane was.

"Price," Ilya said calmly. "What's up?"

Shane was blushing furiously and smoothing out the front of his camp director polo shirt.

"I have some paperwork. Wyatt gave it to me. For you."

"Thank you," Shane said. "You can put it on the desk. And, um, about what you just saw . . ."

Ilya rolled his eyes and took the paper from Ryan. "He's not going to *tell anyone*, Shane. Fucking relax." He shot Ryan a questioning look that said *you're not going to tell anyone, are you?*

"No. I won't tell anyone. That you're, um . . ."

"Making out at work? Yes. That would be bad," Ilya said with an amused grin. Shane looked like he would never smile again.

"I don't know what I see in you," Shane grumbled.

"Yes. You say that every day."

Ryan couldn't help but smile at them. Suddenly things made a lot more sense. "Your secret is safe with me," he promised.

He left in a hurry, feeling embarrassed but also very keen to see his own boyfriend. He and Fabian were here for the week, and then they were heading to Atlantic Canada so Fabian could play some shows and they could both have some family time.

Ryan wasn't sure how it was going to go with Fabian's family. The Salahs knew they were dating, but Fabian said he didn't think they would actually believe it until they saw them in person. Whatever happened, Ryan would be right by Fabian's side.

He found Fabian sitting on a bench outside their hotel. He looked fucking gorgeous in his blue floral-print romper, enormous black sunglasses, and bright yellow espadrilles. Ryan was wearing track shorts, flip-flops, and a gray camp T-shirt.

Fabian stood when he saw him, and handed him a small white bag. "I got you an almond croissant."

Ryan looked in the bag. "Weird that they sold it to you with a bite out of it."

"I *know*! I should complain."

Ryan kissed him, right there on the sidewalk. "You smell nice."

"I may have sampled some fragrances at Holt Renfrew."

Ryan buried his face in the crook of Fabian's neck and inhaled. "I like this one. Did you buy it?"

"No, darling. That's your job."

Ryan grinned and kissed his neck. "You had a good day, then?"

"I did, but it's very hot and I was hoping we could retire to our air-conditioned hotel room."

"Sounds like a plan. You have any ideas about dinner? Besides pastry, I mean."

"None. But . . . I do have something to show you." He handed Ryan his phone. "Tell me what you think."

Ryan thumbed through the gallery of images. They were all photos of rooms in a small townhouse near the Village. "This is for sale?"

Fabian bit his lip. "It isn't cheap."

Ryan closed the gallery and looked at the price. It was almost half of what his sky-rise apartment had cost him. "We could do this."

"Could we? Vanessa and Tarek said they would check it out for us and let me know if it's worth pursuing."

Ryan loved the idea of Fabian filling these rooms with color and ornate knickknacks. He loved the idea of building a home and a life with Fabian. He didn't care where they lived, but he knew Fabian wanted to stay close to his friends. Close to his community. Ryan was happy to do that, even if it meant ridiculously high real estate prices.

They walked hand in hand through the sliding glass doors into the hotel lobby, Fabian swinging their joined arms playfully.

"Don't tell Mom and Dad," he said, "but I am extremely grateful that they took in hockey players when I was growing up."

Ryan laughed. "I find that hard to believe."

"I'm sure they didn't intend to play matchmaker for their son, but it certainly worked out."

"It did."

"Maybe I'll thank them at our wedding."

Ryan snorted, dismissing the idea as if it were ridiculous. As if he hadn't been thinking about proposing since the moment Fabian wrapped his arms around him after his album release show.

As they waited for the elevator, Ryan blatantly ogled Fabian in his cute little romper. His lean bare legs and arms were thoroughly distracting. Fabian must have noticed Ryan's interest, because he licked his lip and, presumably, locked eyes with him. It was hard to tell with the sunglasses covering most of his face.

When they were alone in the elevator, Fabian scoffed at the obvious erection that was straining the fabric of his romper shorts. "Great. Look what you did."

Ryan chuckled and thought about all the ways he'd like to alleviate Fabian's problem.

"I hope you're happy," Fabian scolded.

Ryan grinned. "I really am."

Don't miss Common Goal, *the next book in Rachel Reid's Game Changers series, available wherever books are sold.*

BARGAIN BRUNCH
WHEN: Every Sunday morning
WHERE: Marcus's bedroom
aka Tarek & Vanessa's living room
(next to the vape shop)
GOSSIP GUARANTEED
BYO waffle topping
I ♥ NIAGARA FALLS
bad mimosas in tacky mugs!!

ACKNOWLEDGMENTS

First and foremost, I would like to thank Mackenzie Walton for making my books so much better. I really lucked into getting the best editor. I would also like to thank the entire Carina Press team for being great to work with.

I would also like to thank my husband, Matt, for being so supportive and encouraging, especially when I was reading the first draft aloud to him.

And finally I want to give a huge shout-out to all of the professional athletes, especially hockey players, who have spoken or written bravely and honestly about their own struggles with mental health, addiction, phobias, and the culture of toxic masculinity that can make team sports so difficult for so many people.

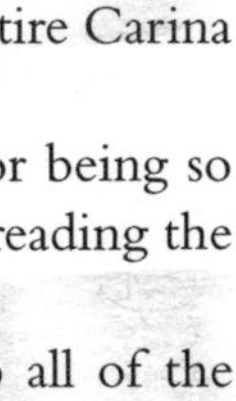